cold reckoning

avril dahl

book one

l.t. ryan

with
biba pearce

LIQUID MIND MEDIA

For information contact:
Contact@ltryan.com
https://LTRyan.com
https://www.facebook.com/JackNobleBooks

chapter
one

FBI Special Agent Avril Dahl breathed in the icy
December air and felt it tingle her nostrils. It was good to be back.

Not good, but something.

Täby, the municipality where she'd grown up, lay in a snowy, white
shroud northeast of Stockholm. The air held the crisp bite of approaching
twilight, the kind that turned breath into visible clouds. Standing outside
the train station, she felt a familiar tug as she stared up at the glass and
chrome architecture of Sweden's biggest shopping mall. How many times
had she gone there with her mother as a girl? Trying on clothes, laughing
over outfits, getting her ears pierced.

The snow-covered streets buzzed with the muted hum of city life.
Commuters hurried by, their faces peeking out from beneath thick scarves
and knitted hats. Holiday lights twinkled from the windows of nearby
cafés, casting a warm glow on the frosty sidewalks. A tram rumbled past,
its tracks clinking rhythmically against the icy ground.

A pang of longing hit her in the gut, and she took a swift gulp of air,
savoring the mingled scents of roasted chestnuts and brewing coffee
wafting from a nearby kiosk.

Memories, who needed them?

She turned and walked away from the mall toward the bus stop. The
streets were clear of snow, but the curbs brimmed with dirty slush, and the
sidewalks glistened with a persistent drizzle. She could call an Uber, a

habit she'd picked up in the bustling metropolis of Washington D.C., but what was the point? The bus would take her directly home, even if it was slower. It would be prudent to save some money, too, since she had a feeling her days at the FBI were numbered.

The bus wheezed into the terminal, and Avril climbed on, hauling her suitcase behind her. It felt surprisingly light, considering how long she'd been away, but then again, she'd left most of her smart work outfits back in D.C. She wouldn't need them here. All she'd packed were jeans, a couple of tops, sweaters, and one winter coat, which she was wearing, even though the weather in Stockholm was currently milder than the unforgiving mountains of Colorado, where she'd spent the last few weeks.

Cringing, she tried not to think what a wasted trip that had been. Two weeks chasing the Frost Killer around a tiny south Colorado town only to find out he was a copycat.

Avril let out a bitter laugh. The copycat had done a great job of emulating his namesake. He'd fooled her, but not the wily sheriff with whom she'd been working. Or rather, whose department she'd muscled in on with her FBI credentials and superior attitude.

Heat spread to her cheeks, and she laid her forehead against the frosted bus window. How could she have been so blind? She, who'd hunted the diabolical murderer for a decade, who knew his MO like the back of her hand, knew each victim by name. Yet, she'd missed all the tell-tale signs. The snowflake pendant that he left on the bodies of his victims —his chilling calling card—had been different. Nothing immediately noticeable, but on closer inspection, the paper cutouts had been more commercial and less homemade.

The way he'd pursued his victims, even sleeping with one of them, was out of character. The real Frost Killer would never do that. He was far too disciplined. Her only excuse was that she'd been so desperate for news after his two-year hiatus, she'd missed crucial evidence. Seen what she'd wanted to see. They even had a name for it in the profession. Confirmation bias. She gave a heavy sigh. Lesson learned.

This December marked three years without a kill. For a man who had murdered four women every year for the last fifteen, that was significant. Sheriff Savage had probably been right when he'd said the original killer was in prison or dead. A man like that didn't stop killing. He didn't wake up one morning and think, *I've had enough of this,* and go back to a regular nine-to-five. She'd worked with enough criminal profilers and behavioral experts at the FBI to know he would never stop. Not unless he had to.

As the bus trundled northwest past snowy nature parks, stark landmarks and frozen waterways, Avril tried to shake off the gloom that had befallen her since leaving Colorado. She'd failed, that much was clear. Her boss and her colleagues whispered behind her back. The pitiful, obsessed field agent who couldn't let go.

That's what this trip was all about. Letting go. In all the ways that entailed.

She'd never come home for her father's funeral two years earlier. Those who knew him would have found that odd. Then again, she wondered how many of the people they used to socialize with, if any, had been at the funeral. After her mother's murder, family friends had dried up and disappeared. Funny how that happened when there was a tragic event in a community, like it was contagious or something. Like they'd be tainted by association.

At school, her peers had stopped playing with her, warned off by their parents. *Don't talk to that girl, her mother was murdered.* Like it was a dirty secret. After that, she'd retreated into herself, closed off her emotions. Trained herself not to mind, not to care. She didn't need them. She was quite happy being alone.

Avril dreaded the task ahead. Her father's house—now hers—hadn't been touched since he passed away. Clearing it out would be a mammoth undertaking. But going through all his things seemed fitting in the wake of her current professional disappointment. There was a strange satisfaction in kicking herself while she was down. Like she deserved the punishment. For not being a better daughter. For not trying to reconcile with her father after her mother had died. For not finding out the truth about what happened all those years ago.

The truth.

She scoffed, startling the woman beside her. The truth had eluded her for so long, she'd forgotten it existed. Beneath this sordid journey to discover who the Frost Killer was and why he'd murdered so many women, there was a purity of thought. An honorable aim. The truth.

Her shoulders slumped. Now she'd never know.

The bus shuddered to a stop. This was her. Standing, she grabbed her suitcase from the luggage rack and carried it off the bus. The frigid air slapped her in the face, making her eyes water—or that's what she told herself. Out here, it was several degrees colder than in the city. The natural parks and nature reserves didn't retain the heat like the concrete buildings. There was nothing to hold on to.

The wheels of her case growled in protest as she lugged it down the street. Around the corner, and she'd be home. How many times had she hopped on and off this bus as a teenager? It was all achingly familiar—the houses and the corner store that used to sell those hard, sugary sweets with the toffee inside, and even the trees lining one side of the street, bare and scraggly now winter had hit.

And there it was. Home. She stared at the rectangular house with its faded yellow exterior, white-rimmed windows, and gray sloping roof. There was a solar heating panel on top—that was new. Her father must have been trying to save energy, or he'd become eco-friendly in his old age. All the shutters were closed, as if the house didn't want to see out anymore. It had shut itself in, just like her. Reaching into her coat pocket, she pulled out an old set of keys. The metal tag was rusty with lack of use. In fact, she'd had a hard time finding them amongst her things in her apartment in D.C. where she'd stopped just long enough to catch up on sleep, pack, and head back to the airport.

The small front garden was overgrown with dead weeds that flopped over the path and swiped at her jeans as she walked up to the front door. If she wanted to sell this place, she'd have to sort out the garden, but that could wait until the spring. Smatterings of unmelted snow lay on the ground, glistening in the dull, afternoon light. It would be dark soon, this far north. She'd forgotten how the nights crept in this time of year. A dark veil, descending on the day, blotting out the sun. Heavens, when had she gotten so morbid?

Mentally shaking herself out of her slump, she slotted the key in the lock. To her surprise, the door swung inwards. That wasn't supposed to happen.

Frowning, Avril pushed it open and stood on the doorstep, peering into the darkened interior. At first glance, everything appeared normal.

Whoever was here last must have forgotten to lock it. The paramedics? Her neighbor? The police?

It had been two years ago when the Swedish officer had called to give her the news. It would have been late in the evening in Sweden, but early afternoon in D.C. She'd been at the office, doing research into the latest spate of killings, his last spate, as it turned out, before he dropped off the grid.

Your father had a heart attack this morning. Paramedics were dispatched, but they couldn't save him. I'm sorry for your loss.

Avril had broken into a cold sweat at hearing the news, much like now, as she stepped into her father's empty house. It was eerily quiet, only the floorboards creaking beneath her feet as she crept down the hallway toward the living room.

"Hello?" she called out. Maybe someone was here. A friend of her father's, perhaps?

No answer, just another creak as she stepped forward.

Rounding the corner, Avril gasped.

"What the—?"

Pulling her glasses out of her coat pocket, she put them on to survey the confusion. The cushions had been upended and lay sprawled on the floor. The rug had been pulled up, the ornaments swept off the mantelpiece, some of them smashed on the hard brick of the fireplace, and the lamp was on its side. Blinking, her brain tried to make sense of what she was seeing.

Had she been burgled? There's no way the police would have left the house in this state, surely? A chill crept over her as she surveyed the chaos of the living room. Yes, someone had broken in here and ransacked the place. With a shaking hand, she pulled out her cellphone and called the police.

chapter
two

"Everything okay?"

Avril jumped, then spun around. A man in his early thirties stood behind her. He wore faded black denim jeans, a thick jumper and had longish, wayward hair that curled at the ears.

"Who are you?" she spluttered, her hand going to her hip. Then she remembered she'd left her gun back in D.C., so she staggered backwards, out of grabbing range.

A large hand went up. "Whoa, Avril! It's okay. Don't you recognize me?" He broke into a lopsided grin. "I suppose it has been a while."

She frowned, but then a memory flickered at the edges of her mind. Pedaling through the woods on bikes, swimming in the lake in the summer. Laughing.

"Krister?"

"Ja." He looked around the room. "Looks like you've had some unwanted guests, or one hell of a party." That grin again.

She didn't smile back.

"The former, I guess. I've just called the police."

He nodded. "Just as well. There's been a spate of burglaries in this neighborhood lately, although I thought they'd caught the guy."

She blinked. "You mean there have been others?"

"Earlier in the year." He stepped into the room. "Has this just happened?"

"I—I don't know." Frazzled, she smoothed a hand over her hair. Goodness knows what she must look like. A ten-hour flight and little, if any, sleep. Her clothes had deep rumples that only a good wash and iron would get out. Not that she cared. "I've just got back."

"I know, I saw you get off the bus."

"Oh?"

He cleared his throat. "I mean, I was shoveling snow off the driveway and saw you get off the bus. I recognized you straight away. You haven't changed a bit."

"Since I was twelve?"

He grinned. "With a few noticeable differences."

Avril felt the heat steal into her cheeks. Turning her back on him, she gazed at the mess. "I wonder what they were looking for?"

"Valuables, jewelry." He shrugged. "Anything they could sell. Must have realized the place was empty."

She gave an awkward nod. "We should probably wait outside so we don't disturb anything."

A questioning look.

She cleared her throat. "You know, in case the police want to dust for fingerprints."

"How long are you around for?" he asked, as they walked back outside.

"I'm not sure yet." She inspected the front door. It hadn't been forced, and the lock was intact.

"You here for Christmas?"

"What?" She was still frowning at the unforced entry.

A sideways glance. "You know, the holiday? Sleigh rides, jingle bells, Santa?"

"Oh, yeah. Probably." She couldn't remember when she'd last celebrated Christmas. It always coincided with the Frost Killer's latest killing spree, which meant she was working the case. The last two years, she'd been trawling crime reports, newspaper clippings and online blogs and podcasts searching for mentions of women found lying in the snow. This year would be different.

"You got any plans?"

"I want to clean out the house, put it on the market."

He raised an eyebrow. "You're selling up?"

"No point in keeping it. I don't live here anymore."

He gave a slow nod, studying her through his darkly lashed eyes. She remembered he'd always had long lashes as a kid. "Where *do* you live?"

At that moment, sirens filled the air, getting louder as they approached. A police vehicle pulled over outside her house, and two officers climbed out. They both wore the standard uniform of the Swedish Police: dark-blue combat-style trousers with a police duty belt, a long sleeve button-up shirt, a heavy-duty jacket with the Swedish Police emblem on the pocket, and a side-cap embellished with a metal badge.

Avril stepped forward to greet them, but they noticed Krister and immediately straightened up. "Afternoon, sir," the taller one, obviously the lead officer, said. "We didn't realize the Regional Investigation Unit was involved."

"It's not. I happen to live next door. Carry on."

He gave a quick nod and turned back to Avril. "Are you Ms. Dahl?"

"Yes." She shot Krister a curious glance. "I called in the burglary."

"May we take a look inside?"

"Of course."

She left her neighbor in the overgrown yard and took the officers into her father's house. The lead officer pulled out a small notepad and began jotting down details as they walked. "Do you notice anything immediately missing, Ms. Dahl?"

"I haven't had a chance to check thoroughly. I just arrived from the States and found it this way."

"Understood. We'll do a preliminary walkthrough, but a more detailed inventory will be needed later."

After checking every room, most of which were disturbed to some degree, the living room and master bedroom being the worst affected, the officer radioed in for a forensic technician. "We'll have our expert come in and dust for prints. They should be here within the hour. In the meantime, please avoid touching anything."

Avril nodded.

"Is there anywhere else you can stay, Ms. Dahl?"

"No, I've just got here. I'm not going anywhere else." A shower, a nap, and some decent food would make her feel better. Traveling always wore her out.

"Well if you could avoid the living room and main bedroom, that would be helpful. We'll need those areas undisturbed for the forensic analysis. The expert will take photographs, collect evidence, and dust for fingerprints."

"Okay." She knew the drill. There was her old room she could sleep in. It didn't look like that had been ransacked. There was also a spare room that her father used to bunk in from time to time, usually when he'd had too much to drink and didn't want to wake her mother with his snoring.

The officers left. As she walked them out, she glanced around for Krister, but he'd disappeared, presumably back inside his house with the newly swept driveway.

Krister Jansson. After all these years.

Standing in the weak midday sun, she surveyed the property. His, not hers. It was well kept, the garden was neat and looked after, the old tree near the gate was still there. Didn't they used to climb it? No, there had been a swing hanging from one of the branches, but that was long gone. He must have inherited the house from his parents. What were their names again?

She frowned, wracking her brains, then it hit her. Hilda and Linus Jansson. They'd joined in the search for her mother the night she'd vanished, along with several other neighbors and friends. Even strangers had joined the search party—not that it did any good. Little did they know that twenty-four hours later, they'd find her mother's body in a clearing less than a mile from where she'd gone missing.

Avril swallowed, forcing the unpleasant memory from her mind, and went back into the house.

chapter
three

SHE DIDN'T HAVE TO WAIT LONG FOR THE FORENSIC EXPERT TO arrive. A tall, gangly man, he wordlessly dusted all the surfaces in the living room and master bedroom for prints. "You got here fast," she'd commented when he'd first arrived, but all she got was a "this job got moved to the top of the pile," in reply.

She suspected that living next door to a lead regional investigator might be the reason, but she didn't say as much. After the two officers had left earlier, she'd powered up her laptop and Googled Krister Jansson. To her surprise, he'd had quite a distinguished career in the Swedish Police Force, moving from Robbery, which had been his first posting, to the Regional Investigation Unit, and then to lead detective the year before last.

Unlike her.

Her boss in Washington had been only too happy to sign off on her leave. "Take all the time you need," were his parting words. Officially, she was due back mid-January, but she suspected they'd try to shunt her to a different department where she couldn't make a fool of herself or the bureau.

The fingerprint expert left, taking his equipment with him. "You get anything?" she asked, as she saw him out.

"Too many," he replied with a shrug.

Great.

Avril knew from working her own crime scenes that too many fingerprints were as useless as no fingerprints. How many people had walked through this living room over the years? Not just family and friends, but police officers, medical examiners, forensic technicians. How many medics and emergency personnel had come in when her father had suffered his heart attack?

The bedroom might be easier as not many people would have been in there, apart from her mother, father, herself and the burglar. Perhaps they'd get lucky.

After locking up, Avril stared at the mess that was the living room. She'd managed a shower and a short nap while she'd been waiting for the fingerprint expert, and she'd eaten a sandwich that she'd brought with her from the airport. It hadn't tasted too bad after she'd washed it down with some strong, black coffee that she'd found in the cupboard, which, remarkably, was still in date.

"Where to begin?" she muttered, as she bent down to pick up the scattered cushions. After plumping them back into shape and placing them on the sofa, she picked up everything that wasn't broken and put it back where she thought it belonged, although why she bothered, she wasn't sure. It would all be packed away in boxes or taken to a charity shop soon anyway.

After an hour of cleaning, she heard a knock on the door. She could guess who that was. Peeking through the peephole, she saw she was right.

Krister, her neighbor, the homicide detective.

"Hi," she said, after opening the door.

"You busy?" he asked.

"I'm tidying up."

"I thought you might be. I came to see if you wanted some help."

Didn't he have a wife at home? Kids? Her gaze dropped to his left hand. No wedding ring. Still, why was he here offering to help? They hadn't spoken in over ten years, and even back then, they'd only been childhood playmates. Neighbors, thrown together because their parents were friends. They'd been close at one point, but it wasn't like they were best buddies or anything.

"Oh, thanks. That's very kind of you, but I'm fine."

"You sure?" He peered around her into the hallway. "Because it looked like quite a mess when I saw it."

"I'm almost done," she lied, still holding the door half open.

"Alright, then." He took a step back, giving her space. "Sorry to disturb."

"It's okay. Thanks again."

"See you around, Avril." She gave a half-wave as he walked away.

After locking up and pulling the bolt across, she got back to work.

The first thing that caught her eye was an old box of vinyl records that had been upended. She remembered her mother playing classical music while she did the housework. They'd had a record player that was still in the side cabinet, but it hadn't been used in years. Carefully, she righted the box and picked an LP up off the floor. It had fallen further than the others.

Beethoven. Piano Concertos Nos. 1-5. Mahler Chamber Orchestra.

Intrigued, she took it over to the cabinet. Would the old record player even work after all this time? She dusted it off, slipped the LP onto the turntable, and after blowing the dust off the needle, lowered it onto the vinyl.

It crackled, then settled into a groove and started playing. Avril stood back and listened as the soft murmur swelled into the room like a gentle tide. The clear, crisp sounds of the piano, the vigorous allegro con brio, full of drama and yet with an underlying promise of resolution.

As the piano danced through the intricate cadenza, Avril was transported back to her childhood, playing with her toys in her room while the sheer power and beauty of the music reverberated through the house.

Feeling emotional, she sat down, closed her eyes, and allowed the waves of the allegro, the adagio, and the rondo to wash over her. How long she sat there, she didn't know, but when the music stopped, she opened her eyes and found her cheeks were wet.

"Silly me," she murmured, wiping her face on her sleeve. It wasn't often she gave in to tears. Of frustration, maybe, but hardly ever emotional. Sniffing, she got up and took the record off the player. No more of that nonsense or she'd be a blithering wreck before the night was over.

The living room took most of the evening, and it was past eleven o'clock when she finished. Thank goodness she'd taken that nap earlier. Unable to keep her eyes open a moment longer, she stumbled upstairs to her bedroom and collapsed onto the bed. In seconds, she was fast asleep.

THE MORNING SUN blasted through the curtainless window and hit her full in the face. For a minute she didn't know where she was. Then she remembered. Sweden. Stockholm. Home.

She turned away from the glare. The sun was always low in the sky at this time of year. It set early, too. If they got six hours of daylight, it was a lot.

Reaching over to the bedstand, she picked up her phone and checked the time. Nine a.m. With a groan, she got out of bed.

She had an apple and a squidgy chocolate bar for breakfast, followed by more black coffee. Not ideal. She needed to go to the grocery store after she'd tackled her father's bedroom. Funny how she didn't think of it as her mother's anymore, even though for most of the time she'd been here, her parents had shared it.

The dresser had been ransacked, which wasn't a surprise. It was the first place a burglar would look. The drawers were open, the contents sifted through. They wouldn't have found anything, though. Her father had gotten rid of most of her mother's things after she died. Unable to accept that she hadn't been having an affair, he'd packed up all her jewelry and taken it to the pawn brokers.

The twelve-year-old, Avril hadn't realized what was going on, but the sixteen-year-old did. They'd had a blazing argument when she found out what he'd done. He hadn't even asked her if she'd wanted any of it. The only piece of jewelry she had with any connection to her mother was the snowflake pendant the Frost Killer had hung around her neck.

There was a stale scent in the drawer. Avril leaned forward and sniffed. Jasmine, or was it violet? It smelled like a long-forgotten memory. Like her mother. Startled, she stood up straight and took a deep, steadying breath. The nostalgia passed.

By mid-day she was starving. The chocolate and coffee made her queasy, so she took a walk to the grocery store, less than a mile away. The fresh air helped. Once her father's stuff was cleared out, she could put the house on the market and that chapter of her life would be closed. No more haunted memories. No more hunting for a man she would never find. She could move on.

It was on the way back from the store that she began to feel uneasy. Nothing she could put her finger on, just a vague sense that someone was following her. Turning, she didn't see anything unusual. The street was scattered with people, but she didn't know any of them. Still, her sixth sense told her something was up.

A colleague in the FBI used to say that a person's gut shouldn't be ignored. He would often remind the team that our instincts were the result of millennia of evolution, finely tuned to detect danger even when our conscious mind couldn't. The brain was capable of picking up and processing multiple patterns of information that weren't consciously perceived, like a supercomputer running in the background. It could be a fleeting shadow, an unusual sound, or a subtle shift in someone's body language. These seemingly insignificant details could trigger a gut reaction, a primal sense of unease that something wasn't right. If more people listened to their intuition, especially women, there'd be fewer muggings and random attacks.

A bus stopped beside her, and on a whim, she hopped on. Nobody else got on with her. If anyone had been following her, she'd left them behind. Avril stayed on the bus as it went up her street, past her house, and around the parkland toward the next suburb. Twenty minutes later, she got off and called an Uber. The driver took her home.

It was getting dark when she unlocked her front door. Shivering, she made a mental note to leave the lights on next time she went out. She couldn't detect any unfamiliar sounds in the house, but she still felt nervous.

For the second time since she'd arrived back in Sweden, she wished she'd had her service pistol, but since she was officially on leave, she hadn't been able to bring it with her. U.S. federal regulations and international laws were strict about transporting firearms, especially for law enforcement officers traveling abroad. Bringing it to Sweden, where she lacked jurisdiction and legal authority to carry a firearm, was out of the question.

Same went for the taser and pepper spray. While non-lethal, these items also fell under strict regulations, and she didn't want to risk any legal complications. Here, she was just another civilian, bound by the local laws and protocols.

Closing the front door, she flipped a switch, and the hallway flooded with light. Some of her nervousness dissipated. Tiptoeing into the living room, she picked up a poker from its spot next to the fireplace. The metal felt cold and hard in her hand and gave her a much-needed sense of security.

Avril spent the next ten minutes systematically checking the entire house, weapon in hand. She peeked under the beds, opened the wardrobes, and even checked the attic, but nothing appeared amiss. All the doors and windows were locked, and nothing looked out of place. Perhaps she'd imagined the creepy sensation on the way back from the store. It could be residual unease from arriving home and finding her house had been burgled.

After supper, Avril went back to her father's bedroom. He didn't have much in the way of jewelry, but she found his watch and a box of cufflinks on the floor beside the dresser with a small card inside. It read, *from Olivia*. Her mother. The burglar must've known they weren't valuable.

Under the bed, she found an old shoebox. In it were a bunch of yellowed documents, folded and stored and forgotten about. Probably her mother's doing. Sitting on the floor, she went through them one by one. Her parents' marriage certificate, her mother's passport, her father's passport, her birth certificate. She studied them for a long time. How young were her parents when these passport photographs were taken? Neither had been renewed over the years.

Her birthday was on January 6th, just over two weeks away. She'd be turning twenty-eight in the new year. It hardly seemed real. Inside, she was still that tragic little girl who'd lost her mother. The anger and resentment hadn't left her, but after ten years of seeking justice— or was it vengeance?—she was tired. Ten years running after *him*. Like a relationship that had gone sour, she'd woken up and realized she'd thrown away a decade of her life on someone. Years she couldn't get back.

Looking up, she noticed a framed photograph on the dresser. She was standing between her smiling parents and must have been about nine or ten when it was taken. They were on holiday at the seaside. She remembered that day. Windswept smiles, ice cream and sunbathing. They looked happy. An idyllic summer.

Avril stared at the carefree smile on the little girl's face. She'd had no idea then that it would all come to an end. That her life would fall apart, and nothing would ever be the same.

The photograph was skewed in the frame. Unable to ignore it, she stood up, picked it up and took off the back to straighten it. That's when she found the second photograph. It was tucked behind the first. Another smiling picture, but this time of her mother... with another man.

Blinking, Avril gaped at the stranger in the photo. Who on earth was he? The man stood side-on to the camera so she couldn't make out his features, other than the dark glossy hair brushed off his forehead, an angular jawline, a dimple in his left cheek, and the crease in his face that told her he was smiling. But it was the enamored look on her mother's face that said it all.

Her mother's eyes, usually a steely blue, sparkled with warmth and affection as she gazed up at him. The corners of her lips turned up in a soft, almost shy smile, a look Avril had rarely seen on her. It was a smile reserved for someone special, someone who had captured her heart.

Exhaling, she stared at the man. The long, tailored coat looked expensive, its fine wool draping perfectly over his broad shoulders. He seemed to exude a quiet confidence. Her mother's dress glittered in the soft lighting, the sequins catching the light and casting tiny reflections around them. Her blonde hair—the same color as her daughter's—was swept off her face in an elegant chignon, the way Avril sometimes wore hers. It was the kind of hairstyle her mother reserved for special occasions.

Their body language spoke volumes. His arm was wrapped around her waist, pulling her close, while her hand rested lightly on his chest, her fingers splayed as if she could feel the beating of his heart. There was a natural ease and closeness between them, a silent conversation conveyed through their touch and expressions. The way he leaned slightly towards her, the protective stance of his body, and the gentle tilt of her head towards him painted a picture of mutual affection and connection.

Avril didn't recognize the man, not from the parties they used to have when she was younger, not from the neighborhood, and not from her mother's work. Yet, it was clear they shared something profound. The photograph captured a fleeting moment of pure, unguarded emotion, a glimpse into a side of her mother's life Avril had never known.

Olivia Dahl had been a personal assistant for a firm of architects. On the odd occasion, she'd accompany her mother to work, though she couldn't remember why. She'd sit quietly at a desk in the corner reading or doing her homework while her mother answered the phone, typed up reports, and made countless cups of coffee.

Occasionally, her mother would be invited to an event, and her father would accompany her. They'd get dressed up, and her mother would style her hair and apply red lipstick to her pale face. They'd come home late, laughing and breathless, and go straight up the stairs to their bedroom. She didn't know when that had changed, but before her mother's death, her father spent more and more time in the spare room.

Avril turned the picture over and stared at the faded words on the back.

Michael?

And there was an address.

chapter
four

IT WAS THE TELEPHONE CALLS THAT CONVINCED THE POLICE and her father that Olivia had been having an affair. Multiple calls in the month before she'd died to a man listed in her phone only as Michael. That, and the necklace.

Nobody could understand where the snowflake pendant her mother had been wearing when they'd found her body had come from. She hadn't had it on earlier in the day, and none of her friends or family had seen it before. It was unusual too, not something you'd easily forget. A delicate paper cutout encased in glass, attached to a silver chain.

It was several years and countless victims later before Avril had pieced it together. The necklace was the killer's calling card. A parting gift to stamp his mark on the women whose lives he'd taken. Even now, the thought gave her goosebumps, and her hand rose automatically to her own neck.

Still, her father hadn't believed her. Didn't *want* to believe her. He'd insisted Olivia's lover had given it to her.

Avril pulled out the thick, dog-eared folder containing the fifteen-year-old police report. The folder was battered and worn, its edges frayed and its corners bent from years of handling. The once crisp manila cover had yellowed with age, and the ink on the tab labeling the case number had faded to an almost illegible smudge.

Handling it was just a habit, she knew the details by heart. Inside, the pages were a mix of brittle, yellowed reports and more recent notes she had added over the years. The original documents bore the characteristic typewritten font of the early 2000s, interspersed with handwritten annotations in the margins. Coffee stains and smudges hinted at many late nights spent trying to piece together the puzzle.

Michael Forsberg. Colleague. 40 years old. Married. Four children.

Michael Olsson. Family doctor. 45 years old. Married. Two children.

Michael Brolin. Reporter. 34 years old. Single. Gay?

These are the notes she'd made when she'd looked into it as a fresh-faced cop straight out of the National Police Academy in Stockholm—before she'd left Sweden for the U.S. and joined the Bureau. She'd revisited the report numerous times over the last decade, and every time it was the same. There was no new information, and the three possible Michaels she'd found in her mother's life all had alibis for the time of death. None of them had left Sweden, and since the Frost Killer had left Scandinavia and taken his brazen acts of killing to America, it couldn't be any of them.

She paused, gnawing on her lower lip. Why had the killer left Sweden? That was something she'd never figured out. Was it because she'd been onto him? Had she gotten too close? Or had he, as the Colorado Sheriff's partner, the psychologist Becca, had said, tried to give up, to reinvent himself and put his sordid past behind him, only to find he couldn't? The urges ran too deep.

She massaged her forehead. Now they'd never know.

Avril scanned the names on the list. Michael Forsberg had been one of the partners in the architect firm. Avril remembered him as a tall, slender man with long, pale fingers. On the rare occasions her mother had taken her into the office, she'd watched him work at his desk, etching out complicated drawings and angles and layouts. It had fascinated her. The precision, the attention to detail. She'd even considered architecture herself for a while, but after her mother's murder, all thoughts other than law enforcement had flown from her head.

Forsberg had been on holiday in Sardinia with his family when her mother went missing. He'd come home to the news that his personal assistant had been murdered a week later. Avril hadn't seen his reaction, but they'd spoken at length several years later when she'd grown up and been assigned to the case. He'd been devastated to hear the news. "Olivia was such a lovely woman," he had said. "Bubbly, good-natured, but also efficient and hard-working. She performed her job well, and they couldn't fault her. She'd be sorely missed."

Sorely missed. What an awful phrase. It was what everyone said. Avril doubted any of them remembered her mother now—sorely or otherwise. She checked the address she had on file for Michael Forsberg. Neither his work nor his home address matched the one in her father's jerky scrawl on the back of the photograph.

Yawning, she reached for her coffee. Jetlag was setting in, and she struggled to keep her eyes open. The early darkness didn't help. It was only five o'clock in the afternoon, but already it was pitch-black outside. She drew the curtains, the same ones that had been in her father's room for as long as she could remember. Old and hopelessly out of date, they had an olive-colored paisley design on them. Why had he never changed them? Like most men, he probably hadn't thought about those things.

Next was Dr. Michael Olsson, the family doctor. Avril recalled being taken to him when she'd sliced open her foot playing on a construction site. With Krister, in fact. It was summer, and a house was being renovated down the road. Builders had left piles of bricks and bags of sand on site, a magnet to two young, adventurous kids—until she'd torn her foot on the corner of a brick and had to be rushed to surgery for stitches. She still had the scar, all these years later.

She wondered if Krister remembered that. He'd carried her home, gasping under her weight. Not that she'd been heavy, but because he'd only been about ten at the time, possibly younger. The edges were a little hazy.

Avril looked up the surgery address. Not a match. The same went for the doctor's personal residence where he had lived with his wife and two children. In any event, she remembered the doctor had been at a medical conference in Denmark during her mother's disappearance. He'd been back when her body had been found, however, because he'd come around and given her father a sedative before checking on Avril. Kind words, a sympathetic look, an awkward tussle of the hair.

It had only been later that she'd met Michael Brolin. He hadn't been part of their life before her mother's death. As the first reporter on the scene, Michael Brolin had covered her mother's disappearance and then her murder. It had made his career. Strange how one person's misfortune could be another person's blessing. Like a predator, preying on the victims of a crime. That's how she'd seen it at the time anyway.

Now, her views were different. She still didn't like reporters, but she knew the crimes would keep happening regardless, and they felt they had a duty to the public to report it. A bit like law enforcement officers, really. They were there to analyze the damage, build a case, and find those responsible. At least there was some form of retribution there, a justice that may come too late for the victim, but it was better than not at all.

She sniffed and glanced down at his address. Neither the newspaper he worked for nor his home address matched the one her father had jotted down.

Sighing, she opened her laptop and Googled the address. Nothing. Not a property listing, not an area code, just a map reference. Clicking on it, she went to the street view, but the images were too small or set back from the road to see the numbers on the doors.

Rubbing her eyes, she got to her feet. Stiffness from inactivity made her sluggish. What she needed was some fresh air.

Picking up the photograph, she slipped it into her jean pocket and then retrieved her coat. It was time to find out where the mysterious address on the photograph was.

Avril had just got into the Uber when her cellphone rang. Expecting the police, she was surprised to find it was an international number.

"Hello?"

"Avril, is that you? It's Sheriff Dalton Savage from Hawk's Landing."

"Oh, Sheriff." She frowned. "It's good to hear from you."

Not really.

Hawk's Landing was one place she wanted to put firmly in her rearview mirror. "I saw you got your man. Congratulations."

She'd followed the case in the news. His department had managed to catch the copycat killer before he'd murdered his fourth victim.

"Thank you, but that's not why I called."

"It's not?" She couldn't figure out why he wanted to speak to her. She'd messed up his investigation, thrown his team off the track of the true killer because she'd been so adamant it was the Frost Killer up to his old tricks. If that's how you'd describe drugging and leaving young women outside in the cold to freeze to death, that is. Closing her eyes, she tried to blot out the memory.

"No, there's something else. Something I think you should know."

"Oh?"

"I received a letter yesterday. It came to my home address, via the mail, but I think it was meant for you."

"What did it say?" Her pulse ticked up a notch.

"It's hard to explain. I'll send you some photographs. They're going through now."

Her phone beeped.

The first was of an envelope with his name and address on it. Sheriff Savage, Apple Tree Farm, Hawk's Landing, and the zip code. It had been postmarked Stockholm. That gave her pause. Who would send him mail from here? Certainly not her.

Heart in her throat, she opened the next picture. A postcard with an image of Stockholm on the front. The image was vibrant, almost garishly so, with bold splashes of yellow, red, and blue. It depicted the city's iconic skyline in an art deco style, with exaggerated lines and curves that gave the buildings a surreal, almost dreamlike quality. The Royal Palace stood majestically in the foreground, its turrets and spires rendered in bright, almost neon hues. In the background, the famous Ericsson Globe loomed large, painted in a striking shade of azure, standing out against the deep blue of the surrounding water.

Above the skyline, a brilliant sunburst design radiated outward, its rays fanning across the top of the postcard, adding to the retro, nostalgic feel of the artwork. She shivered, unsettled. This was a city she knew intimately, but it suddenly felt alien and threatening.

The third picture was of a snowflake cutout laying on a wooden table. Her hands trembled as she zoomed in. It was identical to the Frost Killer's other designs. The same pattern that had been placed on the frozen bodies of his victims. Four a year, for twelve years, barring the last three.

"Oh, God," she whispered into the phone.

"Look at the last image," Savage said quietly.

Quaking, she followed his instructions. Her breath caught in her throat. Hand-written, in capitals, on the back of the postcard was: THIS ONE IS FOR AGENT DAHL.

chapter
five

THE WORDS SEEMED TO PULSE ON THE SCREEN, EACH LETTER A hammer blow to her senses. She glanced around the darkening street through the window of the Uber, half-expecting to see a shadowy figure watching her. Her skin crawled, and the hair on the back of her neck stood up. "What does it mean?" she croaked, her voice barely above a whisper.

"Avril, he's coming for you," Savage said grimly. "I don't know why he sent this to me, and not to you directly, but it's got to be from him."

Avril couldn't speak. Couldn't think. The sides of the Uber seemed to close in on her, and she began to hyperventilate.

"Stop the car!" she demanded.

"But we're not there yet," the driver insisted.

"Stop the car. I need to get out."

He pulled over. Gasping for air, she scrambled out of the vehicle, her hands shaking as she fumbled with the door handle.

"Want me to wait?" the driver asked, concerned.

Shaking her head, she waved him off. He shrugged, and pulled away, muttering something about a crazy lady.

"Avril?" Savage asked from the phone, his voice distant and tinny. "Avril, are you there?"

"I'm here." Her voice was weak. She took a few more deep breaths, trying to steady herself. "I'm here," she repeated, stronger now.

"You should show this to the police. You have no jurisdiction outside of the U.S., no protection. If you're on your own, you're vulnerable."

"I know." She thought for a moment, the weight of the situation pressing down on her. "Could it be a joke? A message from the copycat?"

"He was in custody when I received this. It's postmarked Sweden. He's there, Avril. He's in Stockholm."

Her legs buckled, and she sank onto a low wall outside a row of houses. The driver had dropped her in a wide avenue lined with bare trees, their twisted branches grappling at the sky, reaching for something that wasn't there. Kind of like her.

"Why now?" she whispered.

"I think he's pissed," Savage said. "The copycat killer stole his thunder and didn't do a particularly good job of it. He was sloppy. Got some of the details wrong. Ended up getting himself arrested. The real Frost Killer didn't like that."

A surge of something she couldn't identify coursed through her veins. Adrenaline? Anticipation? Excitement? "This means he's alive," she hissed. "Dalton, he's not dead or in prison. He's alive."

There was a pause.

"It also means he's got his sights on you, Avril. Remember, you're just his type. You fit the profile too."

But she wasn't listening. All she could think about was that he was here.

He was here.

Her mother's murderer. The man she'd been hunting for ten years, who'd been killing for fifteen, was here in Stockholm, and he wanted her to know it.

She felt a strange, almost euphoric relief wash over her. Her entire life had been defined by the hunt for this man, and now he was within reach. It was as if a fog had lifted, revealing a clear path ahead.

She felt giddy with relief.

AFTER SAYING goodbye to the Sheriff and promising to be careful, she walked down the avenue toward the bus stop. The wind whipped her hair around her face, stinging her eyes, but she didn't care.

He was alive.

For the last two years—three, if you counted this winter—she'd thought she'd lost him. That, for whatever reason, he'd stopped killing, and her chance to catch him had disappeared. She now knew that wasn't true. The copycat had drawn him out.

Who would have thought that stupid wannabe serial killer with his outsourced snowflakes and messy preparation had actually served a purpose? He'd rankled the real killer enough to come out of hiding.

A chill passed over her that had nothing to do with the steel-colored clouds moving in. Was that who had been inside her house? Had he ransacked the place to make it look like a burglary? One thing she knew for sure was that the Frost Killer stalked his victims before he killed them. He learned their routines until he was familiar enough with their pattern to ambush them without anyone seeing.

He often broke into their houses to take a look around. Made it personal. It heightened the excitement for him. She shivered as she imagined him standing in her living room, his cold eyes scanning her belongings, touching the objects she held dear. What had he seen? What had he touched?

What if he'd been watching her ever since she arrived? She pictured him lurking outside her window, his breath fogging the glass as he observed her tidying up, sitting on the sofa, eating, crying.

But he couldn't have found the photograph with the address on the back. Her father had hidden it too well. Was he Michael? Was that the Frost Killer's real name?

She scratched her head. So many unanswered questions.

As she walked, Avril tried to decide what to do. If she called her boss at the FBI headquarters in D.C., he'd just tell her he'd had enough. The case was closed. How many times had she convinced him to reopen the investigation only for it to go nowhere? Five or six times. Years of fruitless chasing, of pointless travel expenses and expensive hotel bills, countless resources wasted. *No more,* he'd said, after she'd lost *him* yet again. *You've been reassigned.*

Would he reopen it one last time? She doubted it. He certainly wouldn't send anyone to Sweden to help her. Nobody wanted to be involved in a career-ending investigation. That's what he'd called it the last time they'd spoken.

Gnawing on her lower lip, Avril walked down the street. She passed the bus stop but barely noticed. The exertion helped her think. The address was only a couple of blocks away now. She'd keep going until she got there, despite the cold making her eyes water and her glasses mist up.

There was one man who could possibly help her. A childhood friend who now worked for the Swedish Police's Regional Investigation Unit in Stockholm. A man who'd tried to be nice but whom she'd shut down, not wanting any personal connection right now.

Krister.

Would he understand? Would he believe her? Her stomach twisted with doubt. Reaching out to him meant exposing herself, admitting that she needed help. But she was all out of options, and the revelation that he was here, in Stockholm, meant she had to act.

Making her mind up, she rubbed her hands together and upped her walking pace. She'd go around to Krister's the moment she got back. Right now, she wanted to check out this location her father had thought important enough to write on the back of an old photograph of her mother with a handsome stranger.

THE STREETS GREW NARROWER as Avril ventured deeper into an unfamiliar part of the city. The afternoon light was fading, casting long shadows that stretched across the pavement. The neighborhood had a rougher edge, with more apartment blocks than free-standing houses. Litter clogged the gutters, and the fences and walls surrounding the properties were either broken or covered in graffiti. She could hear the distant hum of traffic, but the streets themselves were eerily quiet, with only a few pedestrians hurrying along, heads down against the cold.

This wasn't an area she was familiar with. She'd never had any reason to come to this part of the city before, didn't even know what it was called. The address on the photograph led her here, and she hoped it would provide some clue.

Glancing down at the address again, she double-checked the number. Nine.

She looked up, eyes searching the properties. That was number five and that was number seven, so the next house should be number nine. Except it wasn't. There was a vacant plot, and the next one was number eleven.

Avril stared at the empty plot for a long time. It looked like the property standing there had been bulldozed to the ground many, many years ago. There was no debris from the remnants of the building. Nothing left behind but cold, hard dirt punctuated with small mounds of snow.

A realtor sign creaked and strained in the wind. *Karlsson Real Estate*. There was a contact number.

Retrieving her phone, Avril took a photograph of the signpost. Maybe the realtor would know what had happened to the structure that used to stand here.

Like everything else in this case, the building that had been at this address was an apparition. A phantom piece of evidence that had disappeared along with everything else she'd ever found. And like the others, it would haunt her until she uncovered the truth or gave up trying.

But she wouldn't give up, not now that she knew *he* was here. In Stockholm.

There'd been a shift in the killer's motivation, she could feel it. Something had changed. Whether it was the copycat, or the fact that she'd come back to Sweden, she didn't know, but for the Frost Killer, this had become personal.

Well, it had been personal for her right from the start. This was what she'd been waiting for.

"I'm going to get you now," she muttered, balling her hands into fists. "You're not going to get away this time."

Avril took some pictures of the vacant lot to show the realtor, and then after a last, lingering look, she tightened her coat around her slim frame, pushed her glasses up her nose, and hurried away.

chapter
six

It was the flashing lights that first grabbed her attention. They lit up the inky sky like a strobe. As she got closer, she realized there was a fervor of emergency vehicles at the end of her street.

"Keep going," she told the cab driver, who'd slowed right down. He crawled past her house and dropped her next to the ambulance.

"You sure?" he asked, uncertainly, peering out of the window at the emergency personnel scurrying around.

"Yes, thank you." She climbed out and followed two paramedics carrying a stretcher down a snow-covered track and into the dark woods that began at the end of her street. Someone had placed battery operated lamps along the route to show the way.

Heart thumping, she muttered, "It can't be. Not again. Not here."

Yet, inside, she knew the truth.

She was running now, overtaking the paramedics, her shoes crunching on the snow. She knew this path so well she could navigate it blindfolded, so the darkness didn't bother her. Through the dense woods, around a bend where the snow had been packed down into a slick, glassy surface. She slipped, catching herself on the gnarled trunk of a tree that seemed to lean in, hovering over her like a silent sentinel.

Picking herself up, she hurried along the straight where the trees evened out, shadows from the small lights loomed around her. Through a narrow, rocky bit, where she slowed down, avoiding the jagged stones that jutted out from the ground, partially covered by snow.

Finally, she reached a small creek, the water frozen against the rocky bed. She stepped across it with practiced ease and kept on going. The path opened into a clearing, a small, almost perfectly circular area where the trees pulled back to reveal the night sky. The area was lit up by powerful police lights and cordoned off. Yellow police tape wound around the trees, encircling a troop of uniformed officers hunched in the middle.

Avril steeled herself. She knew what she would see before she saw it. Heart pounding, she inched closer.

There it was. The body. Encased in snow.

Blonde hair, pale face, hands folded over her chest. A sleeping corpse.

"Oh, God!" she cried out, causing heads to turn.

One of the officers approached her. "Miss, this is a restricted area. You can't be here."

She ignored him, wrapping her arms around herself to fend off the cold.

"Miss, I must ask you to—"

"It's okay." A familiar voice interrupted. Blinking, she saw it was Krister. "She's with me."

"It's the same, isn't it?" she whispered, coming forward.

He took her aside. "Avril, what are you doing here?"

"I saw the lights. It's happening again, isn't it? Just like before."

He stared at her for a moment, then nodded. "Yes."

"Oh, God." She closed her eyes. "It's him."

He frowned. "You know who did this?"

She nodded, then with a trembling hand, reached into her coat pocket and pulled out her FBI badge. He gazed at it for a long time, then he said, "You and I need to talk. Now."

They went back to his house with its freshly scraped driveway and the neat front yard. A black SUV with a police number plate stood outside. It had to be his. The police got standard issue patrol cars. Lead detectives got those.

"You're freezing," he said, seeing her shaking.

"I'm fine."

"Do you want some coffee?"

She shook her head.

Shrugging, he sat down opposite her at his dining table. It was large and rustic, standing on a thick woven rug. Avril traced one of the striations in it with her finger.

"Avril," he said, making her look up. "What are you really doing here?"

She bit her lip. "I'm on leave. I came home to sort out my father's things, to sell the house."

"Really?"

"I thought that was it, that it was over, that he'd gone. But now he's here. Killing again."

"Look, you need to start from the beginning. I remember what happened to your mother. I watched the search party go into the woods the night she disappeared. I saw them come back emptyhanded."

Avril felt hot tears burn her eyes. Blinking furiously, she said, "I've been hunting him, the man who killed her."

He stared at her. "What? All this time?"

She nodded. "When I left home, I joined the police academy. I qualified, then worked on the beat for a few years, but all the time I was investigating my mother's murder. I knew he was still killing. Different girls, four a year, in various locations around Scandinavia. The police hadn't linked the murders."

"But you had?"

She nodded. "I presented my case to the District Chief, and he recruited me on the spot. I worked the case with his team, until the killings stopped."

"They stopped?" He frowned.

"Well, they stopped here, but they started up again in America. Identical killings. Exactly the same MO. Wyoming came first. Then Washington. Then Minnesota. After that, he moved to Oregon, followed by New Hampshire. Each year, four girls, frozen in the snow."

He stared at her. "How many has he killed?"

"Fifty-two, fifty-three if you include this one."

His eyes widened. "Fifty-three women?"

There was a brief pause as Krister struggled to absorb what she'd told him.

"That's why you joined the FBI," he finally murmured.

A nod. "I was on loan to them in the beginning, but then they offered me a permanent position on condition that I did the training at Quantico. Twenty weeks later, I became a special agent."

He pursed his lips, clearly impressed, except it wasn't about the title. She would have done anything to keep hunting her mother's killer.

"Ever get close?"

"Once." She glanced down at her hands. A few weeks ago she'd told this exact same story to Sheriff Savage and his deputies in Colorado. "In Chicago. A girl got attacked, but she managed to fight him off."

"That was lucky. Did she get a look at him?"

"Briefly. She described him as having dark hair, dark eyes, and being good looking." She shrugged. "We had her sit with an artist, but the attack was too quick for her to remember much. He came at her from behind, so she only got a fleeting glance before she passed out. That's his MO, you see. He uses chloroform to knock out his victims. Once they're unconscious, he positions them in the snow so they freeze to death."

Krister gave a low whistle. "What makes you so sure this is him? I mean, apart from the fact the victim was found in the same clearing as your mother."

"Because he told me."

"He what?" The homicide detective blinked at her.

"Indirectly," she corrected, pulling out her phone. After bringing up the photographs Sheriff Savage had sent, she passed the device to him. "This came for me."

Krister studied them in silence. When he was done, he fixed his hazel eyes on her. "What's with the snowflake?"

"He leaves them on his victim's bodies." She sighed. "You'll find one on her, too." She nodded toward the window.

"Why?"

"It's his calling card. He handmakes them. Painstakingly carves them himself. Four, every year. One for each victim."

"That's sick." Krister shook his head.

Avril didn't respond.

He inhaled sharply. "He broke into your house, didn't he? Yesterday, that wasn't a random burglary."

"I don't know that for sure."

"But you suspect it's him, don't you?"

She shrugged. "He stalks his victims before he attacks them. Sometimes he breaks into their houses or apartments. I think it's his way of getting to know them."

"You knew this, yet you stayed alone last night."

She didn't respond.

Krister worked his jaw, his gaze burning into hers. "And the positioning of the body. Here, in the woods, where your mother was found? I'm guessing that's significant too?"

She nodded. "He wants to get my attention. This is his way of sending a message."

Krister's eyes narrowed. "What message would that be?"

"That he's coming for me."

chapter
seven

THEY ARRIVED BACK AT THE CRIME SCENE IN THE WOODS, JUST as the victim was being placed in a black nylon body bag.

Krister went over to speak to the medical examiner, leaving her at the edge of the police cordon. Avril shivered, breathing in a lingering scent of pine and wet snow. The bag was then lifted onto the gurney, and she watched as the medics wheeled it away, the metal wheels crunching on the frozen ground.

The once pristine snow in the clearing was pockmarked with footprints and a large dent where the body had lain. It sparkled under the harsh, artificial light of the police lamps, which also cast long shadows across the frozen ground.

Krister came back over, his breath billowing in front of him. "You were right about the pendant. We found it around her neck." He held up the snowflake necklace in a plastic evidence bag.

She gave a tight nod. "Tell the M.E. to test for chloroform residue on her lips. It'll be easier to pick up than in the bloodstream."

"I'll be sure to mention it."

"Do you have an ID on the victim?"

"Not yet." The corners of his lips turned up. "I forgot how focused you can be when you get fixated on something."

Avril faltered at the familiarity. "She—She'll probably be a young mother. If he's sticking to his original pattern." Which meant there'd be a child out there, like her, bereft. A father, distraught with grief. A family destroyed. Her gloved hands bunched into fists.

Krister pursed his lips. "We don't know it's him yet."

"*Yes,* we do."

"We still have to follow protocol. You know what that's like, right?" He offered a wry smile, but she didn't return it. There was nothing funny about this situation. Shoving his hands in his pockets, he said, "Anyway, I've got to get back to the station."

She nodded.

He hesitated. "What are you going to do?"

"I'm heading home."

"Are you sure that's wise, with a killer on the loose?"

"It's my house. Where else would I go?"

"You could stay at mine," he said, then at her surprised look, cleared his throat. "I mean, I have a spare room. Or ... I could stay at yours, if you like?" When she didn't reply, he added, "For protection."

"Right." She bit her lip. "Thanks, but I'll be fine."

A curt nod, and his gaze hardened. She'd hurt his feelings, she could tell. It couldn't be helped. She didn't want or need a protector. Ever since she could remember she'd lived alone, been alone. It was the only way she knew how to be. "Well, if you need anything, you know where to find me."

"Likewise."

He looked taken aback. She nodded to the evidence bag. "I meant with the investigation."

"Oh, sure."

"I mean it, Krister. I've been hunting this man for years. Nobody knows this case better than me."

"I know that. The problem is you're out of your jurisdiction. This is not an FBI case, it is the Regional Investigation Unit's case, and I don't have the authority to give you access."

Avril bit her lip. "You could ask the Chief. I used to work in the department, remember?" The Regional Investigation Unit investigated Stockholm's more serious crimes. Murder, Rape. Domestic Violence.

"That was a long time ago."

She hesitated. "I'll still be on file somewhere."

He sighed, and rubbed his jawline, shadowed with stubble. "I might be able to use you as a consultant."

She took a sharp breath, but he held up a hand. "I can't promise anything, but I'll make a few calls. Your prior knowledge of the case could be useful."

"It *will* be useful," she corrected. "I know this killer."

He grinned. "You haven't changed."

She didn't know what to say.

"I'll be in touch, Agent Dahl. You take care now."

"I will."

DESPITE WHAT AVRIL had said to Krister, she didn't go home. Instead, she flagged down a patrol car, persuading the officer to drop her off a few streets away from Karlsson Real Estate. The late afternoon air was piercingly cold, a chill that gnawed at her bones, and made her eyes water as she trudged down the dimly lit street.

The agency's storefront, nestled between a bakery and a hardware store, emitted a warm, inviting glow, a stark contrast to the bleak twilight outside. Avril pushed open the door, a wave of heat hitting her and making her cheeks tingle. She stripped off her gloves, ignoring the stylish, minimalist décor, and made her way to a desk where a short, heavyset man peered up from his paperwork.

"Can I help you?" His tone was more curious than welcoming.

Avril came to a stop in front of him. "I hope so. I have a question about one of your properties."

"Please, sit." He gestured to an empty chair.

Avril sat down, leaning back. The warmth was relaxing her. "I'm looking for someone who used to live at 9 Morgonsgatan. When I walked past, I noticed it's a vacant plot."

The realtor nodded. "I know the place you mean. It was knocked down over a decade ago, after a bad fire."

Avril straightened up. "A fire?"

"Ja, it was horrific. A man died, burned to death in his bed in the middle of the night. What a way to go, eh?" He shook his head.

"That's terrible," Avril mumbled, a cold dread settling in her stomach. "Do you have a record of who was living there at the time?"

"No, I don't. Sorry."

Her heart sank. This couldn't be the end of the line. "Is there anyone else who might know?"

The realtor thought for a moment. "There was a landlord. He might have a record of who the tenants were, but I wouldn't get your hopes up. You know those kinds of places, so many people go through them."

"What kind of places?"

"Hostels. Bedsits. Attract all kinds of transient types."

She wasn't ready to give up yet. "Do you have his contact details."

"I might, but I'd have to search the database. Why do you want to know?" He gave her a probing look.

"It's part of a police investigation."

He raised an eyebrow. "I see... and you are?"

"Agent Dahl. FBI." She showed him her ID card.

"FBI. Wow. It must be important." Nodding, he turned to his computer.

She waited, the tension in the room thickening as he tapped away at the keyboard. Nearly two minutes passed before he gave a loud grunt. "Got it."

Avril breathed a relieved sigh.

The realtor scribbled the details on a notepad and tore off the page with a flourish. "Here you go, Agent."

"Thank you." She took the paper, her grip firm.

She had a name.

KRISTER JANSSON WALKED into the Stockholm Police Station where the investigation division was housed and went straight to the coffee machine.

Avril Dahl.

She was one of a kind, alright. He remembered her as a child, a whirlwind of platinum blonde hair and frenetic energy. Running faster than him through the woods, swimming farther out in the lake. A forest nymph, a mermaid. Independent, strong-willed and bright. Very bright. Possibly even cleverer than he was, and he'd come top at his class at the academy.

It was no surprise to find out she'd joined the FBI. He'd always wondered what had happened to her after she'd moved away. They were the same age, but he'd joined the academy after college, one of the conditions his father had set for him upon learning he wanted to be a policeman.

First get a degree, then you can do what you want.

So he had. Criminology. A modern degree—he was one of the first intakes. In later years, he'd wondered whether he'd done it to piss off his father, or because he was truly interested in it. Probably a little bit of both.

Avril's mother's death had changed things between them. She'd gone from being impulsive and spontaneous to introverted and melancholic. He'd gone to a different high school, and they'd lost touch. In retrospect, their childhood had ended the day of her twelfth birthday party.

Fitz, one of his officers, came up beside him. "What are you smiling about?"

He hadn't realized he had been. "Nothing. Where are we on the ID of our victim?" Despite the late hour, the office was full. The entire team had been pinged and were arriving in drips and drabs, their Saturday evening ruined.

"Nothing yet. She just got to the morgue."

"Autopsy?"

"Tonight. Eight p.m. Vali will do it."

Krister nodded. Vali Blomgren was one of the city's top examiners. Brilliant, if a little odd. Still, he'd rather Vali be on the case than anyone else. He checked his phone. It wasn't yet eight. There was still time to write up his report, do some research, and head over to the lab.

First, he pulled up Olivia Dahl's murder. He remembered that day, although the events were a little blurred. He'd been twelve, old enough to comprehend what was happening but too young to make any sense of it.

The party at Avril's house had been fun. They'd had an indoor celebration with sandwiches and cakes, and several families from the neighborhood had attended. They'd been a close-knit community. Once.

Funny how the events of his life could be separated into before the

37

murder and after, even though he hadn't thought about it in almost a decade.

The incident had sliced through the community like a wrecking ball, shattering everything in its path. The families didn't get together anymore after that, except to talk in hushed voices about what had happened, or to speculate over whether Hans, Avril's father, had had anything to do with his wife's death.

Even the idea seemed to taint the man. People avoided him, not knowing what to say. They couldn't meet his eye. The poor man was ruined. Then it came out about the affair and rumors flew, spreading like wildfire. Had Hans found out about his wife's indiscretion and killed her after their daughter's party? Perhaps he'd hidden her body in the house and dumped it a few days later? Made up the part about her taking the dog for a walk. The police hadn't searched the house, as far as he could recall.

He scanned the police report from that day. Actually, they had searched the house, but only later, after they'd found her body in the clearing.

It had been a brutal winter. A vicious snowstorm had meant most people had been hunkering down in their houses the day of the murder. No witnesses. No one crazy enough to go out in the storm.

A dog walker had stumbled upon the body and called the police. A detective, Lars Ekberg, had responded. He'd reported that the victim was lying in the center of the clearing, surrounded by deep snow. There had been no footprints or any way to prove she'd been placed there by anyone else. It was as if she'd simply gone for a walk, laid down, and died. Olivia Dahl had frozen to death.

The initial ruling had been suicide.

There was a statement by twelve-year-old Avril Dahl.

Avril: Mummy took Roffe for a walk and didn't come back.

Ekberg: Did you see her leave?

Avril: Um, no, but I heard Roffe barking as they walked down the garden path.

Ekberg: Where were you at this time?

Avril: In my room.

Ekberg had further noted that Avril's bedroom overlooked the garden, and it would have been feasible that she'd heard the dog barking as Olivia Dahl took it for a walk.

The interview continued.

Ekberg: Was your mother happy?

Avril: Yes, it was my birthday.

Ekberg: She wasn't upset about anything? Angry with your father?

Avril: No. They were always happy.

Krister cringed at Avril's naivety.

Apparently, Olivia Dahl had been calling a man named Michael for the last month, often more than once a day. General speculation was they'd been having an affair. As a detective, he knew there could be any number of reasons she'd been speaking to an unidentified man, but he had to admit, an affair made the most sense. Still, he wouldn't have been so quick to draw a line underneath it as the lead investigator had at the time.

Lars Ekberg.

He wondered if he was still around. Krister didn't recognize the name, but then again, it was some time ago and the old guy had probably retired.

"Boss, Vali wants to know if you're heading to the autopsy?" Freddie asked.

"Yeah." He closed his laptop and got up. "Tell him I'll be there in twenty minutes."

KRISTER HATED THE MORGUE. It was cold and industrial, with a sterile smell that made him nauseous. It felt like a meat processing plant, and the deadpan faces of the pathologists and their lab techs only made it more perfunctory. Thank God for Vali. The eccentric medical examiner was a splash of color on a stainless-steel canvas.

"Krister, my man!"

He high-fived the medical examiner, who was dressed head to toe in blue scrubs, a mask, and latex gloves. His thick, unruly hair was as untamable as ever, contrasting with his neat, graying beard, which was perfectly trimmed. "How are you, Vali?"

"Can't complain. Can't complain. Won't get me anywhere."

That much was true.

"You've brought me a beauty today."

Krister cringed. Could a corpse be described as beautiful? Was it even appropriate to say that? He didn't know. Vali was a law unto himself. The only reason the director tolerated him was because he was so damn good at his job.

"Shall we get started?" Krister asked, wanting to move this along.

"Ja, I'm ready to go."

He recalled Avril's suggestion. "Oh, could you check around the victim's mouth for chloroform residue? We think that's how the killer knocked her out."

"Chloroform? Interesting. I haven't come across that in years. Wouldn't necessarily show up on a tox screen either, not unless we were specifically looking for it."

"So I've been told."

Krister took several steps back and watched as Vali did his preliminary observations. The pathologist inspected the body from top to toe, noting every detail with a practiced eye. He paused, examining the hands and fingernails, then looked up. "She's in perfect form. Not an abrasion or contusion on her."

Krister nodded. He'd been able to see from the crime scene that she hadn't been physically injured in any way. "What about sexual assault?" he asked.

Vali pulled the magnifier further down the table and bent over the body. "Nope, everything looks normal. I mean, she's obviously had children, and judging by her wedding ring, I'd say she's sexually active, but there isn't any trauma to the genital area."

Another nod. It was as Avril had said. The victim was a young mother. "Any chance of an ID?"

"I take it you've run her prints?"

"Not yet."

"Okay, let's do it now."

Vali got the digital fingerprint scanner and placed the victim's forefinger on it. It registered with a biometric beep. Krister would now be able to download the print and run it through the various police and criminal databases. Since the signing of the new fingerprint agreement with America, they also had access to millions of international suspects at the tap of a button.

"Thanks." Pulling out his phone, he messaged Freddie back at the station to get the process going. Hopefully, they'd know who she was before long.

"I'm going to do the chloroform test first," Vali said, "before we get started on the wet work."

Krister wished he hadn't drunk quite so much coffee. It was threatening to come up again. "Okay."

He watched while Vali took a swab and rubbed it around her mouth and over her lips. Then he placed it in a test tube and handed it to his assistant, who walked over to a machine in the corner. The assistant, a young technician with dark circles under his eyes, inserted the tube into a mass spectrometer, a machine that hummed with a low, almost soothing sound.

"That should tell us in a few minutes," Vali said, nodding at the technician.

Krister took a few more steps backward as Vali began the incision. This part always left him queasy. For a few moments, the only sounds were a scalpel moving through flesh and the steady hum of the machines. The fluorescent lights cast a harsh, unwavering light on the scene, making the stainless-steel surfaces gleam.

"That's a positive for chloroform," the technician called, waving the swab in the air. "Strong positive."

Krister nodded. Avril had been right. Why wasn't he surprised?

Vali continued his work, now examining the internal organs with meticulous care. "Her lungs are clear, no signs of inhalation injury, which fits with the chloroform theory. Heart looks good, no signs of struggle or panic."

Krister averted his eyes, focusing on the wall behind the body. In his peripheral vision, he could see Vali's hands moving deftly, revealing the layers of the victim's body, each one telling a silent story.

"I'm seeing no signs of a struggle," he continued. "She was probably unconscious when the killer moved her. No defensive wounds."

Krister's mind raced, piecing together the puzzle. The killer was methodical, calculated—just like he had been all those years ago when Avril's mother Olivia had been murdered. The autopsies were practically identical. He watched as Vali completed the Y-incision, his skilled hands unwavering.

"Cause of death is hypothermia," Vali concluded. "No other trauma. She didn't suffer."

Krister exhaled, long and slow. "Thanks, Vali. Let me know if anything else comes up."

Vali nodded, already turning back to the body, lost in his work.

Krister left the morgue, the cold air slapping him in the face. It was a brutal wake-up call. Avril had been right about the chloroform; could she be right about the perpetrator too? Was it even remotely possible that they were dealing with the same person who'd murdered Olivia Dahl over a decade ago?

chapter
eight

After visiting the realtor, Avril decided she'd had enough junk food and took herself out for dinner. Nothing too fancy, just a cozy Italian place she'd spotted earlier. Inside, the restaurant buzzed with life. Candlelight flickered on red-checkered tablecloths, and in the background was the sound of clinking glasses and laughter. The air was thick with the mouthwatering aroma of garlic and fresh basil.

She took a seat, her stomach rumbling. A waiter rushed past balancing a tray of pasta, baskets of bread, and glasses of wine. In the corner, a group were celebrating, joy etched on their laughing faces. When last had she felt like that? She couldn't remember.

The waiter returned and she ordered, adding a glass of red wine as an afterthought. While she waited, she turned to the tattered manila folder she'd brought with her, the one that contained all the important case documents, reports and analyses on the Frost Killer investigation.

Knowing she was rubbing salt into the wound, she re-read the dog-eared reports on her mother's disappearance and murder. The sounds around her—laughter, conversation, the clinking of cutlery—faded into a distant hum.

When this was over, she promised herself, she'd burn the damn folder and everything in it. But only once *he* was caught and behind bars. When his many victims had justice, she could put it behind her and move on with her life.

She wouldn't fail this time. Not now that she had his attention.

The food came and she paused to eat. Not bad. While she sipped her wine, she carried on reading. The number of the mysterious man her mother had been calling was not a registered number, but a prepaid or burner phone. Her father's statement indicated he thought Olivia may have been having an affair.

Avril frowned. Why had he said that? Michael could be anybody. Other than the phone calls, had there been any other indication of her mother's infidelity?

She thought back but nothing came to mind. As far as she could remember, her parents had been happy. They hadn't argued. There'd been no screaming matches or silent treatment. Nothing that would raise an alarm. Why, then, did her father have a photograph of her mother smiling into the eyes of another man?

Her thoughts turned to the dead girl in the woods. It didn't matter so much who she was, but where she'd been found. Avril felt sorry for the family, especially if there were any children left behind. She knew what it felt like to lose a parent in such a way.

The Frost Killer was meticulous in his attention to detail. If he was going to emulate a crime scene, he would do it properly. All the details would be on point. The victim was under thirty, blonde, and slender—a perfect fit for the profile. Her body was positioned in the same place, in the same pose, wearing a snowflake pendant that he would have made himself. Not outsourced like that copycat in Colorado. Avril shuddered at the memory.

This killer was precise. That's why she knew the victim would have had a kid. Probably only one. A girl.

Like her.

Sheriff Savage in Hawk's Landing had said there was always a pattern, even if the killer himself wasn't aware of it. There didn't seem to be any pattern to how this killer had chosen his victims, until now. He was emulating that first murder, going back to his roots, where it all began. He was getting her attention. This was him saying, *I'm back*, and waving a big, red flag in her face.

Avril drank what was left of her wine and asked for the check. Two could play that game, and this time, she was ready.

. . .

THE LIGHTS WERE all on inside the house when she got home, putting her at ease. The hair she'd laid across the crack in the front door was still intact, so she knew nobody had opened the front door. Even so, she still did a quick poker check, just to make sure.

Kicking off her shoes, she decided to sort through all the paperwork she could find and look for something that might give her an indication of who this Michael was, or what had made her father suspicious.

Where had that photograph come from? Either her father had followed her mother and taken it himself, or he'd hired someone to do it. A private investigator, perhaps?

Buoyed by red wine and determination, Avril went to work. Soon, however, it became obvious there was an alarming lack of documentation in the house. Either her father had led a paper trail-free existence, which was unlikely, or he'd thrown a lot of stuff away. Apart from the shoebox under his bed, she couldn't find anything other than instructions for the long non-working dishwasher and various appliances, the deeds to the house, which were in the bureau in the living room, and a couple of receipts. There weren't even any photo albums.

It was almost as if he'd known he was going to die.

Feeling emotional, Avril stacked what she had found together and took it upstairs to the shoebox. At least then everything would be in one place. She really should have come back to see him before the heart attack, but how do you undo seven years of silence?

Hey, Dad. I'm home. Let's hang out.

She hadn't spoken to him since the day she'd walked out on her seventeenth birthday. That's how old she'd been when she'd joined the police academy. They wouldn't let her join any younger—she'd asked.

A loud knock on the front door made her jump. She glanced at her phone. Nearly midnight. Who would visit this late? Grabbing the poker, which went everywhere with her now, she tiptoed downstairs. "Who is it?"

"Krister."

"Oh." Placing the poker in the corner, she opened the door. "Hi."

"Hi." He hesitated. "Can I come in?"

"Sure." She held the door open, and let him in, mostly because she wanted to find out what had happened with the investigation. He looked tired. His eyes were bloodshot, and his jaw had even more shadow than earlier.

"I thought you might like to know we ID'd the victim."

"Oh, yeah?"

"Yeah. We ran her prints, but she wasn't in the database. Her husband called the station to report her missing."

"Who is she?"

"Agnes Hellgren. Married, has a daughter, age ten."

She nodded. It was as she'd expected.

Krister went into the newly cleaned living room and sank down into her father's armchair. "What type of monster does this?" he asked, rubbing his eyes.

How many times had she asked herself that same question?

"Did you go and see them?"

Krister nodded. "The husband came in to ID her." The muscles in his jaw popped with strain, and she knew it couldn't have been easy. Witnessing other people's grief wore you down. After doing it for so many years, she'd steeled herself against the emotion. Her empathy had worn thinner with every new victim. Fifty-three vics later, and she barely reacted anymore. It wasn't a good thing.

"Did he say anything?"

"I didn't question him. That can wait until tomorrow."

"Sometimes it's better to question them when it's—"

"You should have seen him, Avril." Weariness dripped from every word. "The man wasn't in any state to answer questions."

She raised her hands. Unlike her, he still had empathy. Another ten years of this, and he'd begin to understand how she felt.

He sniffed. "I do have some good news, if you can call it that."

"What's that?"

"The Police Commissioner agreed to bring you in as a consultant."

A surge of adrenaline. "That's great. When can I start?"

"Tomorrow." He snorted. "The weekend's canceled, thanks to your Frost Killer."

She nodded, already planning her strategy to catch him. "I've been thinking. If he re-enacted the first murder to get my attention, maybe he'll do the same with the second."

Krister raised a hand. "It's been a long day, Avril. Can we talk about this tomorrow? Right now, I need to take a hot shower and go to bed."

Avril gave a hurried nod. She didn't want to think of him in the shower. "Can I catch a lift with you to the station in the morning?"

"Sure. Meet me outside at eight."

He got up and walked to the door. Turning to face her, he said, "What's your number?"

"What?"

"Your cell number? What is it?"

"Oh." She gave it to him, and he immediately dialed it. Somewhere in the living room, her phone buzzed.

"Now you've got mine. Call me if anything happens, okay? I'm right next door."

"I know."

He gave her that look that he used to when they were young. She remembered it now. The look that said, 'Don't argue. Just trust me, okay?'

She sighed. "Fine. I'll call you—*if* anything happens."

He gave a satisfied nod. "Good. Night, Avril."

"Night, Krister."

chapter
nine

THE CAR HUMMED STEADILY ALONG THE HIGHWAY, THE rhythmic thrum of the tires on the asphalt blending with the low murmur of the engine. Outside, the sky was a dull gray, heavy with the promise of snow. The landscape blurred past, a mix of bare trees and frost-covered fields, stark against the overcast sky. The windshield wipers occasionally swept away the light flurries of snow that began to fall, their steady swish grating on her nerves.

"The second victim, Lene Hansen, lived in Bergen. She was killed two weeks after my mother. I was thinking—"

"This victim isn't even cold yet, Avril," Krister interrupted, taking his eyes off the road to look at her. "Let's just concentrate on her for now, shall we?"

"Once they're dead, it's too late," she said resolutely. "He's moved on to his next target by now. He's already stalking her, getting to know her routine."

"We have to follow protocol," Krister insisted, signaling before overtaking a stream of slower vehicles on the highway into the city. "Interview her family, document her last movements, look for witnesses. Someone might have seen something."

"The killer will be in Norway by now."

"You go to Norway, if you want," he said, irritably. "But you're on your own. I'll stay here and work the case."

She'd upset him, she could tell by the tightness in his jaw. "I'm sorry," she murmured. "I know you had to pull some strings to allow me to work as a consultant, and I appreciate that. But I know this guy. I know how he operates."

"That might be true," Krister said tightly, "but this is my investigation. I'm the Senior Investigating Officer, which means you work for me. Got it?"

She gave a sulky nod, looking out the window at the blur of passing cars and snowy landscape.

"I know you're a bigshot FBI agent, and I'm just the boy you used to boss around when we were kids, but you're in Sweden now. On my turf."

She almost smiled. "I did use to boss you around, didn't I?"

A smirk. "You tried, but it didn't always work. I humored you, most of the time."

"Oh, yeah? Is that what it was?"

"Of course. I knew you'd do exactly what you pleased, anyway."

She did laugh then, a short burst that surprised even her.

His eyes crinkled. "Now that's more like the girl I remember."

Her smile faded as the city drew closer. "I've been chasing this man for a long time, Krister. I thought he'd gotten away, that he'd eluded me, but now I've got another chance. I can finally catch my mother's killer and let her rest in peace."

He concentrated on the road, the buildings of the police department just visible through the snowflakes dancing in the air. "There are no guarantees here."

"I'm ready for him this time."

"How? You have no backup. No gun. You don't even have the backing of your boss."

She looked over. "I have you."

He paused as he turned into the Swedish Police headquarters parking lot. "Yes," he murmured. "You have me."

The car came to a smooth stop, and they both sat for a moment, gathering their thoughts. The large, imposing structure of the headquarters loomed ahead, reminding her of why she was here. They stepped out into the biting cold and walked briskly toward the entrance.

Inside, the lobby was bustling with activity. Officers and staff moving with purpose, their conversations a low hum that filled the space. Avril wasn't usually one for nostalgia, but the familiarity and sense of urgency brought back memories of her early days in this very precinct.

As they reached the elevator, Krister pressed the button for the third floor. The ride up was silent, the only sound the soft ding of the elevator as it ascended. When the doors opened, they were met with the organized chaos of the serious crimes division. Desks cluttered with files and computers, whiteboards covered in scribbled notes and timelines, and the constant buzz of phone calls and hurried discussions.

"Follow me." Krister led her through the maze of desks to a conference room where his team was already assembled. Avril stood quietly at the back while he addressed his team. He was so easy being the lead investigator, so confident in his presentation, but then knowing him as a child, she wasn't surprised. He'd always been the one taking control, the voice of reason amidst her chaos.

"Alright, everyone, listen up," Krister began, his voice cutting through the noise. "We have a high-priority case on our hands. The victim is Agnes Hellgren. I need everything you can find on her. Start with her recent movements—trace her last known activities. Check phone records, bank accounts, credit cards, social media interactions. I want a comprehensive timeline from the last 72 hours."

There were nods all around, and more than a few curious glances her way. "This is Special Agent Avril Dahl," he continued, beckoning to her. "She used to work here at HQ, but now she's based in the USA with the FBI. She has specialized knowledge of this case, or rather, of the killer, which is why she's here. Feel free to treat her as one of the team."

A few eyebrows went up, and Avril sensed their curiosity as she moved forward. She nodded at the team, despite not knowing their names or roles, but it didn't matter. Their purpose was the same.

She didn't recognize anybody from her rookie years, but then that wasn't surprising. A decade was a long time to be a cop, especially in the serious crimes department. The relentless tide of human tragedy wore on you, etched lines into your face, and hardened your soul. The ambitious officers had long since moved on to greener pastures, seeking promotions and less grim duties. Some old-timers clung on, more out of habit than dedication, unsure of what else to do with their lives.

Many, however, grew dejected and cynical, eventually leaving because they couldn't bear to face another dead body, another grieving family, another scene of senseless violence. In this division, it wasn't just the cases that got to you—it was the sheer, unyielding accumulation of them. Each one took a piece of you, leaving behind a void filled with sorrow and a gnawing sense of futility.

Or, like her, you became immune to it.

As Krister spoke, the team quickly fell into a well-rehearsed rhythm. Officers were already pulling up computer screens, scrolling through databases, making calls. One officer stood by a whiteboard, marking out the timeline of Agnes Hellgren's last known movements, adding notes and photographs.

"Check the CCTV footage from her neighborhood," Krister added. "I want eyes on every entrance and exit from her building. Coordinate with local businesses to see if they have any external cameras that might have caught something."

"On it," replied a detective, already dialing a number.

"Also, follow up on her workplace. Talk to colleagues, find out if anyone noticed anything unusual. Any new acquaintances or relationships that stood out?"

A detective near the front raised a hand. "We've got her phone records coming in. Should be here within the hour."

"Good. Cross-reference those with her social media activity. Look for any discrepancies or unusual contacts."

Krister then turned to Avril. "Agent Dahl, anything you'd like to add?"

Avril stepped forward, feeling the weight of their expectations. Clearing her throat, she said, "This killer is meticulous and patient. He stalks his victims, learning their routines before he strikes. We need to be thorough in our interviews. Someone might have seen something they didn't realize was important. Pay attention to the details, no matter how small they seem."

There were a few nods and murmurs. She fingered the lanyard around her neck which housed the temporary ID badge Krister had organized when they'd arrived. She could sense the skepticism.

A young detective came up and shook her hand, his eyes wide with curiosity. "A real FBI agent, wow!" She nodded, keeping her expression neutral.

"I'm Detective Karlsson." He gave her a flirty grin. "But you can call me Dave."

Avril forced a smile. She should have worn one of her suits, but she'd left them all in D.C. The jeans, T-shirt, and winter sweater didn't command the same level of respect her suits did, and the tennis shoes meant every man and most women in the department towered over her.

"Special Agent Dahl," she said, releasing his hand.

He leaned against the wall. "Where in the States do you live? My uncle's in—"

"Karlsson, back to work," barked Krister, striding toward them with an air of command.

"Yes, sir." The young detective shot her an awkward look and hurried away.

"You can use the other side of my desk," Krister offered, leaning over and clearing off a bunch of folders. "We don't have much free space around here."

They were squashed into a small department on the third floor of the police headquarters. The squad room was home to eight detectives, including Krister, while the rest of the floor was taken up with a kitchen, an evidence room filled with lockers, and several offices for the top brass.

"Thanks." Avril sat down and put her folder on the desk.

"What's that?" He eyed the dog-eared corners and faded label.

"It's my file on the Frost Killer investigation," she said. "Not everything, only what I brought with me."

He raised an eyebrow. "Care to share?"

"Sure." She pushed it over the desk. "I've noted the second and third murders back in 2006." She pointed to the colorful dividers sticking out of the file. "In case you want to read about those."

He gave her a hard look. "You really think he's reenacting his first crime wave?"

"I do."

"To get to you?"

"Yes."

"Why?"

"Because of what happened in Colorado. It pissed him off."

Krister arched an eyebrow at her choice of words. "What happened in Colorado?"

She took a deep breath. "There was a copycat killer mimicking his MO. This copycat made mistakes and got caught, which gave the real Frost Killer a bad name."

"That's why he's active again? To prove to the world it wasn't him?"

"I think so, yes."

"But what has that got to do with you?"

She shook her head. "Other than I was in Colorado, I don't know. He knows I've been hunting him for a decade. I've gotten close a few times, too, but he's always managed to stay one step ahead of me. I think this is his last murder spree, and then we'll never hear from him again."

"You think he's going to quit?"

"I can't explain it, but I do. It's almost like he's come out of retirement for one last show, and he means to attract my attention with it."

"So he can kill you."

She nodded.

He studied her for a long moment. "Why don't you look scared?"

"I've waited my entire career for this moment. If it means using myself as bait, so be it. This is the reason I became a cop, Krister. To catch him."

He frowned. "Don't you care that you might die in the process?"

"We'll be ready for him." She gave a determined nod. "We'll catch him in the act. The notorious Frost Killer will finally be behind bars."

THEY SPENT the morning going over Agnes Hellgren's last moves.

"She dropped her daughter off at her mother-in-law's, then went to the gym and met a friend for coffee. When she didn't collect her daughter later that afternoon, the mother-in-law called her son to fetch the child." Krister read out the feedback he'd gotten from his team.

"Makes sense." Avril nodded. "By that stage, she'd already been abducted. When did her husband call the police department?"

"Later that night. He was worried something had happened to her."

She gave a knowing nod. A missing daughter or partner, a worried parent or spouse, a frantic call to the police. The process was all too familiar.

"He's coming in later today to help us with our investigation. Nice guy. Helpful, considering ... I mean, he didn't have to come in."

"That's good," Avril said, already thinking ahead. "You can get his alibi and rule him out."

The husband came into the station and Krister went downstairs to meet him, Avril went too, but not because she was interested in what the husband had to say. She was going out.

"I'll be back later," she told Krister. "I've got a meeting with a realtor." She didn't say what it was about, even though she knew Krister would assume it was her father's house. She didn't want to burden him with this. He had enough on his plate. Besides, it might turn out to be a dead end, and she'd learned over the years that there was no point in saying anything until you had something worthwhile to say.

The landlord, Anders Elmander, lived in a three-story townhouse in one of Stockholm's better neighborhoods. He was an effeminate man in his fifties with streaked silver hair and soft, delicate features. His moist brown eyes followed Avril as she entered the house. "Can I offer you a drink?"

"No, thank you." This wasn't a social call.

"So what can I do for you, um?" He'd forgotten her name, even though she'd introduced herself when he'd opened the door.

"Avril Dahl."

"Miss Dahl."

"I'd like to talk about a property you used to manage, Morgonsgatan, number 9." She watched his face, but there was no reaction, apart from one eyebrow lifting slightly.

"What about it?"

"I believe it burned down in a fire?"

"Yes, back in 2007. It was a terrible thing. One of the residents fell asleep with a lit cigarette, or so the police said, and he burned the place down. The tenants lost everything."

"But you were insured, right?" She looked up at him.

A pause.

"Yes, yes I was. Thankfully. Although it didn't stretch to cover the tenants' belongings. They're responsible for that themselves."

"I see." She pretended to consult her notes. "Would you be able to provide me with a list of tenants living on the premises at the time of the fire?"

He thought about that. "I should be able to. If you can come back tomorrow—"

"I don't mind waiting."

He hesitated. "Could I ask why you require this information?"

"We're looking into someone and think he may have stayed in your property at the time of the fire."

"We being?"

"The Swedish Police, Regional Investigation Unit."

"Ah, I see. Excuse me for saying this, Miss Dahl, but you don't look like a detective."

"I'm not. I'm an FBI agent." She held up her ID, irritated that he had questioned her, even though he was in his rights to do so. "Now, if you'll get me the names, I can be on my way."

He didn't argue, simply rose from his chair and walked out of the room. She heard his footsteps recede down the wooden hallway and into what she assumed was an office or study at the other end of the house. About five minutes later, he came back.

"Here you are. Seven tenants in that block when it burned down."

She took the list of names. "Do you know which one died?"

"That one." He pointed to one of the names. "Mikael Lustig."

chapter
ten

MIKAEL.

Michael.

"He's the one who died?" Avril tried but failed to keep the disappointment from her voice.

"Yes. Did you know him?"

"No, I don't think so, but he might have been the person we're looking for."

He gave a sad nod. "Mikael was a charming young man. Articulate, educated, musical. He studied Classics, if I remember correctly. I was sorry to hear he'd died in the fire."

Avril fished in her coat pocket and pulled out the photograph her father had hidden. "Mr. Elmander, can I ask you if you recognize this man?"

The landlord stared at it for a long time, then gave a little nod. "Yes, that's Mikael."

Avril left Anders Elmander's house and walked back to the train station in something of a daze. It was dark outside, but she barely noticed.

She'd found her mother's lover.

SHE PULLED out the photograph and studied it again. The glossy hair, erect stance, elegant cut of the coat. She pictured him as a musician, a lover of the finer things in life. Had he wooed her mother with his interesting conversation? Trips to the art galleries and the theater? She could see her mother falling for someone like that.

Olivia Dahl had always longed for more.

"One day, darling," she'd say to Avril. "You'll leave Sweden and travel the world. There is so much to see."

Her father was a simple, hard-working man. He was loyal, but he wasn't exciting. Maybe her mother craved adventure, and Mikael offered it to her on a charming, silver platter.

Avril shook her head. At twelve, she'd existed in her own world, learning new things at school, hanging out with her friends, and running wild with Krister on the weekends and holidays. She hadn't paid her parents much mind. They'd always just been there.

Now she wished she had.

Still, there were six more names on the list. Six people who might be able to tell her more about the mysterious Mikael and his relationship with her mother. One thing was for certain, however, Mikael couldn't be the Frost Killer.

KRISTER SAT ACROSS THE COLD, metal table from Olaf Hellgren, the only light in the room casting a harsh shadow on the suspect's face. The interrogation room was sterile, its walls a bland shade of gray. No windows. The scent of disinfectant and sweat lingered in the air, mixing uncomfortably with the stench of booze wafting from Hellgren.

The man looked broken. His red eyes were sunk into dark circles, his clothes rumpled and stained. Nicotine-streaked fingers trembled slightly as he clenched them on the table.

"Mr. Hellgren, thanks for coming in. I know this isn't easy for you." Krister kept his voice even, a practiced calm that had taken years to perfect. It helped put the suspect at ease—or lured them into a false sense of security. Either worked.

"I want to help find my wife's killer," Hellgren said through gritted teeth.

"Of course. Could you tell me when you last saw your wife?"

"Yesterday morning. I play golf every second Saturday. There's an indoor driving range on Enhagsslingan. It gives Aggie time to go shopping, meet up with her friends, get her hair done. You know, girl stuff."

Krister nodded. For some reason, his mind flicked back to Avril. He couldn't imagine her doing any of that.

"I left home around ten in the morning. We said goodbye, and that was the last I saw of her." He gulped, his Adam's apple jumping in his throat. "I'm still trying to understand what happened."

"We'll get to that," Krister said, keeping his tone neutral. "Could you talk me through the rest of your day?"

Hellgren's bloodshot eyes widened. "Wait, you don't think I had anything to do with this, do you?"

"It's standard procedure," Krister replied, flipping open a fresh page in his notepad. "We have to rule you out as a suspect."

A stony nod. "The spouse is always the prime suspect, right?"

A shrug.

Mr. Hellgren sighed. "It doesn't matter. I've got nothing to hide. I drove to the golf center, met my friends, and went out to the driving range. We broke for lunch, then practiced our putting for another few hours. That's when I got the call from my mother saying Aggie hadn't arrived to collect Ellie."

"What time did you leave the golf center?" Krister's pen moved swiftly across the page.

"I'm not sure. After the phone call. It must have been sometime after four o'clock."

Krister slid a piece of paper and a pen across the table. "Could you write down the names of your golfing friends and their phone numbers?"

Hellgren hesitated. "You checking up on me?"

"I'm afraid we have to." Krister's tone was firm but not unkind.

With a disgruntled nod, Mr. Hellgren drew the paper toward him and picked up the pen. "What time did my wife die?"

"I'm afraid we don't know yet. We're still waiting on the autopsy report." Even if he knew, he wouldn't give the time of death to her husband in case he was fine-tuning his alibi. "Mr. Hellgren, I hate to ask, but were you and your wife happy?"

Hellgren scowled. "Of course we were happy."

"It's just that you had some financial troubles, didn't you?" Krister had inspected the Hellgrens' bank statements, noting the strain. Aggie didn't work, and Hellgren's income barely covered their expenses. They'd defaulted twice on their mortgage repayments.

The scowl deepened. "Ellie has special needs," he murmured. "Aggie quit her job to stay home with her. Things have been a bit tight recently."

Krister nodded, absorbing the new detail. He hadn't realized the daughter had developmental issues.

"Was your wife acting unusual leading up to her death?"

The man finished writing and put the pen down. "What do you mean?"

"Was she herself? Did you notice any anxiety or change in her behavior?"

He pursed his lips. "Now that you mention it, she was a little uptight."

"In what way?"

"She said she thought she'd seen someone outside the house, watching Ellie."

Krister sat up straight. "Really? When was this?"

"Recently, but I just put it down to the break-in."

"What break-in?" His pulse accelerated.

"We had a break-in two weeks ago. You know when all those burglaries were happening? Someone picked the lock on the back door."

"Did you report it to the police?"

He shook his head. "Nothing was taken as far as we could tell. I repaired the lock and that was that, but Aggie couldn't settle. She kept saying she thought someone was watching the house."

"Did your wife see this person?"

"I don't think so. She said she saw a shadow outside the window one day, and in the garden one evening. Each time I checked, there was nobody there. I thought she was imagining things."

Unlikely. In all probability, Aggie Hellgren had seen her killer. As Avril had said, he liked to stalk his victims before he grabbed them.

"Thank you, Mr. Hellgren. You've been very helpful."

"Is that it?"

Krister nodded. "For now. We'll get in touch if we have any other questions."

"So my wife was telling the truth? She really did see someone outside the house?"

"I don't know," he replied. "We're following every lead right now."

Hellgren stood up, his chair scraping loudly against the floor. "You will find him, won't you? You will catch the man who murdered my wife?"

Krister gave a stiff nod. "I'm certainly going to try."

chapter
eleven

Avril showed her ID badge to the security officer in the lobby and was allowed into the building. She took the elevator, along with several other officers, to the third floor.

Krister looked up as she walked into the squad room, and beckoned her over with a nod. A female officer, whose name Avril couldn't remember, glanced up and frowned. Avril had seen her talking to Krister earlier, laughing too loudly and thrusting her chest out—blatant signs of flirting. She supposed she was pretty, in a well-groomed kind of way. A bit like a show horse, designed to attract attention, rather than demonstrate any particular skill set.

"How was the interrogation?" She dropped into the chair opposite Krister's desk.

He leaned forward, elbows on the desk. "Did you know their daughter has special needs?"

"No." Avril exhaled heavily. "That's tough."

"Yeah, the guy's devastated. The family were having financial troubles too, because the victim had to stay home to look after the kid."

Avril nodded, tapping her fingers on the edge of the desk. "Makes sense. Specialist childcare is expensive."

Krister sighed. "He's got an alibi for the afternoon of the murder. We're checking it now."

She nodded, distracted. "He didn't do it."

"I know, but you understand we've got to tick the boxes." He studied her, his gaze roaming over her face. "Where have you been?"

"The realtor, remember?"

"Oh yeah. Did you get a quote?"

"A quote?" She blinked, drawing a blank.

"For your father's house."

"Oh, yes. They're going to do a valuation." She waved a hand in the air. "It's not important."

Krister tapped his pencil on his notepad. "There's something else. Hellgren said his wife thought there was someone watching the house."

Avril's head shot up. "What?"

"They also had a break-in a few weeks back. Nothing was taken."

"It's him," she hissed. "Did she get a look at him?"

"No. A shadowy figure outside in the garden. That's what she told her husband."

Avril gritted her teeth in frustration. "Ugh, it's always the same. He stays just out of reach."

Just then, the female officer sauntered up. "Sir, you asked me to look up Lars Ekberg?"

He glanced up at her. "Yes?"

"I've got an address for him." She bent over the desk giving Krister a good look down her impressive cleavage. Avril, who'd lost so much weight her breasts had almost disappeared, grimaced with disapproval and, if she were honest, a tinge of envy.

Krister made a point of not looking. "Thank you, Ingrid."

"Lars Ekberg?" Avril mused. The woman's perfume lingered over the desk, annoyingly potent. She must have applied it right before coming over to talk to Krister, but he didn't appear to notice. "Wasn't he that useless detective on my mother's case?"

"That's right." He grinned. "Good memory. I asked Ingrid to track him down. I thought we could pay him a visit."

She took a sharp breath in. "I've talked to him before, but it was a long time ago."

"He probably won't remember anything new," Krister said, "but you never know. It would be good to get his insight into the murders."

Avril took out the names the landlord had given her and placed them in the folder. "What's that?" Krister asked.

"Oh, it's a list of people I want to check out. Contacts my mother may have known."

He frowned. "Where'd you get them?"

"I found them in my father's things. They probably mean nothing, but I thought I'd check them out in my spare time." If they led to anything, she'd come clean and fill him in. For now, he had enough to be getting on with. He didn't need to worry about the tenants in a hostel that burned down over a decade ago, and who may have nothing at all to do with the case.

He shrugged. "Are you coming with me to speak to Ekberg?"

Avril jumped up. "Of course. Wouldn't miss it."

Ingrid stared after them as they left the office.

"SHE LIKES YOU," Avril remarked as Krister drove them to Uppsala, forty-five miles north of Stockholm, where Lars Ekberg lived.

"Who?"

"Ingrid."

"Ingrid at the office?" He raised an eyebrow.

"Don't tell me you haven't noticed her flirting?"

"Well—" He shrugged. "I try not to notice those things. I don't want to be nailed for inappropriate behavior or sexual harassment."

Avril nodded. The woman irritated her, but she didn't know why. Maybe it was because they were so different. She glanced down at her jeans and jumper. "I really should get something more fitting to wear."

He laughed. "What's wrong with what you've got on?"

"It's not suitable for office work."

He kept his eyes on the road. "I like what you're wearing. Jeans look good on you."

She glanced across at him. "Thanks."

"But if you want to show off your legs and fall out of your shirt, go for it. I won't complain."

"That's not what I meant." She scoffed. The last person on earth she'd want to look like was Ingrid. "I left all my suits in DC."

"I take it the FBI has a no jeans policy?"

"They have a reputation to uphold."

He snorted. "Of course. It's the FBI."

She shook her head. "I didn't leave under the best circumstances."

"Oh?" He waited for her to continue.

"I was reassigned two years ago when the Frost Killer stopped his murder spree, but I kept going. I kept looking for his next victim, who I was sure was out there somewhere. I couldn't believe he'd just quit. Killers like him don't just stop killing."

"Did you get into trouble?"

"No, but they weren't happy about it. As long as I worked the cases I'd been assigned to, they didn't argue."

He nodded.

"Colorado was a mistake."

He glanced at her. "You mean your going there was a mistake?"

"Yes. I was convinced it was the Frost Killer. The MO was the same. The pendant was there. I was so intent on making the murders fit my narrative, I failed to notice the differences."

"The copycat?"

She gave a rueful nod. "I derailed the entire investigation because I pointed them in the wrong direction."

"It happens," he said quietly.

"I should have known better."

"Don't be so hard on yourself. You made a mistake, big deal. Who hasn't?"

She sighed. "I guess so. Anyway, my boss was only too happy to give me extended leave. I don't think he wants me back."

"If we catch this guy, you won't have to go back."

She studied him, but his gaze was fixed on the road. Strong jawline, a straight, aquiline nose, full lips. She didn't know why she'd noticed his lips.

Taking a quick breath, she said, "*When* we catch this guy."

Krister smiled.

. . .

As they left the city and approached Uppsala, the landscape shifted dramatically from urban sprawl to the more serene suburbs, and finally to the tranquil countryside. The fields and forests, blanketed in snow, stretched endlessly on either side of the E4 highway. The low winter sun cast long shadows from the few structures they passed, creating a stark contrast against the white expanse. Avril admired the traditional Swedish cottages, their iconic red or yellow siding and white trim standing out like jewels in the snowy landscape.

"It's so different from Washington D.C.," she murmured.

"Do you miss it?" Krister asked.

"I've been too busy to miss it." It was the truth. Her head had been filled with the Frost Killer for so long, there was no room for anything else.

It was hard to imagine her life without him in it.

The closer they got to Uppsala, the more pronounced the rural charm became. Lars Ekberg's house came into view, a detached home with a modest garden, surrounded by snow-dusted trees.

As they pulled up beside it, Avril noted the traditional Swedish architecture, its clean lines and functional design standing firm against the winter's harshness. The house, well insulated and built to withstand the cold, exuded a sense of warmth and sturdiness. Smoke curling from the chimney was a sure sign someone was home.

"You ready?" Krister said.

"Is he expecting us?"

"I called ahead, yes."

Krister parked the car, and they both stepped out, their boots crunching on the frozen ground. It was colder out here with fewer buildings to retain the heat. Avril was grateful for her long, woolen coat, even though she knew it hung off her like an older sister's hand-me-down.

"He wasn't very nice when I spoke to him before."

"Lars?"

"He didn't want to talk about the case." She hesitated, "And I may not have handled it as well as I could have, but I was young and inexperienced."

"This was after you graduated from the academy?"

"Yeah, I went straight into investigating my mother's murder."

Krister rang the doorbell. The chimes cut through the quiet of the late afternoon. Avril looked around. Out here, there was minimal traffic, no airplanes, no train lines. Just the odd squawk of a bird flying overhead. A frozen lake glittered across the field.

Then they heard footsteps, heavy and plodding.

Krister glanced at her. "Let's see if he's mellowed over the years."

She gave a soft snort, but stood beside him, waiting for the door to open.

"You must be the detectives from Stockholm?" A middle-aged man stood there frowning, his hair white and a stomach that suggested not enough exercise in his retirement years. He didn't extend a hand, simply held the door open for them to enter.

"I'm Detective Jansson, and this is Agent Dahl," Krister said, before stepping over the threshold into the warm interior. "Thank you for seeing us."

He grunted and gestured for them to sit down. The living room was cozy, with a worn carpet, a fluffy rug, and a log fire burning in the fireplace. Krister sat on a vacant armchair, while Avril perched on the edge of the sofa.

"I believe you wanted to talk to me about a cold case." He didn't spare Avril a second glance. He hadn't even reacted to her last name.

"The murder of Olivia Dahl," Krister said.

The man was about to sit down, but he stood again, with some difficulty. "You're wasting your time coming here for that. The case ruined my career. It was a disaster from start to finish. I have nothing to tell you about that investigation."

Avril had been expecting this. She glanced at Krister, whose jaw was tense. "Detective Ekberg, we'd still like to go through what happened with you. It's important."

"Why? I spoke to a young lady about it a decade ago. It wasn't important then and it isn't now. I have nothing to add to what was a botched investigation."

"Botched by who?" Avril asked, quietly.

He turned to her as if seeing her for the first time. "You! You're the lady that came before." He shuffled toward the door. "You really must leave."

"We're not going anywhere, sir," Krister said with a steel edge to his voice. Avril glanced at him in surprise. She hadn't heard that tone before. "If you'll sit down, we can get through this as quickly as possible and leave you in peace."

Begrudgingly, the retired cop returned to his chair.

"Now, Olivia Dahl," Krister began. "Why don't you tell us what you remember about her murder?"

The man gave a hefty sigh, as if to emphasize how little he enjoyed this. "A young mother from Täby. Married with one kid." He frowned at Avril. "You, I'm guessing."

She managed a stiff nod. This guy wasn't any friendlier than last time.

"Anyway, she takes the dog for a walk one evening and disappears. Vanishes, into thin air. The dog is found later that night wandering around the woods. A search party doesn't turn up any sign of her. She's gone."

Avril found she was clenching her gloved hands into tight little balls.

"The next evening, a dog walker finds her body in a clearing, not a mile from where she went missing."

Krister frowned. "You think her body was dumped there?"

"Must have been. We searched that entire area the day before, and I swear she wasn't in that clearing."

"So the killer brought her back? Why?"

"To pose her," Avril cut in. "He wanted to preserve her in her own environment."

Both men turned to look at her.

"Why wait twenty-four hours?" Krister asked.

"Because everyone was out looking for her," she explained. "He couldn't leave her to freeze to death. There wasn't enough time. In those temperatures, death occurs in about an hour. She would have been found before she died."

Krister nodded slowly, while Ekberg gritted his teeth. "We ruled it a suicide."

"What made you think she'd killed herself?" Krister asked.

"The manner in which she died. She'd frozen to death. There were no marks or bruises on her body. It was like she'd laid down and fallen asleep in the snow."

Avril scoffed.

Krister sent her a warning glance.

"There were no footprints around the body," the old detective continued. "No signs of a struggle. No evidence that anyone else was involved other than the victim."

"I can see how it might have looked that way," Krister said.

It was Avril's turn to shoot him a dark look.

Krister cleared his throat. "Was there any other evidence that suggested she was unhappy?"

"Sure." He paused, thinking. "The weeks leading up to her death, she'd been acting strange."

Avril opened her mouth to object, but Krister held up a warning finger. She shut it again. "In what way?" he said.

"Erratic behavior, secretive, out a lot. Her husband thought she was having an affair."

"He thought what?" Avril blurted out, unable to help herself.

"Avril, please," Krister began.

"Did he tell you that?"

The old detective fixed his jaded eyes on her. "After his wife's body was found. When we arrested him."

Her poor father had been arrested following the discovery of the body. They'd barged into the house, put him in cuffs and hauled him down to the police station in front of all his family and friends. Krister's mother had stayed with Avril until he'd gotten back, much later that night. She didn't remember where Krister had been.

"I don't understand. Why would he say that?"

The photograph.

"He caught them together, as far as I can remember."

Avril stared at him, open-mouthed. "He actually saw them together?"

"That's what he said, yes." Ekberg scratched his chin. "Then there was the pendant."

"The pendant found on the body?" Krister asked.

Avril's head was spinning. Her father had found her mother and Michael together. When? How? And why hadn't he said anything?

"Yes, we concluded her lover had given it to her."

"Why wasn't this in the police report?" Avril whispered. She'd gone through that report a hundred times. There was no record of her father mentioning an affair in his statement.

Ekberg glanced at his hands. "Because I took it out."

She gasped. "Why? That's withholding evidence."

"What are you gonna do? Sue me?" He gave a dry laugh.

Krister frowned. "Why did you take it out, Detective Ekberg?"

"Because when it came out that she'd been murdered, and that there were others like her, left to die in the snow, the suicide verdict was off the table. We tried to find this mysterious lover—Michael, I think his name was—but he was dead. Died in a house fire shortly after the incident, if I remember correctly. It was a dead end, if you'll excuse the pun, and not relevant. Going further down that path only made us look bad."

"So you removed it from the police report?"

He gave a resentful nod.

Avril shook her head. "You could have saved me so much trouble."

Krister shot her a curious look but didn't question her. She knew he'd wait until they were in the car to do that.

"As it was, the failure to recognize that Olivia Dahl's death was part of a wider serial killer's MO forced me to resign my post."

"They blamed you?" Krister asked.

"Someone's always the fall guy." He nodded at Avril. "You'd better watch yourself, young man. This one's trouble."

"I can handle it," Krister said, jutting his chin into the air.

"And he's unlikely to be as narrow-minded as you were," Avril bit out.

"Look where I ended up." The former detective spread his hands. "Uppsala. They offered me a desk job here. That's what I did for the last ten years of my career. Pushed paper around. If you're not careful, you'll get the same treatment."

A career-ender, her boss had said.

"That's not going to happen." Avril turned to Krister. "I won't let it."

"I know." He met her gaze. "We're going to catch this guy."

chapter
twelve

THE CAR HUMMED STEADILY AS THEY SPED DOWN THE E4 highway, passing snow-blanketed fields and forests. The sun was beginning to set, despite it being early afternoon, turning the winter scenery a pale gold, yet the atmosphere inside the car was tense, the silence only broken by the rhythmic thrum of the tires on the asphalt.

"Okay, tell me about Michael," Krister asked, his voice steady. She could tell he was annoyed, but holding it in. She closed her eyes, just briefly, as if she could block out the question, but of course, she couldn't. He deserved to know.

"Michael was my mother's secret lover." She struggled to keep her own voice even. "I found a photograph of them together in my father's bedroom when I was tidying up after the burglary."

Krister's eyes widened, momentarily darting from the road to her face. "Why didn't you say anything?"

"Because he died, Krister. Michael died in a house fire right after my mother's death, like Ekberg said. That's where I was today. I went to speak to the landlord. He told me."

Krister was silent for a moment, the weight of her revelation settling in the car. "Do you think Michael had anything to do with her death?"

Avril shook her head, her gaze fixed on the passing scenery. "How could he have? He died so soon after it happened. I don't even know if he was aware that she'd died. I mean, he must have been, but..." She shrugged.

"Have you looked into him?"

"I haven't had time. I only just found out who he was. Mikael Lustig. I got a list of names of the other tenants in the house that burned down. I thought maybe some of them might remember him or my mother."

"It's worth exploring, I guess." Krister fixed his eyes on the road, the headlights of oncoming cars flashing by. "I'm sorry about your mother. I had no idea she was having an affair."

"Neither did I. She kept us all in the dark."

"Your father must have known."

Avril gave a sad nod. "He knew, yes. He hid this picture behind another photograph, one of the three of us." She held out the photograph of a smiling Olivia and a dark, elegant Mikael.

Krister glanced down briefly, taking in the image before returning his gaze to the road. They were back on the E4 now, heading toward Stockholm. "Looks like the National Museum," he said. "I recognize the statue of Psyche being carried by the cupids in the courtyard. See, behind the glass doors."

Avril squinted through the hazy glass in the background. She'd been so focused on her mother and her lover that she'd neglected to study the rest of the photograph.

"You have good eyesight."

"I used to go there when I was doing my degree. Art history was one of my subjects," Krister replied, a hint of nostalgia in his voice.

She frowned. "I thought you did criminology."

"That was to irritate my father, but I took a few additional credits in my first few years." He gave a wry smile, his eyes momentarily distant.

She chuckled. "I remember he wanted you to become a lawyer, like him."

Krister pulled a face. "Yeah, that was his dream, not mine."

"How are your parents?" she asked, a pang of guilt clutching at her chest. She'd been so obsessed with the investigation that she'd forgotten to ask him about his family.

"He and my mother moved to France a couple of years ago. The weather is kinder to my father's leg."

"I'm sorry." She remembered his father had lost part of his leg in a bad motorcycle accident when Krister was young. It acted up in the cold, making winters in Sweden particularly painful.

"It's okay. I go see them whenever I can, which, admittedly, isn't as often as I should."

"It's a good excuse for a vacation," Avril said, trying to lighten the mood.

"That is true." He looked across at her, a soft smile playing on his lips. "Maybe when all this is over, we can take one together. Somewhere by the sea, like we used to when we were kids. Remember?"

Avril didn't reply immediately. What was he suggesting? That they holiday together? As friends? Or something more? She hadn't had anyone interested in her for so long, she'd forgotten what it felt like. Now her head was spinning, and she had no idea what to say.

He glanced across at her face. "Too soon?"

She let out a breathy laugh. "A bit."

"Okay, that can wait. We'll revisit it when we catch this bastard."

She liked that he said *when* and not *if.*

Krister's hands relaxed on the wheel. "It's just, you've only been back for a couple of days, and it already feels like old times. You know what I mean?"

"I do." Krister had always been quick to talk about his feelings, whereas she'd kept hers buried, preferring to lose herself in action rather than words.

"Sorry if it made you uncomfortable. I didn't mean anything by it. It's just nice to have you back."

"I know."

The car sped toward Stockholm, while Avril thought about what Lars Ekberg had said. "I can't believe he left that bit of information out of the report. I've wondered for years who Michael was."

"I thought you said you'd just found out about him?"

"My mother's phone records. She made several calls that last month to a man in her contact list called Michael. It's why the police thought she'd committed suicide, because her affair had ended."

"I haven't had time to read your file yet," he said.

"You can take it with you tonight, if you want. I know it all by heart anyway."

"Did they trace the number?"

"No, it was a burner phone."

"Convenient."

"Very." She hesitated. "But now I have a name."

Mikael Lustig.

The city was in darkness when they got back, the wet streets illuminated by pools of sticky yellow light. Mushy snow had built up along the edges and on the sidewalks, but the roads were glistening with inky blackness.

"It's after five, do you want me to drop you at your place?"

"No, I'll come back to the station. I want to start looking into those names. I thought I'd track them down tomorrow."

He nodded, and ten minutes later they pulled into the police station parking lot. Avril was pleased to see Ingrid had gone home for the day, along with about half of the detectives. Karlsson, however, was still at his desk, along with Freddie, Krister's right hand man.

"Boss, I've got something for you," Freddie said, before Krister had even taken off his jacket.

"Oh, yeah?"

"Remember you asked me to check into Hellgren's alibi for the afternoon his wife was murdered?"

"Yep."

"Well, he wasn't at the golf center like he said. I spoke with his golfing buddies. He was there until lunch time, but then he took off. Said his wife needed his help."

Krister frowned. "He said that?"

"Yeah, those were his exact words."

Avril was shaking her head. "It's not him. It can't be him."

Krister put his hands on his hips. "Bring him in, Freddie. Let's find out why he lied."

"HERE WE ARE AGAIN," Krister said to Olaf Hellgren. They were back in the interrogation room, but this time Olaf was under arrest. The sterile room felt even more oppressive now, its gray walls closing in, the single overhead light uncomfortably bright.

"Why am I here?" Olaf demanded, his voice rough with desperation. "My daughter needs me."

"YOU LIED TO US, OLAF." Krister studied him closely. Olaf's hands were callused and rough, his shoulders broad and muscular. He was a strong guy. Strong enough to carry a woman Agnes's size along that icy track to the clearing. But there was a problem. Olaf was in his late thirties, while the Frost Killer had been active for fifteen years. The timeline didn't fit. This man was not the Frost Killer—but was he his wife's killer?

"I did not," Olaf insisted, but his eyes flashed with fear.

"You said you were playing golf all Saturday, but your buddies confirmed you left at lunch time." Olaf hung his head. "Did you think we wouldn't find out?"

"I hoped."

"Why did you lie?" Krister asked quietly.

"Because I didn't want anyone to know what I was doing on Saturday afternoon. What I do every Saturday afternoon." Olaf's voice cracked.

"What is it that you do?"

"I work at the fish market. It's minimum wage, but we need the money." He hung his head, clearly ashamed that he'd sunk so low.

Krister's heart went out to the guy. "You should've told us, Olaf. We had you pegged as a suspect in your wife's murder."

"I didn't kill her." He broke down and sobbed, his head in his hands. "I loved my wife. We were going through a tough time, but we'd have made it. We'd have been okay, I would have made sure of it."

Krister remained silent for a moment, letting Olaf's words sink in. "Can we have the name of the company you work for?" he asked.

Olaf sniffed but nodded.

Krister passed him a piece of paper and he wrote it down.

"We'll need to verify this."

Cold Reckoning

Olaf looked up, his gaze bleak. "Can I go home to my daughter now?"
"Yes, go home. Just don't leave town, okay?"
Olaf spread his arms. "Where would I go?"

chapter
thirteen

"You look tired," Krister said to Avril when they met to drive to the station the next morning. "Didn't you sleep well?"

"I'm fine."

The truth was, she'd lain awake thinking about the Frost Killer, and wondered whether he was outside watching her. Several times in the night, she'd gotten up and peered through the crack in the curtains, looking for a shadowy figure out in the street.

"You're welcome to stay at my house," Krister said. At her annoyed look, he raised his hands. "Just saying."

In truth, she was only irritated that he'd seen through her attempt at bravado. "Thank you, but that's not necessary."

"Suit yourself."

Krister didn't talk much after that, and once they got to the squad room, he went straight to his desk. Avril watched as Ingrid's heavily made-up eyes tracked him across the room. It wouldn't hurt to be a little less obvious, she thought, as she sat down.

"Hi, Agent Dahl." Detective Karlsson grinned at her as he walked past, a cup of coffee in his hand. She nodded, glancing across at Krister, but he didn't look up.

The first thing Avril did was log into the police database, using Krister's password, and check the incident report for the house fire back in 2007. At the top of the page was the incident particulars, date, address of incident, how the call was received, and a list of the responding officers.

One name she recognized. Gunnar Mellberg. He'd been a serving officer when she'd joined the police force in 2012. She'd served under him for a year before she'd moved to the Regional Investigation Unit.

She looked up. "Hey, Krister, is Gunnar Mellberg still around?"

He scratched his chin. "I think so. Freddie, isn't Gunnar still in the Robbery division?"

"Yeah, I think he heads it up now."

"Great." She lowered her voice. "He was a first responder at the house fire back in '07."

"Robbery is on the first floor," he said.

Avril took the stairs down two floors and walked along a cold corridor toward the Robbery Division squad room. This had been her floor, and not much had changed in the decade she'd been away. Passing a door, she spotted the name Gunnar Mellberg on a plastic strip on the outside.

Knocking, Avril waited for his deep baritone voice. She remembered him well. He'd been patient with her, a determined young rookie eager to prove herself. Fixated with moving to the Regional Investigation Unit and doing everything in her power to get there.

"Come in."

She pushed open the door and forced a smile. "Hello, Gunnar."

"Holy smoke!" He jumped out of his chair. "If it isn't little Avril Dahl. How the hell are you? Geez, it's been a while."

"Ten years." She came forward and shook his hand, negating his attempt to hug her.

"Ten years, my God. You haven't changed a bit."

"Thank you. I think."

He laughed. "Take a seat, Avril. Tell me what you've been up to."

Where to start?

She sat down, deciding to spare him the gory details of her endless hunt for the Frost Killer. "I'm working with the FBI now. In Washington D.C."

"I heard you'd gone abroad. You were always too good for this place." He waved his hands around. "Best recruit I've ever had the pleasure of mentoring."

"Pleasure?" She raised an eyebrow.

He laughed again, a deep rumble from his belly. "You weren't the easiest graduate, I will admit, but you more than made up for it in closed cases."

"Thank you, Gunnar."

"Now, what are you doing back here? You're not looking for a job, are you?" He winked. "Because you've got one if you want it."

She couldn't help but grin. "No, that's not why I'm here. I'm working with Detective Krister on a murder case."

"Ah, yes. The woman in the woods."

"That's the one."

"Awful business. I remember something similar years ago." He frowned, scratching his head.

"We think there might be a link to a house fire that occurred back in 2007," Avril said quickly, hoping he wouldn't remember the series of events that began with her mother's murder. He would have been younger then, and in a different division, so he might not connect the dots.

"'07? Hmm...."

"You were the first responder. It was a hostel, the address was number 9 Morgonsgatan. One man died. Apparently one of the tenants fell asleep with a cigarette in his hand."

"Ah, yes. It's coming back to me now. Geez, that was a long time ago."

"I know."

He pursed his lips while he thought back. "Yes, that was quite a horrific fire. Obliterated the building. The fire department managed to contain it, so it didn't spread to the neighboring buildings, but it was touch and go there for a while."

"Was there anything unusual about the blaze?" she asked.

"You mean was it suspicious?"

She nodded.

"Well, the findings were that it was an accident, but I had a friend in the fire department, and he said he'd never seen a fire spread so fast. The entire house was incinerated, and it burned hot, too."

"Why did they rule it an accident then?"

"There was no real evidence to the contrary. Even though they suspected foul play, there was no sign of an accelerant, the individual who died was still in his bed, and they found a burned-out zipper lighter on the floor beside him."

"What about the victim? Remember anything about him?"

"Not really. You'd have to look up the police report."

"I did. His name was Mikael Lustig."

He clicked his fingers. "That's it. Popular guy, as I recall. Everybody was devastated when he died."

"Did you interview the other tenants?"

"Not all of them. There were a couple we couldn't find after the fire. They were all fairly transient types, you know. Hostels are like that."

She nodded. "Okay, thank you. You've been extremely helpful."

He studied her, his eyes twinkling. "It's been good to see you, Avril."

"You too, Gunnar." She got to her feet.

He gave her another wink. "Glad I could help. You take care now."

FIRST, she logged into the police department's secure network and initiated a general internet search, combing through various social media platforms. Out of the six tenants, she found profiles for four. There were limits to what she could access without following or liking their profiles, but she managed to match their profile pictures with their driver's licenses in the police database to get their addresses.

The fifth name on the list, a woman called Anna Frieberg, was harder to find. She didn't appear to be on social media, unless she'd gotten married or changed her name, which was possible. A search through the Swedish Transport Agency came up empty as well. Avril felt a twinge of frustration but didn't let it slow her down.

Eventually, she decided to run Anna's name through the police database, hoping for a break. To her surprise, she got a hit. Anna Frieberg was the victim in a domestic violence report filed in 2016. No charges were brought against the abuser, who appeared to be a boyfriend rather than a husband, as Anna had kept her last name. But there was an address listed in the report.

Avril wrote it down next to Anna's name on her list. It was on the outskirts of Stockholm, so it wouldn't be too hard to get to. She noted the case file number and jotted down a few more details from the report—statements, dates, and the name of the investigating officer.

She'd pay the woman a visit that afternoon.

Nils Henemark was the sixth person on the list, and despite multiple attempts, Avril could not find anything about him. He wasn't on any social media platforms, didn't own a business, wasn't listed as an employee on any company profiles, didn't appear to have a driver's license, and didn't have a criminal record. It was as if he didn't exist.

Frustrated, she tapped her fingernail on the keyboard, staring at the blank search results.

"What's up?" Krister asked, dropping into his chair after being away from his desk most of the morning. He began writing up some reports, glancing over at her.

"I can't find any trace of this man, Nils Henemark. It's like he doesn't exist," she replied, exasperation clear in her voice.

"Have you tried the church records? Sometimes births are registered by the church. They're all online now."

Her eyebrows shot up. "I haven't, no."

She dove back into her search, following a complicated trail of links to various websites, some of which were 'not found.' Eventually, she managed to pull up a list of people born in Stockholm from 1901-2006. There were a lot of names.

Exporting the list, she pasted it into a spreadsheet and searched for Nils Henemark. Bingo! There he was, born 1973 in Lännersta, a small town to the east of Stockholm.

"Okay, so he exists," she said, glancing up. "But there's nothing else online about him."

"Must be a school record somewhere?"

"Nothing I can find."

Krister shrugged, unconcerned. "Is it important?"

"Probably not. I'm going to see this woman, Anna Frieberg, after lunch. She was one of the tenants who lived in the building at the same time as Mikael, or Michael as he was known, lived there."

He grimaced, a look of concern crossing his face. "I'd come with you but I'm going to be tied up here for the rest of the day."

"That's okay. I'll be fine."

Krister worked his jaw, clearly uneasy. "Please be careful. There is a killer out there with his sights set on you, remember?"

How could she forget? "I know."

But he wasn't coming for her yet. There were two other women to get out of the way first. If he was sticking to his original cycle of murders, there would be more deaths before he came for her. The Frost Killer didn't deviate. He wasn't impulsive or spontaneous.

No, she was pretty sure he would save her till last. A shiver shot down her spine, and she exhaled quietly. Until then, she was relatively safe.

Or so she hoped.

chapter
fourteen

ANNA FRIEBERG LIVED IN AN APARTMENT BLOCK IN THE
center of Stockholm. She answered the door in her dressing gown, despite
it being early afternoon and not yet dark, and her graying hair was up in
curlers.

"Mrs. Frieberg?"

"Ms. I've never been married, dear. Not my thing. And you can call
me Anna."

Avril nodded. "I'm Avril Dahl. We spoke on the phone?"

"Yes, the FBI agent. I remember. Come in."

She entered the apartment. It was fairly spacious for an inner city flat,
and it was clear Anna Frieberg had lived here for some time. The furniture
was old and stained, the carpet worn and fraying at the edges. The curtains
looked like they'd been there since the seventies, and the walnut sideboard
was almost retro. An old-style record player sat on one end, the cover up,
and underneath was a pile of LPs.

"You like music?" Avril asked, eyeing the records.

"I love music," she corrected, in a husky voice. "I used to sing, you
know. Bluesy stuff, mainly, but my voice isn't what it used to be."

"I'm sorry to hear that," Avril said.

She shrugged. "You wanna drink?"

"No thank you."

"Oh, alright then. Sit down." She lowered herself onto the sofa and studied Avril. "What did you want to talk to me about?"

"9 Morgonsgatan."

Anna's eyes widened. "That place. Why on earth do you want to talk about that place? It burned down, you know. I was there."

"Will you tell me about that night?" Avril asked.

Anna put her hand on her chest as if to still her heart. "It was a long time ago now," she murmured. "Must be at least ten or twelve years."

"Fifteen," Avril corrected.

The woman gave her a suspicious look. "How come an FBI agent wants to know about that night?"

"It's an ongoing investigation so I'm afraid I can't comment. Please, can you tell me what happened?"

Anna took a deep breath. "It was a very cold January night. I remember because a few days earlier we'd celebrated the New Year. Now that was fun." She shook her head. "I was sleeping when I heard a commotion, and somebody screaming. It was Felicity, another woman on my floor. There were flames coming down the staircase. The entire top floor was on fire." Her body shuddered, and she wrapped her arms around her waist.

"Who lived on the top floor?" Avril asked.

"Mikael," she said softly. "And Nils."

"Nils Henemark?"

"Was that his last name? I didn't know. Did you know him?"

"No, I didn't."

She waited for Anna to continue.

"We evacuated, taking what we could, which wasn't much." She scoffed. "I think I managed to grab some knickers and my guitar. Strange what you reach for in an emergency, isn't it?"

Avril nodded. "Panic makes us behave erratically."

"You can say that again. We got out of the house and then stood there, in the road, and watched it burn. I was in my nightgown, barefoot, even though it was snowing outside."

"Did you lose everything?" Avril asked.

She sniffed and gave a short nod.

"What about Mikael?"

"He didn't make it." She hung her head. "Such a shame, a handsome young man like that."

"Did you know him well?" Avril asked.

"Fairly well." She snorted. "I would've liked to have known him better, if you know what I mean. We all would've. The ladies used to go mad for Mikael. He was so charming, you know, with his posh accent and cultured ways. Never did understand what he was doing in that dive."

"Was he there for long?"

"A couple of years. Him and Nils." Her eyes grew cloudy. "I remember he used to play classical music up in his room. It filled the house. We'd never heard music like that before. I was into jazz and blues, you know, 'cause of my singing, but I didn't know much about that type of music."

"Classical music?"

"Mikael loved it. Always used to say his favorite composer was Mozart." She bit her lower lip. "No, Beethoven. That was it. He loved Beethoven. Said he was a genius."

Avril raised her eyebrows. "What about work? Do you know what Michael did for a living?"

"Not really." She frowned, thinking back. "He used to paint occasionally. Had some lovely pictures on the walls in his bedroom. Shame they were all destroyed in the fire."

"He was an artist?"

"I don't think he sold any. It was more of a hobby, if you know what I mean."

Avril nodded. "Did Mikael and Nils arrive together?"

"I think they met at the hostel, but Nils latched on to Mikael. Followed him everywhere like a puppy dog."

Avril frowned. "Whatever happened to Nils?"

"I don't know," Anna said with a shrug. "He wasn't in the house at the time of the fire, and he never went back there. Not much to go back to. I think he saw what had happened and got spooked. Nils was, well, a bit different."

"As in intellectually challenged?"

"I think they said he was on the autism spectrum. He was smart. That's why he and Mikael were buddies. They used to discuss history, art, and politics. The rest of us didn't know what they were talking about most of the time."

The woman pulled a vape out of her dressing gown pocket and sucked on it.

"How long were you at the house for?" asked Avril.

"I arrived in 2005. I'd got a job at a record store down the road, so it was convenient—and cheap. After the fire ... Well, I floated around for a while before I moved in with my boyfriend." She snorted. "What a mistake that was."

Avril recalled the domestic abuse charge. She didn't want to talk about that, however, so she steered the conversation back to Mikael.

"Were you at the house when Mikael arrived?"

She nodded. "I tried to befriend him, but Mikael was funny like that. I thought he might be gay, at first, so many of those artsy types are, but there was this one woman." She shook her head.

"What woman?" Avril blurted out.

"I can't remember her name now, but he was crazy about her."

Avril found it hard to breathe. "What did she look like?"

"She was blonde, slim...." Her dark eyes roamed over Avril. "A bit like you, actually."

"Did you meet her?" A whisper.

"Oh, yes. Before Christmas. We had a party at the house, and she arrived."

"She came with Mikael?"

"No, Mikael was already there with the rest of us. She stormed in and confronted him. That's why I remember. They had a massive fight. It was intense. I'd never heard Mikael angry before. That's when I knew he really loved her and nobody else stood a chance."

Avril caught her breath. "He loved her?"

"The way they were arguing. You can just tell, can't you? She was crying, and he was trying to hold her, but she was having none of it."

"Did you hear what they were saying?" Avril croaked.

"Everybody did. It was impossible not to. She said to leave her alone, that she was married, and it was over."

Her heart sank. "So, they'd been seeing each other?"

Anna shook her head. "I don't think so. She said it was over a long time ago. Those were her exact words. I remember because it surprised me, but given their passion, it made sense that they had a history."

Avril's heart thumped so violently in her chest she thought she was going to have a heart attack.

A long time ago?

"Mikael begged her not to go. He said they needed to talk, but she wouldn't listen."

"What happened after that?"

"She left. Stormed out as quickly as she'd arrived. Mikael ran after her, yelling at her to come back, but she jumped into her car and drove away, leaving him standing on the sidewalk. I've never seen him so angry. I went to him, then, but he shook me off. He only had eyes for her." She shook her head. "Damn shame."

Avril found she was hyperventilating. With shaking hands, she reached into her pocket and pulled out the photograph. "Was this the woman, Ms. Frieberg?"

The woman gasped. "Why yes. That's her." She stared at it for a long time, her eyes flitting over Olivia's smiling face and coming to rest on Mikael's head. "That's Mikael. Isn't he gorgeous? Gosh, they look so happy there."

Avril nodded. They did. She wished she knew when the photograph had been taken. That December, before her mother had died?

Or was this an older photograph from "a long time ago"?

chapter
fifteen

THE KILLER BLINKED AS HE STARED OUT OVER THE STORMY white caps of the North Sea. The biting wind tugged at his hair, or what was left of it, but he didn't care. It felt good. He relished the sensation of the spray hitting him in the face, the cold, unrelenting metal of the railing beneath his gloved hands, the sharp, briny smell of the sea.

He was alive.

If only you could take memories with you into the afterlife. He scoffed. That was almost sentimental.

"Sir, it's rough out there. You should stand back. Health and safety."

The killer spun around, annoyed at the intrusion. A young ferry operator in a yellow, high-visibility jacket gestured to him. He glared at the youngster until the man shrugged and hurried back inside, unwilling to get into an altercation with a crazy passenger.

Health and safety, bah!

He'd be dead soon, anyway. What did it matter if he was swept overboard?

The ferry's bow lifted as it surged over a swell, then dropped sickeningly down the other side. The killer gripped tighter onto the railing.

Actually, it did matter. He still had work to do. He couldn't leave without finishing what he'd started. His grand finale.

Like a musician, each life he had taken was a note in his own macabre composition, each scream a crescendo in the dark music he composed. His hands, now clenching the railing, were instruments of precision, guiding the fates of his victims with the same finesse with which the maestro arranged his orchestrations.

The comparison pleased him. Just as the conductor had led the orchestra through the tumultuous waves of Beethoven's 5th Symphony, he had orchestrated his deeds with impeccable control. Every movement was calculated, each decision as deliberate as the pauses between the movements in the music. He reveled in the power, the absolute command he held over life and death, the ultimate expression of his artistry.

As the ferry plowed its way through the heaving sea, the killer contemplated his final opus. It had to be a masterpiece, the climax of all he had done before. The final crescendo. The finale would be his legacy, the ultimate testament to his life's work. It would be talked about, analyzed, and feared, long after the last note had faded into silence.

He closed his eyes and inhaled deeply, the salt-laden air filling his lungs. When he opened them again, a determination had settled in his gut. The finale was near, and he would conduct it with the same control he had exercised all his life. The final movement of his symphony was about to begin, and it would be *grand*.

chapter
sixteen

"S<small>UCH A WASTE</small>," A<small>NNA</small> F<small>RIEBERG</small> <small>MUTTERED</small>, <small>NOT FOR THE</small> first time.

"Anna, I'm trying to locate Nils Henemark. Do you have any idea where he could be?"

"Dear, I haven't seen that man since the fire."

"You said he wasn't at the house?"

"That's right. He went out that evening to look at the trains."

"The trains?"

She nodded. "He liked to do that. Would stand at the station for hours watching the trains go by. It was a hobby of his. He even had a toy train set in his bedroom. Took it everywhere with him."

Avril frowned. "Did you see him leave the house?"

"I think so." She scratched her chin. "I can't remember. I must have done, 'cause how else would I have known he'd gone out?"

"Maybe someone told you?"

She shrugged. "Maybe. Anyway, he wasn't there when the fire broke out, thank God."

"Anna, is there any way Nils could have started that fire?"

She jerked her head back. "No, of course not. Nils wasn't like that. He was a soft-hearted fellow. Wouldn't hurt a fly. Besides, he didn't smoke."

The lighter.

"It just seems like a lucky coincidence that he wasn't there when the fire broke out." Almost too lucky. Who goes trainspotting at night? There aren't many trains that run at night.

"I told you, he liked to—"

"Yes, I know. Watch the trains." Avril drew in a deep breath and let it out slowly. Something about this didn't make sense. She couldn't put her finger on it, but it felt odd. "Where did they find Mikael's body?" she asked.

"In his bed, sleeping. Hopefully the smoke overwhelmed him before he burned to death." She shuddered.

"Is there anything about Nils you can tell me? Something that might help me find him?"

Anna thought for a moment, sucking on her vape. Avril watched as the vapor twirled upwards into the air before dissipating into nothingness.

"He had a social worker. She might know where he went."

Avril's pulse leaped. "Do you have her name or number?"

"Her name was Elin. I remember because it was always Elin said this, Elin said that. He liked Elin. She was kind to him." Anna smiled sadly.

"Last name?"

She shook her head again. "Her office was close by, though, because she used to walk over to see him."

"You met her?"

"A couple of times, yes. She used to pop in to check on him from time to time. A nice lady."

Avril gave a grateful nod. It might still be possible to track down Elin the social worker. How many Elin's were operating in the Stockholm area back in 2007?

"Could you give me a description? I know she'd have changed now, but I might still be able to track her down."

"Petite, dark hair, curvy figure. I liked her," she said again.

"Thank you. You've been very helpful." Avril got to her feet.

Anna Frieberg walked her out. "If you find Nils, will you tell him I say hello? We all wondered what had happened to him after that night."

They weren't the only ones. Somehow, Avril felt Nils was the key. He'd known Mikael the best, and so he might be able to tell her how Mikael and her mother had met all those years ago."

Strange how he'd disappeared straight after the fire, not even coming home to see what had happened. An idea formed in her mind, and she didn't like the direction in which it was going.

Avril hurried back to the police station, her head swirling. She had to run her idea by Krister. He'd know if she was grasping at straws here. He'd always been a voice of reason.

KRISTER STARED AT HER. "You think this Mikael and your mother had an earlier relationship?"

"From what Anna Frieberg said, it sounds like it. They may have known each other from before—when this picture was taken." She laid it on the desk in front of him.

He glanced down at it. "Olivia does look a lot younger here. You could be right."

"It could have been before I was born," she mused, fingering the edges of the photograph. "I don't remember this dress. I don't remember her going out without my father. Not when I was little. She was a very hands-on mother."

"I know."

"Krister, what if Mikael came back into her life before she died? Anna said my mother told him to leave her alone. That she was married, and it was over a long time ago. What if he didn't listen?"

"You think he was angry that she rejected him? Enough to kill her?"

Avril gave a breathy nod. "I do, yes. What if he was obsessed, unable to handle the rejection? It's the only thing that makes sense."

"Her phone records?"

"There are calls both ways. More him calling her than the other way around."

Krister ran a hand over his chin. "So he intercepts her when she's walking the dog, on your birthday."

Avril cringed but managed a tight nod.

"He chloroforms her, drags her back to his car." Krister glanced up. "He must have had some form of transport, otherwise how did he get her out of the woods?"

"True."

"The next day, he takes her back to the clearing and leaves her there for all to see."

"She would still have been alive at that point," Anna whispered over a lump in her throat.

Krister gave a sour nod.

"The search had been called off by then." Avril felt her pulse racing as she extrapolated the data. "The police had concluded that she'd run off on her own accord. I remember them telling my father that."

Krister frowned. "My parents didn't believe it either."

"A few days later, there's a fire at the hostel where Mikael lived. His body is found in the ruins." She tapped her finger on the desk.

"I know that look," Krister said. "What are you thinking?"

She took a shaky breath. "What if Mikael staged the fire so he could disappear?"

Krister shook his head. "They found his body."

"They found a body. There wasn't enough of him to do a DNA test. He was incinerated by the fire. I read the report."

Krister stared at her. "You don't think it was Mikael Lustig who died in the fire?"

Avril leaned forward. "What if it was his housemate, Nils Henemark?"

"The autistic guy?"

"Yeah. It's possible, isn't it? Michael somehow renders Nils unconscious, maybe using the same chloroform with which he'd knocked out my mother. He places him in his bed, puts the lighter on the floor so the police would think it was an accident, then sets fire to the place. In the melee, he gets out and the house burns to the ground."

"That way, if the police ever traced him, they'd hit a dead end."

"Literally."

Krister studied her, the muscles in his lower jaw flexing. "It's a valid hypothesis. Did you have any luck tracing Nils Henemark?"

"None. Other than his birth on the church register, I can't find any record of him, although he might be in the social services system. Anna Frieberg mentioned he was seeing a social worker."

"There must be a record of him somewhere, then."

She picked up the photograph and slipped it back into her pocket. "I'll keep digging."

"Let me know if I can help."

Avril met his gaze. "What if he killed her because she rejected him, and fifteen years later, he's still killing? Killing her. Over and over again."

chapter
seventeen

Nils Henemark had been adopted at the age of two. From what Avril could gather, his adopted parents had taken care of him until he was five, at which point he'd ended up in foster care. It wasn't clear what had happened to his adoptive parents, whether they'd died, or moved away and abandoned him. Either way, Nils had gone into the foster system.

He'd been luckier than most. Placed with an elderly couple who'd looked after him all the way through his childhood and adolescence until he turned nineteen, at which point they'd died, one after the other, and Nils was left on his own.

There were no records of him for the next few years, until he arrived at the hostel in 2003. At that point, he'd been twenty-four years of age. She looked down at her notepad. If he was still alive, he'd be in his early forties now.

Avril blew a stray hair off her face, then looked up the number for Social Services. The woman who answered the phone sounded busy, and there was a rustling in the background like she was multitasking. "Yes, can I help you?"

"My name is Avril Dahl, and I'm with the Swedish Police Authority. I'm trying to trace a social worker. Her name is Elin, but I'm afraid I don't have a last name."

"Without a last name, we can't help you."

"She would have worked in the Stockholm region back in 2007. I know she was visiting a man called Nils Henemark."

A pause.

"Please, it's important I speak with her. It's to do with an active case we're working on."

"Who did you say you were again?"

"Avril Dahl, Swedish Police."

"One moment."

The rustling stopped, and Avril heard the sound of fingers on a keyboard. After several minutes, the woman came back on the line.

"I've got an Elin Gunnersson on file. She's no longer working with the social service, but could she be the one you're looking for?"

Avril's heart skipped a beat. "Yes, she might be. Do you have contact details for her?"

"Yes, but she left over four years ago. I don't know if—"

"Could I have them?" Avril interjected.

The woman read out an address and a telephone number. Avril thanked her and hung up. With a bit of luck, Elin Gunnersson had been Nils Henemark's social worker, and was still alive and would talk to her.

ELIN GUNNERSSON LIVED in a traditional Swedish cottage in a small town called Knivsta, in Uppsala County, 48 miles north of Stockholm. The cottage had thick, dimpled walls, a pitched roof, and cute, white-rimmed windows. A wooden fence surrounded the property, adding a rustic charm and separating it from its neighbors.

As Avril walked up the narrow, cobbled path, the door creaked open. "You the policewoman who phoned?" a voice called out.

"Yes." Avril held out her hand. "Avril Dahl. It's good to meet you."

"Come in," Elin said, stepping back to let Avril through the door. "I don't want to let the cold in."

They entered a cozy living room where a coal fire glowed in a modern grate. The rest of the cottage decor was quaint, keeping with the traditional style. In the corner, a Christmas tree twinkled with mismatched baubles of all sizes, filling the air with the scent of pine. Wooden beams crisscrossed the ceiling, and the floorboards creaked underfoot, even though the place was carpeted.

"You have a lovely cottage," Avril said, taking off her coat and hanging it on a peg near the door.

"Thank you. Would you like some tea?" Elin offered, her eyes warm but curious.

"No, thank you." It had been a long drive from Stockholm, but Avril was keen to get on with the questioning.

Elin led Avril into a small but functional kitchen. On the table were several gifts in various stages of being wrapped, adding a festive clutter to the room.

"Excuse the mess." Elin shifted the presents to one side. "Please, sit down. We can talk here."

Avril took a seat, noticing the worn but inviting atmosphere of the kitchen. "When did you retire?" she asked, sensing that this room was the heart of Elin's home.

"Four years ago." Elin put the kettle on, despite Avril's earlier refusal. "That kind of work wears you down after a while. You see a lot of things you'd rather you didn't."

"I can imagine," Avril said, empathizing with the emotional toll. "Domestic abuse, disabilities, neglect, illness—all the reasons one might need to call on social services. It takes a special type of person to be a social worker."

"You must see it too," Elin continued, fetching cups from a cupboard. "In your line of work."

Avril nodded, trying to build rapport. "We do, and it is tough sometimes. Some things... they don't leave you."

Elin placed the cups on the table, her eyes reflecting shared understanding. "You said on the phone that you wanted to ask me about one of my former clients?"

"Yes, a young man called Nils Henemark. I believe you visited him a few times in Stockholm, between 2006 and 2007."

Elin paused, a look of surprise crossing her face. "Nils. My goodness. I haven't heard that name mentioned in a long time."

"You remember him?" Avril's heart quickened, sensing a breakthrough.

"Of course. What a dear man. Such a shame what happened."

"What did happen?" Avril leaned in.

Elin leaned against the counter, her expression somber. "Do you know about the fire?"

"Morgonsgatan, wasn't it?"

"That's right. Nils lived there with some other young people. It was a type of hostel in the city. It burned down in 2007, a fire completely destroyed the place."

"A man died," Avril said. "Mikael Lustig."

"I remember him. Nils used to talk about him all the time. Such a tragedy."

"What did Nils say about him?" Avril asked.

"It was more the way he talked about Mikael. It was clear he worshiped the man. Mikael is so clever, Mikael showed him this, Mikael did that. Mikael was a role model for Nils, and he looked out for him too."

"You met Mikael?"

"Several times. Charming fellow. Easy smile, twinkling eyes, but...." She petered off, frowning.

"What is it?" Avril asked.

"There was something about him I didn't like. I know that sounds mean, and he never did anything to hurt Nils, quite the contrary, but there was something behind those pale blue eyes. An emptiness. It's hard to explain."

It seemed the social worker may be the only person who Mikael hadn't fooled with his charming act. "Did Nils ever mention Mikael's girlfriend? A woman called Olivia?"

"Now you're asking me...." She frowned, thinking back. "No, I don't think so, although he may have done. It was a long time ago."

"I understand." Avril hid her disappointment. "Elin, when was the last time you saw Nils?"

"Oh, that's easy. It was just before Christmas in 2006. I visited him at the house and we talked. Sometimes we used to take a walk and he'd show me the trains. He loved trains."

"So I've heard." Avril pushed her glasses up her nose. "What happened to Nils after the house burned down?"

Elin set two cups of tea down on the table. Avril immediately wrapped her hands around one of them. The warmth was comforting. "I don't know. That question has haunted me ever since that day."

"Apparently he wasn't in the house at the time of the fire."

She gave a sad nod. "That's what I was told. I looked for him, you know. I went back to the house, nearby hostels, motels, even the street, but he wasn't there. Nobody knew what had happened to him."

"Did you contact the police?"

"No, he wasn't missing. He'd just taken off, probably spooked by the fire. Nils was autistic, but he was able to look after himself. He was incredibly bright. He could argue the socks off you in a debate. And don't get him started on politics." She gave a soft chuckle.

Avril was frowning. "How do you know he wasn't missing? You said nobody knew what had happened to him."

"Because he got in touch," she said. "A couple of days after the fire."

Stunned, Avril spluttered, "He did?"

"Yes, that's why I stopped looking for him. He sent me a postcard from London. He said he'd decided to leave Sweden and see something of the world." Her eyes became glassy. "He thanked me for being his friend. That's how he put it, which was typical Nils. That's how he thought of our relationship, like a friendship. He was very trusting."

"You're absolutely sure this postcard was from Nils?"

"Yes, it was his handwriting and everything."

"Do you still have it?"

She shook her head. "Sorry, no. I threw away a lot of old stuff when I moved."

That was a pity. She'd have liked to verify it for herself.

"But he said he was in London?"

"That's right. Miss Dahl, is something wrong? You've gone white."

Avril blinked. "Yes, I'm fine. Thank you. I'm just surprised he wrote to you, that's all."

"Nils was a considerate person."

"Have you heard from him since?"

"No. The postcard was sent to the office, not my home address. I didn't expect to hear from him again, although I often wondered what had become of him, and whether he was okay."

Avril drew in a shaky breath.

She doubted Nils was okay. In fact, she was willing to bet it was Mikael who sent Elin that postcard back in 2007, and he'd done so to stop her, or anyone else, from looking for Nils. A postcard was proof he was alive and well, and living in London, rather than incinerated in a house fire.

chapter
eighteen

"You think Mikael is still alive?"

Avril stood outside Krister's house, the snow falling gently around her. She could feel it kissing her face, fluttering down her cheeks. A gentle, icy touch.

She'd rushed over to his place the moment she'd gotten back to talk about what Elin Gunnersson had said. His SUV stood in the driveway, the engine cold, which told her he'd been back for some time. "Yes, don't you? I think he sent that postcard from London, before he killed his second victim in Norway days later."

Krister stood back to let her in. "Why go all the way to London?"

Avril walked into the warm, well-lit house. "He couldn't send it from Norway, not with the killings there. It would lead them straight to him." She paused, cocking her head to one side. "Is that Christmas music?"

"Radio," he said, coloring slightly. "It is Christmas Eve."

"Oh, yeah." She cringed, feeling like she was intruding. "Maybe I should go. Have you got friends over? Family?"

"No, it's fine. It's just me. You were saying?"

She refocused her thoughts. "He wanted Elin Gunnersson to think Nils was nowhere near any of the crime scenes."

Krister crossed his arms and studied her. "So, Mikael murdered Nils and took his name?"

"It looks that way. I think he staged the scene at the hostel to make it seem like he'd died in the fire, just in case anyone came looking for Mikael. He must have known the police would find his burner phone number in Olivia's call records. Luckily for him, they didn't connect the dots, and he had time to get away."

Krister gave a slow nod. "The fire was ruled an accident, and he was pronounced dead, effectively ending any search."

"Exactly."

They stared at each other, both contemplating the scenario.

"Come into the kitchen." Krister turned and walked down the hallway. "I'm just making supper."

She hesitated, suddenly realizing how hungry she was. "I won't stay. I didn't mean to interrupt you."

"That's okay. Have you eaten?"

She thought of her empty fridge. "I'll warm something up."

"Don't be silly, it's Christmas Eve. Stay and have dinner with me." At her hesitation, he added, "We can talk about the case."

She couldn't decide whether he was being kind or he knew that would win her over, but either way, it worked. Besides, she only had an empty house to go back to. "Okay, thanks."

They went into the kitchen. There was something bubbling on the stove, and she could smell turkey roasting in the oven. After all the takeout and sandwiches she'd been eating lately, it smelled heavenly. Her stomach rumbled.

"If this is true," he said, stirring whatever was on the stove, "it means your mother was his first victim. Why did he then go on to kill those girls in Norway? He had no history with them."

"I was thinking about that." She sat down at the kitchen table. It was bare except for a ceramic dog-shaped salt and pepper set. Avril had a flashback to when they were children and Krister's mother used to make them lunch. Picking them up, she inspected them more closely. "I think something snapped in him the day he killed my mother. He liked the power it gave him. Up until that point, she'd rejected him. He'd always been on the back foot, chasing her, begging her, pleading with her to get back together. Killing her would make her pay. It gave him the ultimate control."

Krister whistled long and low under his breath. "You have thought about it."

"I work with a lot of behavioral analysts in D.C.," she said. The FBI's Behavioral Science Unit was well-known for analyzing the psyche of killers.

He opened the fridge and took out a beer. Holding it up, he asked, "Want one? I've got some wine somewhere, if you prefer?"

She reached for it. "Beer is fine, thanks."

He handed her the can and a glass. "What about the others? Do you think he was re-enacting her murder?"

A satisfying fizz escaped as she opened her beer. "I do. I think he enjoyed it so much he wanted to replicate the moment, so he looked for another target. Another blonde woman of a similar age whom he could drug and leave to die out in the cold. I think that gave him the ultimate satisfaction, seeing the life drain out of them as they slowly froze to death."

He stood still. "That's sick."

"I know. He's sick." She didn't bother pouring the beer into the glass, just lifted it to her lips and took a long, hard pull.

"According to your file, the Frost Killer murders four women each year, then disappears and isn't heard from again until the following winter where he pops up in a different location."

"That's right." She gave a small smile. "I'm glad you read it."

"It took me most of the day, but then we were waiting for forensics to get back to us. They're understaffed, given the time of year. They didn't find anything at the crime scene, by the way. Ditto for the victim's phone records and bank statements. Nothing out of the ordinary."

Avril gave a knowing nod. She'd been down this road many times before. "The killer is careful. He doesn't leave any clues."

Krister slanted his gaze. "Do you think he's got expertise?"

"Maybe."

"Could he be in law enforcement? Forensics?"

"I wondered that. He's never left any clues as to his occupation." She scratched her head. "The snowflake pendants are pretty intricate. He might work with his hands."

"What about this guy, Michael? What do you know about him?"

She set the beer can on the table. "From what I can gather, Michael was charming, interested in music, had a good knowledge of history and art. He might have worked in the arts, I suppose. He painted as a hobby. Anna Frieberg, a woman who used to stay in the hostel, said he had some nice pictures up in his bedroom."

"That correlates with what you said about the pendants."

"So, he's artsy. It doesn't help much unless I know which industry."

"Maybe he was a gallery owner or a museum curator? That photograph of him with your mother was taken at a museum."

Avril clicked her fingers. "That's right. You know, you could be on to something. I'll look into that. If he worked in a gallery or a museum, they might have records of his employment."

"They might, but it was over a decade ago." Krister put two sets of knives and forks down on the table.

As much as she hated to admit it, ten years was a long time to keep employment records. "I could check in the U.S. I never had a suspect to run through the system before." Her mind was thinking of all the checks she could run now that she had a name. Two names. Michael and Nils. If only she had access to the FBI computers. "I might be able to log in from your computer tomorrow."

"Avril, tomorrow is Christmas Day. Nobody will be in the office."

She scowled, crossing her arms. "There's a murder to solve. There are leads we need to follow up on."

"It will have to wait until after the holiday." Krister got the roast out of the oven, the rich aroma filling the room.

"I'd still like to go in," she said stubbornly.

He sighed as he transferred the food to a serving dish. "Why not take the day off and relax? Have some downtime."

"Isn't that what we're doing now?"

"I suppose." He turned around and put his hands on his hips. "You're impossible once you set your mind on something, you know that?"

She didn't reply, her brain already jumping ahead. "If we can figure out what he does for a living, it might help us figure out how he's finding his victims."

"You think it's related?" he asked, placing the dish on the table and sitting down.

"Could be." She leaned back, deep in thought.

Krister set two plates and a carving knife on the table, then sat down opposite her. "I saw you'd performed detailed background checks into all of the victims, including their habits, jobs, and even their hobbies."

"I was trying to find a connection between them, other than their looks. I know there has to be one, but..." She drifted off, staring at the wall.

Krister began carving the roast. "Fifty-two victims, not including Agnes Hellgren, and no connection whatsoever?"

"The only thing I know is that he must preselect them in advance."

"What makes you say that?" He glanced up, his knife pausing mid-cut.

"His level of preparation. He likes the snow, so he has to go somewhere with a lot of it."

"Can't leave someone to freeze to death without snow," Krister remarked dryly.

"Yes, but snow causes problems. If it's too heavy, the roads close, services don't always work, fewer people are out and about. It's not an ideal hunting ground," she said, her voice trailing off as she gazed at the turkey.

"Fewer people mean fewer potential witnesses," Krister said, nodding as he placed slices of turkey on the plates.

"Four girls every year, apart from the last two."

Krister began to carve. "Why do you think he stopped?"

She'd asked herself the same question over and over again. "I don't know. Maybe he was arrested, or changed jobs, or went on the run. Who knows? The bigger question is why did he start again?"

"And why choose Agnes Hellgren?" Krister handed her a plate piled high with food.

"Other than she fits the profile, I don't know. These murders are different. He's replicating his previous kills, so he's looking for a specific type of person. He won't be following his normal pattern of selection."

"So we dig into Agnes Hellgren's life and find out how she was targeted." Krister placed his own plate on the table.

She glanced up at him. "It'll take time. Meanwhile, he's going to move on to his next victim."

Krister sighed, sitting down. "Then what do you suggest?"

"You know what I think. We should go to Bergen. Pre-empt him."

"We've already gone over that. Without a body—"

"I know." She blinked, finally registering the perfect roast dinner on the table in front of her. "Krister, this looks amazing. I can't believe you cooked this feast for yourself."

"I was hoping it would last me a few days." He gave a self-deprecating grin.

"I'm sorry, now you're having to share it with me."

He chuckled. "I'm glad you're here."

Avril smiled, momentarily distracted. He'd gone through so much trouble, and here she was harping on about the investigation. "I remember your mother was a great cook. I used to love coming over here for lunch."

He laughed. "Who do you think taught me?"

"You must miss them."

"Sometimes, but they're happy in France, so—" He shrugged. "Let's eat."

They dug in. The food was delicious. The Christmas music soothed her nerves, and despite the topic of conversation, Avril felt a glimmer of the festive spirit. It had been so long since she'd celebrated the holiday that she'd forgotten what it was like.

"Thank you," she said between mouthfuls. "For this."

"You're welcome."

I'll give myself tonight, she thought. *One night to be a normal human being.*

Tomorrow was soon enough to go back to the living nightmare.

chapter
nineteen

THE KILLER WATCHED AS THE PRETTY, BLONDE FERRY WORKER got off the ship, backpack slung over one shoulder, laughing with a co-worker. They were both wearing Santa hats, the white fluff pulled low over their ears. He frowned. Not at the festive attire—it was Christmas Eve, after all—but because normally, she was alone.

Her shift ended at six o'clock when the Stavanger ferry docked. She disembarked at half past, after which she walked through Bergen Harbor to the bus station and caught the 484 to her apartment in Loddefjord.

Her routine was etched in his mind, and he hoped this imbecile wouldn't put a spanner in the works. It had to be today. He'd planned for it to be today.

To his relief, the co-worker walked with her through the faint layer of fog to the bus stop, then said goodbye. She waited undercover for the bus, while her friend walked in the direction of the parking lot. After tonight, he was going to wish he'd offered her a lift.

It was snowing, reducing visibility and bringing with it an icy chill. Somewhere behind him, the call of a seagull pierced the stillness, echoing off the steel hulls of the moored ships. She zipped up her jacket, checked her phone, then sat down to wait. The bus came every 41 minutes; he'd checked. Ten minutes to go. Just enough time to get to his rental car, pay the parking charge, and get into position.

The bus drew in. A couple of people got off, a few more, including the blonde, got on. The bus pulled out again, but this time the killer slotted in behind it. He followed as it left the harbor and turned right toward Sotra Bridge—a quiet predator lurking among the urban sprawl.

The suspension bridge, a marvel of modern engineering, was lit up like a Christmas tree. Far below, on the dark surface of the sound, its reflection flickered like a jumble of fireflies. It was pretty, but the killer wasn't thinking about that right now; he was focused on the next step in his plan.

His target would get off the bus at the fifth stop, then walk to her apartment. It was a ten-minute stroll, but it was cold, and he knew she walked fast, which left precious little time for him to get into position. As soon as the bus crossed the bridge, he overtook it and drove the rest of the way to the bus stop as fast as he dared.

On the seat next to him was a rag and a small bottle of chloroform. It was an old trick, but one of the best. Perfect for his purposes. As long as he was careful, it didn't kill the victim, just knocked them out for a few hours.

A few hours were all he needed.

In his experience—and he was an expert—the onset of hypothermia in these sub-zero temperatures could take anywhere from 30 minutes to an hour, although some of the slighter women succumbed faster. As their body temperature dropped below 95°F, their brain and internal organs began to shut down, with death following within a few hours. The beauty was, they didn't even know it was happening. The thought made his pulse quicken, the familiar excitement building inside him.

By the time the bus pulled into the stop, he was buzzing.

The woman got out, raised a hand to the bus driver, and then walked along the dimly lit road toward her apartment. It wasn't a deserted area, but there were few people around. During his reconnaissance, he'd decided this was the best place to take her.

He hid along a dark side road, the shadows cloaking him from view, and waited for her to walk past. She moved quickly, her court heels clacking on the pavement, drowning out the squeak of his sneakers as he slipped out and crept up behind her.

Heart pounding, he lifted the soaked rag, his breath steady despite the adrenaline surging through him. He reached around her body with practiced precision. The rag went over her mouth, preventing her from screaming, while his other arm slipped around her waist, holding her against him.

It took less than thirty seconds before she slumped in his arms. He held the rag against her face for another ten seconds just to be sure, feeling her weight grow heavy as her legs buckled. He knew she was out.

Looking behind him, he double-checked there was nobody around. The street was empty. A pair of headlights were fast approaching from the direction in which the bus had gone, so he half-dragged, half-carried her backwards, down the side street, toward his car.

Opening the back door, he laid her across the back seat. The Santa hat fell off and her hair draped over his hand, soft and silky. Soon, he'd spread it out around her on the snow, like a golden halo.

The drive into the foothills took fifteen minutes. The killer had selected this spot fifteen years ago. Fløyen Mountain overlooked the city of Bergen, its peak often shrouded in mist. He'd spent the previous day reacquainting himself with it, avoiding the funicular that took tourists to the top, instead exploring the many hiking trails that crisscrossed the range.

The funicular was closed now that it was mid-winter, and the hiking trails were deserted. The cold, hostile night deterred anyone from wandering around at this hour. A biting wind swept off the peak, chilling him, but he ignored it. He was well protected.

His victim, however, was not. He removed her jacket and jumper, leaving her in a thin shirt and her jeans. It would be faster that way. He took her shoes and socks off, a deviation from his usual routine, but time was of the essence.

Agent Avril Dahl was no fool. She'd be expecting a second murder, and since he was reliving his glorious, inaugural spree, it was no secret where he would leave the body. He counted on the ineptitude of the Swedish police to stall her. He knew they were still investigating Agnes Hellgren's murder, and despite what the FBI agent had told them, the wheels of bureaucracy turned slowly. That detective who lived next door to Avril would have to follow protocol, which meant so would she.

The risk was worth it. How else would he ensnare her?

For now, however, he had to stay one step ahead.

Invisible in his black clothing and woolen hat, the killer pulled his victim out of the car and slung her over one shoulder. He grunted with the strain. She was heavy—a dead weight despite her slim frame—and he wasn't as fit or healthy as he used to be.

By the time he'd gotten her into position, he was panting. Sweat pricked his brow as it cooled, leaving him weak and clammy. It didn't matter. His heart pumped like he'd sprinted there, and for the second time since his chemo had finished, he felt alive.

Keeping a keen eye out for law enforcement, he lifted the woman's hair off her neck and arranged it around her body, letting it slide through his fingers. He placed her arms on her chest and then carefully took the necklace out of his pocket. The snowflake was so pretty, almost mesmerizing in its glass case. Bending forward, he fastened it around her neck.

There. She looked perfect.

The killer got to his feet, then watched while nature did its work. Her breathing was shallow, the visible puffs of air growing fainter as the cold seeped into her body. Her cheeks, once flushed with life, were now pale, tinged by the icy fingers of death. Snowflakes, falling hard now, settled on her hair and eyelashes, as if covering her in a white funeral shroud.

He looked around, checking for footprints, but the few that existed would soon be covered. The cold dutifully performed its task, slowing her heart rate until it stopped completely.

He knew the minute she was gone. That stillness. There was nothing quite like it.

As the moon peeked through the heavy clouds, casting a ghostly glow on the scene, he finally turned away, leaving her to the night.

chapter
twenty

CHRISTMAS DAY DAWNED FROSTY BUT CLEAR. A THIN LAYER of ice coated the windows, reflecting the pale morning light. Avril lay in bed thinking about Krister and their evening together. It had been fun. Her first real Christmas in nearly ten years. How sad was that?

Except, the Frost Killer was still out there. He wouldn't stop just because it was Christmas. A man like that didn't celebrate the holiday; he was evil. If she was going to catch him, she couldn't rest either.

After a quick shower, she got dressed and went around to Krister's. Frost crunched under her shoes as she strode up the driveway. He answered the door in his sweatpants and a crumpled T-shirt, his hair messy. "Seriously, Avril? It's not even nine o'clock yet."

Still, he got dressed, made them a cup of coffee, and then drove them to the precinct. The streets were eerily quiet, devoid of the usual hustle and bustle. Everyone was at home with their families, opening presents beneath twinkling Christmas trees. There was a sense of stillness, as if the city itself was taking a breath.

As expected, the police station was deserted, with only a skeleton crew manning the front desk and dispatch.

"Use my computer. I've got my laptop." Krister gestured to his desk.

After several attempts, Avril finally managed to log on to the FBI's National Crime Information Center (NCIC) database. The computer screen flickered, the system lagging slightly as she navigated through the layers of security. She typed in "Michael Lustig" and waited. Nothing came up. She tried "Mikael" but got the same result.

"It wasn't going to be that easy," Krister said dryly, standing behind her with a cup of coffee in hand.

She moved on to "Nils Henemark," but the search yielded no useful leads either.

"Damn." Avril slumped back in her chair, frustration evident in her furrowed brow.

"He must be using an alias," Krister rationalized, leaning against the desk. "It makes sense. He wouldn't use anything already known to law enforcement, in any country."

Avril knew he was right. It had been a long shot. "What about Interpol?" he asked, glancing at her screen.

She typed in the details again, this time accessing the Interpol database. The system was slower, the international queries taking longer to process. After several minutes, she shook her head. "No hits. It seems he was only known as Mikael here. If we're going to find anything, it'll be in Sweden."

"Then we'll have to wait until the twenty-seventh. Nothing is open over the holidays."

Avril gave a resigned sigh. "In the meantime, I'm going to look at the victims' social media accounts. There might be something I missed." Even though she'd checked them again and again over the years. With every new victim, there'd been a renewed search, which never turned up any new connections.

Still, she couldn't give up.

"I'll dig into Agnes Hellgren's background," Krister said, turning back to his laptop. "Maybe something there will tell us how he chose her."

They worked in silence for a short while, until Krister said, "Agnes used to do the books for a small gallery. Do you think that's relevant?"

Avril glanced up. "It might be. Where's the gallery?"

"Not far from where they live, actually. We could pay it a visit next week, when they reopen."

"I'll look for any gallery jobs in the other victim's profiles, the ones that are still online." Adjusting her glasses, Avril got to work. It took some time, but eventually she found a photograph on an archived Facebook page of a woman standing in front of a painting.

Hearing her gasp, Krister looked up. "What?"

"I think I may have found something." The post read: *Started a new job today. Wish me luck.*

Krister had come around the desk and looked where she was pointing. "Was that one of the victims?"

Avril felt a chill slide down her spine. "Yes, five years ago in Oregon. I'll have to confirm, but it looks like her job was at a gallery. I'll reach out to the local PD there, see if they can provide any additional information about her employment."

"Good idea. Any others?"

"I don't know yet."

They divided the list between them and trawled the social media pages, mostly Facebook, with renewed vigor.

"Got one," Krister exclaimed, a short while later. "2016. The Red Gallery Chicago. I'll contact Chicago PD, have them pull the case file and send over anything they have on her employment there."

"I've found another one," Avril whispered, her pulse racing. "Salem, 2018." She stared at Krister over her computer, the enormity of the discovery dawning on her. "We've done it. We know how he targeted them. Krister, this is huge. I've never made a breakthrough like this before."

He gave her a cautious smile. "The killer must work in the art world."

She sat up straight. "We're getting closer. I can feel it."

"Well, let's keep going and see if we can link all the victims, then we might be able to find a pattern. It's something to take to the Commissioner, anyway. We'll need to brief him on this new development and get his approval to pursue this lead further."

KRISTER GOT off the phone with his boss, the Police Commissioner, and raked a hand through his hair.

"What?" asked Avril, sitting opposite him.

It wasn't good news. Despite their two days of research, which had turned up at least eighteen victims with possible links to galleries or museums, his boss wasn't interested. "He doesn't think a few social media images warrant racing off to question all the galleries in Stockholm. He wants us to concentrate on closing the Agnes Hellgren case."

"He doesn't think it's related." Avril huffed and leaned back against the desk. It was the day after Boxing Day, and most of the team was back at work.

Krister grimaced but shook his head. "Numbers are down, and the department review is coming up. He wants an arrest."

"We could go to Norway," Avril suggested. "Try to intercept the killer there."

He sighed. "Your serial killer theory isn't holding water with the Powers That Be. They need more than one kill to link it to the other murders."

She threw up her hands. "How can they be so narrow-minded? It's obvious it's the same killer."

"To you, maybe, but don't forget, the Frost Killer hasn't been active in Sweden since 2010."

Avril scowled. "Did you point out the similarities to my mother's murder?"

"Of course, but without concrete evidence—" He shrugged.

Her shoulders drooped.

Krister felt her frustration, but there was nothing he could do. The Commissioner would not sanction a trip to Norway before a murder had even taken place. Preventative policing was not a policy they adhered to. They were there to pick up the pieces after the crime had been committed, dealing with the fallout, the heartbreak, the grief. Interviewing witnesses, questioning suspects, and tracking down the perpetrator. Not using up valuable police budget to traipse across Scandinavia just in case he struck again.

Freddie broke the tight pause that followed, pink-cheeked and out of breath. "Sir, I might have something."

"Yeah?"

"You know the victim worked for her husband's father, Olaf Senior. She did the books for his restaurant business."

"Uh-huh."

"Well, he's under investigation for tax fraud. I've just spoken to the fraud department, and they're looking into his accounts. Suspected tax evasion."

"Really?"

"But—" Avril looked up.

Krister shook his head. "Bring in the father, let's see what he has to say."

"It's not him," Avril ground out.

"I'm sorry, Avril, but procedure comes first. If he has a motive for killing his daughter-in-law, we have to explore that."

She shook her head. "You're wasting your time with him."

Freddie shot her a curious look. She supposed it wasn't often someone spoke to the boss like that. Even rarer that he allowed it.

Krister faced his deputy. "Go get him, Freddie. I don't want to waste any more time on this than necessary."

"Yes, sir." The young officer turned and hurried off.

Krister sank into his chair. As much as he believed Avril, he couldn't ignore a suspect with a motive right in front of his face.

The interrogation took place at three o'clock that afternoon. By the time Krister got to the interview room, Mr. Olaf Hellgren Senior was prepped and waiting, having been read his rights by the uniformed officer who had brought him in.

Krister pushed open the door and studied the grey-haired man sitting in the steel chair. The questioning was being filmed and recorded, as was their standard procedure, with a video camera mounted on the wall and a microphone on the table. "Mr. Hellgren, I'm Detective Jansson. I'll be conducting this interview today. You have the right to have an attorney present during questioning. Do you wish to have an attorney present?"

Olaf Senior grunted. "No, I don't need a lawyer. Why am I here?"

"We just need to ask you some questions, that's all."

"Is it about my daughter-in-law?"

"It is, yes."

He nodded, his expression grim.

Krister sat down and opened his notebook. "Mr. Hellgren, I understand you're being investigated for tax evasion?"

A scowl. Olaf Senior wasn't as amiable as his son. "So what? I didn't do anything wrong."

"According to the Swedish Tax Agency, your sales figures don't comply with your VAT return. That's a serious offense, Mr. Hellgren."

"It's an honest mistake. My bookkeeper isn't experienced."

"Your bookkeeper is dead, Mr. Hellgren."

He dropped his head. "I know."

"When did you last see your daughter-in-law, Mr. Hellgren?"

"She came in two days ago to do the books. She comes in every Friday morning."

Krister noticed he was still talking about her in the present tense, a sign he hadn't fully processed her death yet. It also meant he probably wasn't guilty of murdering her. Still, he decided to push him a bit, see if he could elicit a reaction.

"When she came in, did you argue? Were you angry at her about the fraud investigation?"

"No, it was an honest mistake."

"Are you sure? Maybe she threatened to go to the police with evidence of tax evasion? That would give you motive to want her silenced."

"I told you, she didn't realize what she was doing. She's not an experienced accountant. I had no reason to harm her."

"It might be time you got a professional accountant," Krister suggested.

"I can't afford it. Times are tough, if you hadn't noticed. The hospitality industry is suffering. We'll probably have to close down."

"You will have to close if you've been defrauding the government. That's a felony offense, Mr. Hellgren."

Olaf Senior sighed. "Look, I don't know what happened to my daughter-in-law. She was fine when she left the restaurant on Friday."

"Where were you on Saturday afternoon, sir?" Krister asked, making a note to confirm the time of death with the medical examiner.

"I've just said, I was at the restaurant."

"All afternoon?"

"Yes, from about noon until we closed at midnight."

"Can anyone vouch for you? "

"Yeah, my chef. He was there preparing for the evening shift. We open at six."

"We're going to need his name and contact details, please, so we can corroborate your alibi."

Olaf Senior gave a sullen nod and provided the information, which Krister jotted down in his notebook. He would have uniforms follow up and confirm, but for now, it seemed Olaf Senior was not their prime suspect.

A COUPLE OF HOURS LATER, Freddie approached Krister's desk. "Franco Vertelli, the chef, remembers Olaf Senior being at the restaurant around four o'clock when he got there to prep for the evening, but he said he couldn't swear he was there the entire time. He was busy in the kitchen, while Olaf was in his office above the restaurant. He could have left and come back without the chef knowing."

Krister exhaled. He'd been hoping this could easily be disproved and they could get back to investigating the Frost Killer's victims and the gallery link. Avril had been trying to get through to someone in Human Resources at the National Museum, but it was proving tricky. It seemed the administrative departments were still closed.

"Any cameras in the restaurant?" he asked.

"No, I checked."

"What about his vehicle? If he abducted Agnes, he must have used his car. Let's bring it in for analysis."

"We'll need a warrant for that."

"I'll get the Commissioner to sign off on it."

"Yes, sir."

An unconscious woman would need transporting. They knew she hadn't been abducted from the woods, not like Avril's mother back in 2006, so she'd been driven there. That meant there could be hair or fibers from her clothing in the suspect's vehicle.

"Let's try to figure out where she was taken from," Krister told his team. "What were her last movements? Who was the last person to see her alive?"

"She left the gym at three-thirty on Saturday," Ingrid said. "I spoke to the manager who said she swiped out at that time."

"Right, and where did she go from there?"

Ingrid shook her head.

"Her car was found outside her house, so presumably she was taken from there."

Krister knew there'd been no sign of forced entry. "Okay, so she was either taken from outside the house, when she got home, or someone knocked on the door and she let them in."

Ingrid nodded.

"We couldn't find her purse, so she may have been taken when she got home. If she'd let the killer in, it would still be in the house."

"Good point," Krister said. "Any of the neighbors see or hear anything?"

"Not that we can gather. Herman is going door-to-door to make sure."

"Okay, good work guys, let's keep it up."

Avril gasped and jumped out of her seat. The chair tumbled backwards, causing everyone to look over at her.

"What is it?" Krister asked, clocking her ashen face.

"Krister, we have to go to Bergen."

"Avril, I told you, I can't sanction—"

"There's been a second murder," she breathed, her eyes flashing. "A body has been discovered on the lower slopes of Fløyen Mountain, exactly where Lene Hansen was found in 2007."

Krister felt his stomach lurch. "Is it him?"

She gave an earnest nod. "It's him."

chapter
twenty-one

"IT'S EXACTLY LIKE THE SECOND MURDER," AVRIL SAID, AS they drove to Stockholm's Arlanda Airport. "She was found on the lower slopes, just off the hiking trails."

"Did you visit the site last time?"

Avril gave a grim nod. "After I'd graduated from the Academy. It's an isolated spot, open to the elements but far enough away from the track not to be seen."

"How would he have got her up there?" Krister asked. "Is there a service road?"

"No, not really. From what I can remember it was a walk. He would've had to carry her body up there."

"What's the victim's name?" He'd written down all the details, after speaking to the senior investigating officer in Bergen, but had barely glanced at it. They'd been more concerned with the location of the body, and the position in which she'd been found.

"Erika Fornstedt. Twenty-six years old and from Bergen. That's all we know." There hadn't been time to look into her background. Once they'd confirmed her death matched Lene Hansen's murder fifteen years earlier, complete with snowflake pendant, Krister had told his boss, who'd had a long, hard think about it, then allowed Krister to fly over and take a look.

"You have to pay for your own ticket," Krister had told Avril. "The Commissioner is not in a generous mood."

Avril shrugged. She knew the budget was tight. It was the same for police departments all over the world. "I'm okay with that."

"Don't take it personally. He's annoyed this isn't a simple open and shut case. Multiple homicides and joint operations complicate everything."

Avril pursed her lips. That wasn't her problem. All she cared about was that the Frost Killer was back, and he was playing a game with them.

With her.

He wanted to get her to Norway. She felt a flutter of anxiety. Why? What did he have in store for her?

Whatever it was, she had to be one step ahead.

The flight from Stockholm to Bergen took an hour and twenty-five minutes. On landing, they hired a car and Krister drove them to the police station. Bergen police headquarters was a stark, modern building nestled amidst the traditional Scandinavian architecture. The gray stone facade gave it a somber, imposing presence.

Avril shivered as they walked toward it, the cold seeping into her bones. "You okay?" Krister cast a worried glance in her direction.

"It's cold here," she whispered, drawing her coat around her.

"We'll be inside soon." The victim's body had already been removed from the mountain and was at the morgue awaiting an autopsy.

They walked through the main entrance, the automatic doors hissing open to reveal a vast, open lobby, strangely devoid of police officers. The clicking of heels on marble made them glance up.

"Detective Jörgensen?" Krister asked, as they were greeted by a woman in a suit and blazer, her dark hair framing her face in a severe cut. She gave a curt nod and held out her hand. They both shook it. It was ice cold. Her personality didn't look much warmer, either. "I'm Krister Jansson and this is my associate, Avril Dahl from the FBI."

Detective Jörgensen's eyes flickered over Avril briefly, her gaze cool and assessing, before snapping back to Krister. "Won't you come with me?"

They followed her up a flight of stairs and into the bowels of the building, passing several smartly dressed officers striding purposefully along the corridors. "How much do you know about the murders?" Avril asked, getting straight to the point.

"Not much before your phone call," she replied stiffly. "I've heard of him, of course, but today was the first time I read the case history. He's a long-standing and prolific serial killer. Leaves his victims to freeze to death. His calling card is the snow pendant, which we found on the body."

She beckoned them into a small room which Avril took to be her office. There wasn't much in it, other than a desk and chair, a window and a computer. No personal items, not even a photograph, but then Avril's office in D.C. was the same. Hers was littered with old files, research and anything pertaining to the investigation, while Jörgensen's seemed empty. Maybe it was just a temporary working area.

"Can we see it?" Avril asked.

"It's being processed and is in evidence."

"As soon as possible, then?" Krister asked, smiling.

The stony glare softened a bit, and Jörgensen nodded. Clearly, she was more responsive to Krister than her. Avril knew she rubbed some people the wrong way, and it was something she was trying to work on, although not very successfully.

After they'd told Jörgensen about Agnes Hellgren, and the reenactment of his first murder spree, the Norwegian detective shook her head. "So the third murder will be here too?"

Avril was impressed she'd read enough of the file to know there were four murders every year. "Yes, if he sticks to his original plan, the next victim will be abducted in Oslo, and her body placed near a hiking trail on the Bygdøy Peninsula."

"Like Erika's?"

"Yes, exactly the same."

Jörgensen frowned. "I can notify the Oslo police, but they won't be able to do anything until the woman is actually taken."

"We know." Krister grimaced. "That's the problem."

"But if you know where the body will be found—" She broke off, thinking.

"Exactly." Avril leaned forward. "That's what he's counting on. He's playing a game of cat and mouse with us."

"But why?" Jörgensen looked at both of them in turn. "Why is he reenacting his first murders?"

"We don't know for sure," Krister said carefully.

"It's his final killing spree," Avril cut in. "After this, he's going to disappear, and we'll never hear from him again."

"How do you know that?"

She paused. "I can't explain it. I just do."

Jörgensen glanced at Krister.

"It's a theory," he explained, shooting Avril a warning look. "He disappeared two years ago, and we thought he'd retired then, but now he's back and mimicking his first kills. We think it's his grand finale."

Jörgensen nodded slowly. "Okay, so how do we find this man, this Frost Killer?"

"We need to see where she was found," Krister said. "It's unlikely he's left any clues, but you never know."

Avril spoke up. "Have you traced the victim's movements? Do you know where she was taken?"

A nod. "She worked for a ferry operator at the harbor and had just come off her shift. She caught the 484-bus home—we have her on the bus camera footage. After that...." Jörgensen shrugged.

"She never made it home?" Krister asked.

The detective shook her head. "Her parents are distraught, obviously. We've got a family liaison officer with them."

Avril frowned. "She must have been taken after she got off the bus. Have you appealed for witnesses?"

"Not yet. We're still going through the bus footage and trying to identify them. Someone may have seen something."

"They won't have," Avril said. "He'd have waited until the bus was gone before he took her. He's careful that way."

Jörgensen threw her a hostile look. "We'll check anyway, just to be sure."

"Thank you," Krister said, standing up. "If you'll direct us to the crime scene, we'll get out of your hair."

"You should also check anyone who rented a vehicle in the last few days," Avril said, thinking out loud. "He would need a car in order to move her body. It'll be a fake name, of course, but you might be able to trace it back to a hotel, or the rental company might have security cameras." Then she scratched her head. "Check under the name Nils Henemark."

"You think he'll use his assumed name?" Krister said.

"Maybe. He won't know we've figured that out."

"You have a suspect?" Jörgensen's eyes widened.

"We have a name," Krister said. "But that's a recent development, so keep it to yourself. We can't afford to let the press know. If he gets wind of it, he might disappear again."

Avril thought not. Michael would see this through, no matter what. That's how they would catch him. That's what she was banking on.

chapter
twenty-two

THE SNOWY HILLSIDE TRAIL WAS CORDONED OFF WITH BRIGHT yellow tape. Forensic technicians scurried around, clothed head to toe in white suits, blending seamlessly with the background.

Avril and Krister pulled on booties and navigated the steep slope to where the body had been found by a hiker earlier that morning. On either side, tall frost-covered pines bordered the trail, branches sagging under the weight of the snow.

"Got anything?" Krister asked the Crime Scene Officer, his breath misting in front of him. Jörgensen had called ahead and informed him they were coming.

The officer, his face partially hidden behind a mask, looked up from his work. "There are car tracks in the parking lot," he said, in the gruff monotone of someone who'd processed too many crime scenes. "We've cast the tire's impression. Might just lead us to the vehicle he was driving."

Avril turned to Krister. "He could still be driving the hired car. He's got to get down to Oslo for the next—"

"Jörgensen is contacting the Oslo police," Krister interjected. He turned back to the CSO. "Anything else?"

"A partial footprint off the side of the trail. It's deep, which means he was probably carrying her body at that point."

Avril's heart skipped a beat. "Can we see it?"

"This way."

He led them back down the path to roughly a hundred feet from where the victim's body was found. Sure enough, to the side of the path was a deep indent, the outline partially obscured by fresh snow. The surrounding area had been carefully marked and photographed, with flags indicating points of interest.

The indent was clear, the heel and ball of the foot pressing deeply into the snow. It looked like he'd stumbled under the weight and his foot had slipped off the path, leaving a ragged edge where the snow had been disturbed.

"He's making mistakes," Avril whispered, crouching down to get a closer look. "He's not as careful as he usually is."

"It's a long way up here," Krister mused, surveying the steep, icy trail. "And he's not a spring chicken anymore."

"He'd be in his forties or fifties," Avril guessed. "It's not that old."

Krister shrugged. "True, but carrying a body up this kind of terrain would take a toll on anyone, especially in this weather."

Avril stared at the footprint, gnawing at her lip.

"What are you thinking?" Krister asked. The CSO stood waiting, his hands in his pockets.

"I don't know."

The position of the body was off the trail, in a clearing but beyond a line of trees. The snow around where she'd lain was pockmarked with footprints from the crime scene technicians. "Were there any prints around her body?" Krister asked.

The CSO shook his head. "Not a one. The heavy snowfall last night covered all those tracks. Only the one on the path remained. The Senior Investigating Officer will have the crime scene photographs."

Avril sighed. She'd expected as much. Still, they had the partial. That was something.

When they got back to the Bergen Police Station, Detective Jörgensen was waiting for them in the lobby, her expression as steely as ever. "The pathologist confirmed what you said. Chloroform was found on her lips."

Avril gave a knowing nod. "Are they doing the autopsy now?"

"Yes, they started an hour ago."

"What about the crime scene photographs?" Krister asked. "Are they available yet?"

"Follow me," Jörgensen replied, turning on her heel.

Jörgensen led them to an empty conference room and flicked on the light. The walls were bare, not a picture in sight, only a wide window covered by a blackout blind. She gestured for them to sit at the large table in the center, where a laptop awaited.

"The crime scene photographs are on here," she said, sitting down and opening the laptop. "We're still processing everything, but this is what we have so far."

Both Avril and Krister leaned in, peering over her shoulder as she began clicking through the images one at a time. The photos displayed the scene in stark detail: the deep footprint, the disturbed snow, and the path leading up to where the body was found.

"Hold it there." Krister stared at the body positioned in the snow. Her arms were resting on her chest, her hair spread out around her like a frosty, golden crown. The photograph had been taken from above, looking down at the body. The snow around her was unmarked.

"Do we know the time of death?" Krister asked.

"Hard to say for sure," Jörgensen said, frowning. Avril knew the snowy conditions and freezing temperatures made it difficult to determine an accurate timeline. "The pathologist thinks it was last night, somewhere around nine o'clock, give or take a few hours."

"What time did the victim's shift end?" Avril asked.

"Six. Her bus was at six forty-one and would have reached her stop at six fifty-three."

"If he took her on her walk home, she would have been abducted around seven o'clock," Avril said, thinking out loud. "By the time he'd gotten her up the hiking trail, it would be nearer to eight, and hypothermia would have set in by nine. Yeah, I think that's an accurate assumption." She met Jörgensen's eyes. "Can we see the pendant?"

"This way."

They followed her down another long corridor to a locked room. Jörgensen knocked, and a uniformed officer opened the door. He asked to see their ID and then entered their names into his computer.

"Okay," he said, giving a firm nod. "Go ahead. It's over there on the back table. We haven't stored it away yet."

Jörgensen walked over to the table and opened the box. She took out a plastic evidence bag in which the snowflake pendant had been placed. Avril took it from her and, adjusting her glasses, inspected it through the bag.

"It's the same," she whispered.

The paper snowflake was expertly carved and encased in glass. Avril reached beneath her shirt and took out her own pendant. Lifting it over her head, she compared it to the most recent one. The design was the same, as she knew it would be.

Jörgensen shot her a curious glance but said nothing.

Avril handed the pendant back to Jörgensen. "Thank you."

Krister stared at the necklace she held in her hand. "Is that Olivia's?"

She nodded. "I use it for comparison purposes." She wasn't in the mood to get into why she wore it, not in front of the Norwegian detective.

Krister was quiet on the way back to Jörgensen's office, and she knew she'd shocked him by wearing the pendant. It was a bit macabre. Obsessive, even. But her mother's death was what had determined her path. Everything that had happened had started with her murder. Her police training, the move to America, her job at the FBI. She'd dedicated the last ten years to hunting this man. No one understood what that felt like. No one could, not unless they'd experienced it themselves.

The pendant was a constant reminder of why she was doing this. When her energy sagged, when she felt like giving up, she looked at the pendant and it renewed her. In a weird way, it gave her the strength to go on. To keep searching.

Once they were inside, he turned to her, "Avril, you know this man better than anyone. What do you think we should do now?"

"We should go to Oslo."

"You think he's already there?" Jörgensen asked.

"He'll be on his way. That's the scene for the third murder. He's done here."

"Surely he'll be expecting us to go there," Krister said, studying her. He had that concerned look in his eyes, the one where he knew she was going to do something stupid, and he'd be roped into it whether he liked it or not. Like when they were kids and she'd swam out to the island in the lake, and he'd gone after her, even though the water was freezing, and it was getting dark. Or when she'd snuck onto Mr. Jansson's farm to steal some of his rare, arctic raspberries, and he reluctantly followed. They'd only just escaped being discovered.

"Yes." She felt the weight of her mother's necklace pressing into her chest, as if it were burning a mark there. "I think that's the point."

"He's trying to bait you?"

She met his gaze. "Yes."

"Which means he's going to kill you."

"Maybe."

Krister sighed. Jörgensen was watching them curiously. "Who is Olivia?"

"She was my mother," Avril said. "The Frost Killer's first victim."

A restrained nod. "I thought I recognized the name. Olivia Dahl, Sweden, 2006?"

"That's right." Avril was impressed that out of fifty-four other victims, she'd remembered her mother.

"The first is often the most significant," Jörgensen said, tilting her head. "Does the killer have some connection to your family?"

She was astute, Avril would give her that much.

"We think he was my mother's lover, before she met my father," she added, hastily. "He reappeared when I was twelve and started harassing her. Soon after, she was dead. That's all we know."

"And that name you gave me, Nils Henemark, is that him?"

"That's his assumed name," Krister said. "His real name is Mikael Lustig."

"Why is none of this on the system?"

"It's a recent development," Krister said. "We haven't been able to confirm it yet."

"If he stole Nils Henemark's identity, there's no reason why he wouldn't have stolen someone else's too," Avril mused. "He could have any number of aliases."

"I'll get my team working on the rental car agencies, and cross-check those with the hotels and guest houses in Bergen. If he's using that name, we'll find him."

They followed her down the corridor to the squad room where several detectives and officers sat in three neat rows, working on computers or talking on the phone. There was a gentle electronic hum in the background, and somewhere, a printer spewed out pages with a rhythmic clickety-clack.

When it stopped, Jörgensen asked for everyone's attention. The detectives stopped working and looked up, regarding Avril and Krister with open curiosity.

"Detective Jansson and Agent Dahl are working with us on this morning's homicide. We're looking for a man going by the name Nils Henemark. Please check all the car hire companies, hotels, guest houses, ferries, et cetera in the last week or so. He's a person of interest in the murder of Erika Fornstedt."

A few nods and grunts, and the team got back to work. Jörgensen ran a tight ship, and it was clear she garnered a substantial level of respect. Avril wondered what she'd done to deserve it. A woman in charge had to earn esteem; it wasn't naturally given. Especially by a largely male team.

"You can sit here." Jörgensen gestured to an open desk. "I'll get an extra chair."

"Thank you, but we won't be staying long," Avril said, glancing at Krister.

"I'll book us on an early morning flight to Oslo," he said. "It's too late to drive. It'll take six hours."

"We'd be there by morning," Avril insisted, eager to get on the road.

"I'm not driving through the night." That look again. "Your killer has to sleep too. Tomorrow will be soon enough."

"He's *my* killer now, is he?" She raised an eyebrow.

"You have to admit, he seems to be as obsessed with you as you are with him. It's bizarre, like you have this unspoken connection or something."

Avril fell silent. It was true. He'd stalked her, broken into her house, tampered with her things, and reenacted his first two murders in order to get her attention. Was this how the other victims felt before they died? Scared? Fearful? Anxious?

Did they know they were being watched?

Even now, she had the uncanny feeling he knew exactly where she was, and was laughing at her while he was on his way to Oslo for his next crime. *Catch me if you can* he seemed to say.

She gritted her teeth. "I will," she murmured.

"What was that?" Krister asked, from opposite the desk. He had his laptop open and was running his finger over the mousepad.

"Nothing," she said.

I will.

THE DAY HAD DESCENDED into darkness, and the lights burned bright in the Bergen Police Station when one of the detectives gave a low hiss. Avril glanced up. "Have you found something?"

He ignored her and picked up the phone. Avril waited, seething, but she understood he'd want to tell his boss before he divulged details of the case to a stranger.

Seconds later, Jörgensen strode through the door. "Tell us what you've found, Arne."

Both Avril and Krister turned to him expectantly.

He cleared his throat.

"A guest by the name of Nils Henemark stayed at a holiday cottage in Fyllingsdalen, outside of Bergen."

Avril gasped. "Is he still there?"

"Checked out this morning."

"Damn it!"

A few of the other officers glanced at her in surprise.

Krister frowned. "Can we get a forensic team there?"

Jörgensen nodded. "I'll get on it. Arne, make sure they lock it down and don't let anyone in there, not even the cleaning staff."

"Will do."

She turned to Avril and Krister. "You coming?"

chapter
twenty-three

"YOU'RE SURE NOBODY HAS BEEN IN THERE SINCE THIS morning?" Jörgensen asked the manager of the holiday cottages. They stood on the porch of the main office, overlooking a dark lake. The inky surface reflected the overcast sky, and Avril was sure it was going to snow again. The cottages were scattered around the shoreline, and she was sure it was a pretty spot in the summer, but right now, their windows were dark and lifeless like vacant eyes watching over the water.

The terse, balding man nodded. "I was about to send in the maid when your constable called."

"Good, let's proceed."

They trudged across the gravel-strewn parking area toward a particularly secluded wooden cabin. The maritime-themed lantern by the door flickered, casting an unsettling glow over the deck, illuminating a table with two benches. Beyond the railing, the lake lay in wait—dark, vast, and seemingly endless.

"Is that music coming from inside?" Krister asked as the manager slotted the key into the lock.

He scowled. "Shouldn't be. There's nobody here."

"It certainly sounds like it," Jörgensen said.

Pushing open the door, they stepped into the room. Avril clutched Krister's arm as the hauntingly familiar strains of Beethoven's Piano Concerto No. 1 whirled around her.

How?

"Is something wrong?" Krister asked, staring at her face. "You've gone white."

"This music," she whispered.

"Oh, yeah. You were playing it the night you arrived."

She widened her eyes.

He inhaled sharply. "Shit. He heard you?"

Avril felt her entire body tremble. "He must have. How else would he have known?"

He'd been there, outside her house, listening to her as she went through her father's things. Watching through the window. Her grip on Krister's arm tightened. Had he left the record out on the floor for her to find, knowing she'd pick it up?

The notes that once danced gracefully in the air now hovered with an ominous edge. The allegro, which had previously stirred her to tears, now mocked her. The adagio, instead of providing solace with its slow, reflective melody, dragged out, stretching the seconds into minutes, each one heavy with the knowledge that *he* had orchestrated this moment with chilling intention.

"Where is it coming from?" Krister snapped, looking around the room.

"Over there." Jörgensen strode to the bedside pedestal where a small device lay. "It's an iPod. I haven't seen one of these in years."

Krister frowned. "What's he playing at?"

"He's taunting me," Avril whispered. "He's using my mother's favorite record as a psychological weapon."

Jörgensen turned to her. "But why?"

"I don't know." A cold shiver ran down her spine as the room filled with the ghastly echo of Beethoven's creation. "Turn it off. Please."

Pulling on a forensic glove, Jörgensen picked up the device and hit stop. Silence filled the cottage, the melody replaced with the frantic rhythm of Avril's heart.

Krister turned to face her. She let go of his arm, her legs still unstable. "Why is he doing this, Avril? What aren't you telling me?"

"Nothing."

"Come on, Avril. I know you. I can tell when you're holding back."

"I'm not, Krister, I swear."

"He's watching your every move. He's orchestrating them, for God's sake. He knew you'd be here. The girl in the mountain, the pendant, the cottage, the music," he waved his hands around the room, "were for you. He's telling you something. What is it?"

Jörgensen watched her from across the room.

"I don't know," she whispered again. "I don't know."

chapter
twenty-four

THE KILLER LEFT THE HOTEL IN OSLO, KEEPING TO THE shadows. It had been three days since his last kill, and he was hungry again. Damn, he'd missed this. The thrill of the chase. The anticipation of what was to come. The God-like power he held over his victim.

He watched her walk up the road to the train station. She had an ambling gait, and a slight limp from an old injury, although he didn't know what it was from. Her social media profile hadn't been clear.

Blonde hair up in a tight bun—he preferred it loose—and her navy skirt hugging her slim thighs under that dark coat, her heels echoing on the damp sidewalk. He watched her go, studying the sway of her hips as she disappeared into the station.

The killer waited a few seconds, then followed. Invisible amongst the after-work commuters, he blended into the bustling melee working its way toward the platforms. Her blonde head bobbed and swayed as she navigated her way through the crowd.

Holding back, he waited until she'd moved halfway down the platform, then shuffled onto it, making sure to keep behind a row of commuters. Cap down, he surveyed her from afar, watching as she glanced up at the announcement board. The next train was in six minutes.

The woman checked her phone, her thumbs cavorting over the screen as she typed a message. To whom, he wondered. A boyfriend? That could pose a problem.

This was his first time following her. A fact-finding mission. Would she suit his purposes? On paper, she was perfect. A history of drug abuse, no family, a childhood spent hopping between foster families in the social system. She'd even done a stint as a stripper before securing the job at the hotel, although you wouldn't know it to look at her.

She was a hotel receptionist now. A step up, in his opinion. It seemed Greta Thorstvedt had turned her life around. Pity he was going to cut it short. He felt a tinge of something, but it wasn't remorse. He didn't feel things like that. Oh, he'd tried, but where normal people would cry, laugh or feel regret, he felt only emptiness. A dark hole in his soul that would never be filled. A pit of nothingness.

The closest he got was the thrill he felt now. Anticipation. It made his heart beat faster, a sensation he relished. And afterwards, a quiet delirium. A hunger, satisfied. An urge, sated.

That fleeting buzz that lifted him up and made him feel human for a few short days, before it faded into nothingness, and the emptiness returned.

She'd filled it. Sort of. Once, a long time ago.

Olivia.

Their fleeting, passionate affair.

She'd been older than him. His first. They'd met at a concert in the park. A beautiful summer's day, the smell of freshly cut grass, and her perfume. Jasmine, with a hint of violet. He didn't remember the name, just the creator—Givenchy. The endless daylight had shone on her pale blonde hair and brought a flush to her cheeks. He'd never seen anyone more beautiful.

Their eyes had met, and he'd felt an instant attraction. A jolt of desire, something that had never happened to him before ... or since.

Why it had happened then, with her, he had no idea. Perhaps it had been the stirring melody of the orchestra. Maybe it had been the clear skies, the warmth of the sun, the festive atmosphere.

But it had moved him.

He'd initiated a conversation—he was good at that.

"I love Beethoven, don't you?"

It came from being left to your own devices at a young age, having to fend for yourself. That, and having no sense of shame. No embarrassment, no regard for what others thought. It gave him a confidence that others didn't possess.

"I don't know. This is my first Beethoven." She'd laughed, her eyes twinkling bluer than the summer sky.

"He was a genius. One of the most innovative and influential composers in history."

"I'll have to take your word for it."

"Did you know he eventually lost his hearing and could no longer perform? A terrible fate for a composer of his stature."

A flick of her head. "I didn't know that, no."

He'd taken her arm and led her away from her friends so they could talk. That was the beginning. They'd spent every night together for the next week. It had been illuminating, exhilarating, exciting.

Then one day she'd said goodbye, just like that.

"I'm sorry, Mikael. It's over."

Attempts to contact her had failed. It was clear she'd moved on. A few months later, she'd married someone else, the selfish bitch.

He'd never recovered.

Still, he'd known they'd meet up again one day. When the time was right. It was like that with soulmates.

And he was a patient man.

The train rolled onto the platform. The woman got on. Two carriages down, so did he. He could just about see her from here. A slim figure in a dark coat, the fluorescent lights gleaming on her pale hair. He'd make her pay, just like he'd made Olivia pay.

As the doors hissed shut, he felt a surge of adrenaline.

It was almost feeding time.

chapter
twenty-five

UNLIKE THE QUIET, PICTURESQUE TOWN OF BERGEN, OSLO was alive with activity, the streets filled with the sounds of traffic and chatter. Snow-covered buildings lined the sidewalks, their facades adorned with twinkling festive lights that added a touch of warmth to the cold landscape.

Avril and Krister had left the small coastal town of Bergen and flown to Oslo earlier that morning in hopes of getting a jump on the killer. If he was sticking to his original pattern, this was where he'd be, and the most obvious place to target his next victim was the hotel where his third victim, Helene Basken, had worked fifteen years ago.

"I understand you can't give me the names of your staff," Avril said to the hotel manager, a tall, stocky woman with masculine features. She'd decided to approach the manager alone, thinking that a woman concerned with the security of the female staff might be better received. But she quickly realized she was wrong. Instead of coming across as concerned, she felt she was being perceived as paranoid. Krister's moderating presence would have been useful.

"If you could tell them to be careful, that might help."

"Because a crazy murderer might be stalking them?" The manager gave a doubtful frown. "I don't want to scare them."

"You'd be warning them," Avril insisted, her patience wearing thin. "Just to be on the lookout for anyone who might be following them."

The manager shrugged. "Okay, sure. If that's what you want."

Avril went outside to where Krister was waiting, the icy air hitting her in the face. "She's not going to say anything to them, I know it."

He stomped his feet to keep warm. "Maybe she doesn't want to panic them."

Avril cocked an eyebrow. "Rather that, than one of them turns up dead."

He nodded in agreement, then looked up and down the road. "Hey, you want to grab a sandwich? I'm starving, and it's damn cold out here."

"Sure." They hadn't had breakfast, and it was past lunch time. Besides, she'd left her gloves in Bergen and her hands were going numb. A warm café would help thaw them out.

Krister led her into a nearby deli-style restaurant, the smell of baked bread and fresh ingredients filling the air. The place was bustling, with patrons crowded around small tables and a long counter filled with cold meats, cheeses, and other fillings. They ordered, then found seats at the counter overlooking the street, giving them a clear view of the hotel entrance.

"You sure he's going to target one of the women who work there?" Krister asked, biting into a double-decker sandwich.

"No, I'm not sure of anything, but it does fit the pattern."

Krister sighed. "Would he really target the exact same hotel? Wouldn't he consider that too risky? Surely he'd know we'd be here, waiting for him."

"I'm assuming he'll stick to his original MO, but—" Avril broke off as a young woman with pale blonde hair tied up in a neat bun crossed the road. Her burgundy coat flapped around her long, tapered legs as she walked with purpose toward the hotel.

"That's his type," Avril whispered, watching the girl. "I'm going to talk to her."

"Avril, you'll have to work on your opening line because, at the moment, you sound insane."

Ignoring him, Avril slipped off the stool and darted out of the café. The street was crowded, filled with the noise of conversations, the clatter of footsteps, and the hum of traffic. She navigated through the throng of people, her eyes fixed on the woman in the burgundy coat.

"Excuse me!" she called, raising a hand. The woman kept walking, almost at the hotel entrance now. Avril sped up, stepping into the road. "Excuse me. Do you mind if I—"

There was a loud roar as a car came careening toward her. It was going way too fast for the busy urban neighborhood and was clearly out of control. The engine screamed, the wheels spun, kicking up loose stones and dust.

"Avril!"

She heard Krister yell from the curb but couldn't move. The car kept hurtling toward her, but her entire body had frozen in terror.

Just as it was about to hit her, an arm grabbed her and yanked her out of the way. She fell hard, bumping her head on the pavement. Everything slowed down. Cars trundled by, pedestrians moved in slow motion, sound muted as if underwater.

Faces blurred above her, their voices a distant murmur.

Is she okay?

Is she breathing?

Is she dead?

"I'm okay," she tried to say, but it came out as a croaky moan. Her vision was blurry, colors bleeding into one another. Pink faces, gray clouds, the brown exterior of the buildings. Somewhere in the background, Krister shouted her name, his voice panicked.

A shadow loomed over her, blocking the light. Someone was bending down, their face inches from hers. A gentle hand swept the hair from her brow, the touch almost tender, and a throaty voice whispered, "It's not your turn yet."

KRISTER FORCED his way through the crowd to Avril, his heart pounding.

"Get back!" he yelled, spreading out his arms, his voice trembling. "Give her some space."

Please let her be okay.

The car had hurtled toward her with no attempt to decrease speed when the driver had seen her. If he'd seen her at all. Avril had been jaywalking, but was the driver blind?

"Avril? Avril, can you hear me?" His voice shook as he knelt beside her.

She opened her eyes and looked at him.

Thank God.

"Avril, are you okay?" His voice still unsteady.

She groaned. "I—I think so. I hit my head."

"I know. Can you sit up?"

She tried to push herself up, wincing in pain. "My shoulder, it hurts."

"It might be broken," he cautioned. "Don't move."

"I called an ambulance." A passerby held up his phone. "It's on its way."

"Thanks." Krister nodded gratefully, his attention still focused on Avril. He took off his jacket and placed it under her head. "How's your vision?"

"It's okay, but my head's throbbing."

Krister couldn't keep the worry out of his voice. "I thought you'd been hit. That driver, he didn't even attempt to slow down."

"It was my fault. I stepped out into the road."

"He was going way too fast. This is a built-up area."

"I know, but still."

Shit, he didn't even get a license plate.

Some cop I am.

"Avril—" He hesitated, his voice low. "I think it was deliberate."

A pause. "You mean—?

He nodded.

She tried to sit up again, but he laid a hand on her chest. "Hang tight, okay? The ambulance will be here soon."

She flopped back down on his jacket. "I don't know. Would the killer try to take me out in broad daylight? It's not his style."

"Perhaps he's desperate. He knows we're getting close."

She closed her eyes. "We're not close. He knows exactly what we're doing. He's playing with us."

Krister clenched his jaw. She was right. Why would he try to kill her now when he had the upper hand? It didn't make sense. Krister clawed a hand through his hair. None of it made any sense.

The ambulance arrived, sirens flashing. Two paramedics jumped out and came over to where Avril was still lying on the side of the road.

"You okay, Miss?"

"She's got a head wound," Krister said, standing back to give them access. "And she's hurt her right shoulder."

"Okay. I'm going to shine a torch into your eyes," the paramedic said. "Look at me."

Krister left them to it and looked around at the passersby. Some had moved off, while a couple stood around watching.

"Did you see who grabbed her?" he asked the onlookers.

As the car had come speeding toward her, he'd noticed a middle-aged man grabbing her arm and pulling her out of harm's way. Krister had been racing out of the cafe, but he'd known he'd never make it to her in time. The vehicle was moving too fast.

But someone had dragged her to safety. She'd fallen and bumped her head, but it didn't look too serious. A slight concussion, maybe, and worst-case scenario, a broken shoulder blade. That man had saved her life.

The paramedics were lifting Avril onto a stretcher.

"Where are you taking her?" he asked.

"Oslo University Hospital. You want to ride with her?"

"Yeah, thanks." He waited until she'd been loaded in, then climbed in beside her. She looked so pale, lying there with her eyes shut.

"Is she okay?" he asked.

"Yeah, she'll be fine. Bit of a concussion, but it's not too serious. She'll need a scan though, just to be sure there's no bleeding."

Krister nodded.

"She's dislocated her collarbone," the other paramedic said. "The doc will put it back in when he sees her."

Until then, it looked like she'd have to endure the pain.

"I've given her some methoxyflurane," the paramedic said, as if reading his mind. "It'll reduce the pain."

"Okay, good."

They set off. No need for sirens.

"Krister," Avril whispered, her eyes glassy.

"Yeah?" He took her hand. It was freezing cold, so he wrapped both of his around her small one to warm it up.

"That man? The one who saved me."

"I looked for him, but he didn't stick around."

"He spoke to me," she said, battling to get the words out. The painkiller was kicking in.

"He did?"

"Yeah. But it was weird."

Krister frowned. "What did he say?"

"He said, *It's not your turn.*"

chapter
twenty-six

Avril looked up as Krister walked into the hospital ward.

"Thank goodness," she said, relieved. "I've been here for hours. When are they going to let me go?"

He perched at the end of her bed, one of four in the observation unit. "The doctor said he wants to check your scans before he releases you."

"I wish he'd hurry up."

There was a slight pause. Krister shifted position.

"I know it was him, Krister," she said quietly.

"The hit and run driver?" But she could tell from his face he knew she didn't mean that.

"No. The one who saved me."

"Avril—" He hesitated.

"I know it sounds ridiculous, but I'm sure of it. What he said ... it could only have been him." A shiver passed through her as she recalled his touch. He'd swept the hair off her face before he'd whispered in her ear.

"It was more likely him who tried to kill you," Krister pointed out.

She shook her head, then wished she hadn't as the room span. "I don't think so. That was just an accident."

The look on Krister's face made her reach out and grab his hand. "Think about it. We know he's been watching us. He's got us jumping through hoops. He was probably watching the hotel, knowing I'd go there."

Krister listened, his brow furrowed.

"He saw me step into the road and grabbed me. He was closer than you were."

"That man saved your life. Why would a serial killer do that?"

A chill swept through her that had nothing to do with the pain in her head or the morphine she'd been given earlier. "I think he's saving me for last."

"Geez, Avril." Krister turned away. "This is screwed up."

"I know."

Krister turned back to her. "Why is he doing this?"

She was silent for a while, then said, "I've been hunting him for ten years, Krister. That's a long time. He's known it, right from the start. Now he wants to end it, to end me. And what more fitting way than to make me his final victim?" She'd had time to think about this while she'd been lying in the hospital bed.

Krister shook his head. "It sounds crazy."

"I know, but you have to admit, it does have a poetic irony to it. It's just the type of thing that would appeal to him."

"I think the painkillers are getting to you."

A glimmer of a smile. "Possibly."

Krister took a deep breath. "I have to go back to Stockholm. There's been a development."

She suddenly felt wide awake. "What development?"

"Freddie has arrested Agnes Hellgren's father-in-law for her murder."

She sat up so fast her head spun. "What?"

"He's under investigation for tax evasion. Agnes did his books. She knew about the fraud, and Freddie thought she was about to go to the police."

"He's wrong. You know he's wrong."

"They found an email on Agnes's computer that provided proof of the fraudulent activities. It was in her Draft folder."

"That doesn't mean anything."

"The commissioner thinks it does. Olaf senior is in custody." He gave her a sympathetic grimace. "I have to get back or else he's going to go down for this."

"Krister, please. Mikael Lustig is here in Oslo. He's the man who saved me. He's going to kill again, possibly soon. We have to stop him."

"I can't run after this man anymore," Krister said weakly. She could tell he was torn. He had the same look on his face as when his mother used to call him in for supper and she wanted to stay out, but he had to go back. "My job is on the line here, not to mention a man's freedom."

She groaned and dropped her head back on the pillow. This couldn't be happening. They were so close. "I'm going to stay."

"You're not safe here, Avril."

"I don't care," she said stubbornly. "Another young woman is going to die if I don't stop him."

Krister got up and paced up and down the ward. The other patients eyed him curiously. "How are you going to stop him, Avril? You don't know who his target is. You don't know where he is. You don't even know if he's here."

"He saved me."

Krister huffed. "You don't know that."

"I do. I'm sure of it."

There was a pause as they each fumed. Eventually, Krister said, "Did you ever stop to think this is exactly where he wants you to be?"

She stared at him.

"He lured you here from Bergen. He knew you'd come running to Oslo to stop him. To warn the women who work at that hotel. You're playing right into his hands."

Her chest felt tight.

"For all we know, he could have orchestrated that hit and run in order to act the savior. To give you that message. Have you thought about that?"

She gnawed on her lip. Perhaps the painkillers had clouded her brain.

"If you really want to catch this guy, Avril, you have to change the game, throw him off guard. At the moment, all we're doing is dancing to his tune."

Avril took a slow breath. There was a disgusting metallic taste in her mouth that she suspected was from the medication. "What do you suggest?" she whispered.

"Go home. Rest up and get your strength back. Leave him to do what it is he's here to do. If he really wants you to witness it, he'll have to wait. If he goes ahead, it'll be without you to discover the body."

"What about the girl? Krister, someone's going to die."

"We'll talk to the police, put them in touch with Detective Jörgensen. The Oslo Police Force is perfectly capable of dealing with a multiple offender. At least you'll be out of the picture. This sordid fascination he's got with you has to stop."

Avril pursed her lips as she thought about this. He had a point. The killer was manipulating her, making her react like she'd been doing for ten years. He killed and she came running. He'd gotten used to it. Krister was right. He was the puppet master, and she was the puppet.

Perhaps it was time she changed the rules.

If she wasn't here to witness his crime, would he still kill his next victim? He had to have her in his sights already. Stalking. Watching. Getting ready to strike. Unfortunately, he probably would. He killed because he got some sick pleasure from it. She wasn't arrogant enough to think this was just about her.

The doctor came in carrying a folder.

"Your scans came back." He broke into a grin. "They're clear. You've got a slight concussion, but nothing serious."

Avril looked up hopefully. "Does that mean I can go home?"

"Yes, but keep your arm stabilized in that brace. It'll prevent your shoulder from popping out again."

She cringed at the memory. "Okay. Thank you, Doctor."

"You're welcome. Oh, I think the nurse has some flowers for you."

"Really?" Who would send her flowers? Then, in a dropped heartbeat, she knew. "Where are they?"

"Outside, at the nurses' station. I'll tell her to bring them in." He wished her a speedy recovery and left, clipboard tucked beneath his arm. Avril couldn't wait. She got out of bed, swayed, and clutched the side table."

"Avril, what are you doing?"

"I'll be right back."

Her balance stabilized, and she padded barefoot out of the ward toward the nurses' station. There, on the table, was a big bunch of dark lavender roses.

"Are—Are those for me?" she asked the sister at the desk.

"You're Avril Dahl?"

"Yes."

She smiled. "Then they're for you."

Heart pounding, Avril reached for the card. It had been stuck in amongst the stems so as not to fall out. A thorn pricked her finger as she retrieved it, but she barely felt it. With trembling hands, she unfolded it.

May these flowers brighten your day as the thought of you always brightens mine. Looking forward to when our paths can cross. Until then, please know that you are in my thoughts.

M.

chapter
twenty-seven

"I HATE LEAVING YOU LIKE THIS." KRISTER STOOD IN THE hotel lobby, his face pinched with indecision.

"I'll be fine." Avril straightened her back. She knew the Commissioner had been firm. He wanted to close this case, and they had a worthy suspect with which to do it. It didn't seem to matter that he was innocent. Olaf Senior might be guilty of evading his taxes, but he wasn't guilty of murder. "I'll rest tonight then touch base with the Oslo Police tomorrow. You said Jörgensen's been in touch, right?"

"Yeah, she's spoken to their lead investigator, a man called Morten Henriksson, so they know who you are." She appreciated Krister making the introductions. It was always tricky explaining what an FBI agent was doing operating way out of her jurisdiction. "I explained you're following up on a lead, but I have to go back to Stockholm."

She nodded. "Was there anything on the hospital CCTV cameras?"

"Not that I could find. A delivery worker dropped off the flowers, but we have no way of knowing which florist he was from. He arrived on a motorcycle and wore a helmet, so we couldn't identify him. Anyway, it's unlikely the killer would deliver the flowers himself."

Avril wasn't so sure. It sounded just like the kind of audacious thing he'd do. The motorcycle disguise was clever. No one would suspect a delivery guy.

"If you notice anything strange, you get to safety," Krister was saying. "There's no telling when he'll strike again."

"It won't be me. He wants me alive."

Krister shook his head. "I hope you're right because I don't want to lose you."

She stared at him. The way he was looking at her. A mixture of concern and something else, something she couldn't put a name to.

"You won't lose me." She broke eye contact.

"I'll be back as soon as I can."

"Your job comes first," she said. "My boss in D.C. called this case a 'career ender,' and he was right. It's an endless pursuit, and I don't want to be responsible for wrecking your career."

Except she'd never been this close before. The Frost Killer had been a phantom, a ghost that flickered in and out of her life every year, keeping just out of range. He left no clues, no evidence. Just the pendant as his creepy calling card.

Now she'd actually made contact.

Well, he had.

He'd broken into her house. He'd saved her life. Touched her. Whispered in her ear. The hairs on her arms stood up when she thought about it.

They had a name.

They knew he'd been her mother's lover a long time ago. He'd become fixated on her and couldn't handle her rejection. Then, years later, he'd met up with her again, and when she'd turned him down, he'd killed her.

It was coming together. A full circle. She wasn't about to give up now.

Avril touched the necklace. In a bizarre way, it gave her comfort. "Go on, or you'll miss your plane."

"Take care, Avril," he said softly, then turned and walked out of the hotel, pulling his carry-on case behind him.

SHE GOT IT. She really did. But damn, she wished Krister hadn't gone. The Commissioner was an idiot. All he cared about was how the department measured up on paper. The stats. Someone like that shouldn't be in law enforcement. What was the point when justice didn't get done?

Fuming, Avril paced up and down her hotel room. Each step sent a jolt of pain through her shoulder and head, the lingering effects of her concussion making her feel lightheaded. The painkillers must have worn off. She finally sank down onto the bed, her body protesting every movement.

Fumbling through her overnight bag, she managed to find the pills the nurse had given her before she'd been discharged. She swallowed a couple, washing them down with a complimentary bottle of water.

Not hungry but knowing she should eat, she ordered a hamburger from room service, then sat down with her notepad to go over everything that had happened. Writing things down helped her think, helped her focus through the pain and frustration.

What would the killer expect her to do?

Go back to the hotel and warn the blonde female staff members. Try to convince them they were in danger. How well would that go down?

The hotel manager already thought she was a nutjob. She might even get into trouble for harassing the staff. Perhaps the Oslo Police could help? In her experience, no police officer was prepared to stick his neck out for a murder that hadn't happened yet.

Sighing, she looked out the window at the slate-gray sky. It wasn't snowing, not yet. He wouldn't strike until it did. That gave her time.

If only she could figure out who the target was.

Avril yawned, the pain in her shoulder lessening. Her food came, and she ate, devouring the tasteless burger before washing it down with a Diet Coke. Sated and sleepy, she lay back on the bed, determined to think through her next steps.

SHE WAS WALKING down a dark alleyway, her breath misting out in front of her. It was freezing. She shivered, tightening her coat around her body. There were footsteps behind her. Slow and deliberate. She walked faster, glancing behind her into the gloom, but saw nothing.

Yet she knew *he* was there.

The footsteps quickened. She broke into a run. It was difficult in heels, and she kept wobbling and stumbling on the cobblestones. The ground seemed to tilt, almost as if she was on a boat. She fell to her knees.

A dark shape loomed behind her. Faceless. Only the eyes, like blue fire, burning through a balaclava. She screamed, but nobody heard her.

"Help me!"

The man grabbed her feet and pulled her off the path into the shadows.

"No!"

Her hands grasped at the cobbles, but she couldn't get a grip. Her nails splintered and tore against the rough stones. He kept pulling her into the abyss.

Panic overwhelmed her, and she gasped for breath. Hyperventilating, the biting cold burning her lungs. She felt dizzy.

Oh, God, don't let me pass out.

She knew if she did, it would be over. She wouldn't wake up again.

He'd have won.

Frantic now, she scrambled away from him, grazing her knees, but he held firm. He was stronger than she was.

I hate leaving you like this.

It was Krister's voice.

"Krister!" she cried. "Help me!"

But he didn't come.

I look forward to our paths crossing.

No! Not *him*.

Hello, Avril.

A hand on her forehead, brushing away her hair. Gentle. Terrifying.

"Get away from me!"

She lashed out, opening her eyes with a gasp. Momentarily disoriented, it took her a moment to realize where she was. The hotel. She was in bed. Darkness enveloped her.

Reaching over, she flicked on the light.

Thank goodness.

She was alone. Safe.

Avril wiped her forehead. It was wet with perspiration and felt hot to the touch. She must have a slight fever. Her shoulder throbbed. Taking more painkillers, she tried to calm down.

It's just a stupid dream. It's not real. He isn't here.

You're safe.

Avril sunk back down onto the pillow, breathing hard. Even though her rational brain told her she was safe, her heart still thumped like the rapid-fire of an automatic rifle. It was a long time before she drifted off to sleep again.

chapter
twenty-eight

THE OSLO POLITI WAS HOUSED IN A FOREBODING, rectangular building in Grønlandsleiret, made of gray concrete and glass that matched the overcast sky. It was so straight, it looked like a Lego construction, just without the bright colors.

It was snowing when the taxi dropped her off, and she felt the flakes fluttering against her skin as she made her way to the entrance. An austere uniformed officer holding a rifle stood just inside the door.

"I'm here to see Morten Henriksson. He's expecting me."

With a sharp nod, the man gestured for her to walk through the security scanner. She did so, raising her left hand above her head as instructed. Her right was still in the brace.

"Fifth floor," he said, when she emerged on the other side.

Avril took the elevator up to the fifth floor, wishing Krister was with her. She wasn't good at meeting new people. He always put them at ease, paved the way for her. Without him, she felt like an electric guitar in an orchestra, noticeably out of sync with the rest of the ensemble.

When the doors opened, she found herself in a stark lobby. Bare walls, harsh lighting and a dark wooden block of a reception desk. A female officer sat there, typing on a computer while a throaty electric heater hummed behind her.

"I'm here to see Morten Henriksson," she said again.

The woman glanced up. "Stand in front of the camera."

Avril looked down at the tiny device on the counter. It clicked, and a short while later, her photograph appeared, along with her credentials, spat out from a small, portable printer beneath the counter. The officer slotted it into a plastic sleeve connected to a lanyard and handed it to her. "Wear this."

Avril put it around her neck.

"This way."

The woman got up and led her down a short corridor to an office on the left. She rapped succinctly three times and a deep voice said, "Come in."

Avril swallowed and pushed open the door.

"Good morning, sir. I'm Avril Dahl. I believe Detective Jörgensen called about me yesterday."

A tall, bearded man got to his feet. "Ah, the American FBI agent. Come in." He beckoned to her.

She walked into his office, cold and uninviting. What was it with the Norwegian police?

"Please, take a seat."

She sat. "Thank you for accommodating me."

"No problem." He resumed his position. "I understand you're hunting a serial killer?"

"Yes, sir. He's already killed two women, one in Stockholm and one in Bergen."

"Yesss." He drew out the word, leaving a little hiss at the end. A bad feeling crept over her.

"You understand we haven't had a similar murder here in Oslo. Our police force is vigilant. It's highly unlikely he will try something here."

"Oh, he will," she said, then instantly regretted it.

His eyes narrowed. "When do you anticipate this attack?"

"I don't know, that's the problem. It's most likely he'll target a young woman who works in the hospitality industry, and I think it'll be soon. In the next day or two."

"You know this how?" He eyed her curiously.

"He's following a pattern, recreating a series of murders."

Henriksson stroked his beard. "Like a copycat?"

Avril hesitated. "Yes, although he's not a copycat. He's recreating his own murders."

A frown. "Why would he do that?"

To bait me.

"I don't know, sir."

A pause.

"We appreciate the courtesy call, Agent Dahl, and if you need any assistance, you let us know."

That was it?

"I was hoping you'd help me find him."

"My officers have done a preliminary check for your suspect." He glanced down at a sheet of paper. "Nils Henemark."

"Yes?"

"There is nobody by that name staying at any hotel in central Oslo. We've also checked all flights and ports."

"He could be using an assumed name."

"If he is, we have no way of tracing him."

Avril gritted her teeth in frustration. Mikael wasn't being as open as he had been in Bergen. This time, he didn't want to be found.

Exhaling, Avril got to her feet.

"Sorry I can't be of more help."

Avril nodded. As if by magic, the door opened, and the stony-faced female officer stood there. "Yes, sir?"

"See the FBI Agent out." He crinkled his nose, like she smelled bad.

"Yes, sir."

Great. Avril took off the visitor's pass and dropped it on the reception desk as she left. "I won't be needing this."

She was on her own.

AVRIL SAT AT THE CAFE, in the same position as she had with Krister yesterday, watching the hotel entrance. Festively dressed partygoers with ruddy cheeks bustled along the sidewalk, breath misting in front of them. She'd forgotten it was New Year's Eve and people were celebrating the end of the year. Vehicles raced past, just like they had when she'd been knocked over. A painful twinge in her shoulder reminded her of how close she'd come to disaster.

It had been just before ten o'clock when the hotel receptionist had arrived yesterday morning. Avril checked the time, got up, and left the café. She crossed the road—carefully this time—and proceeded to the hotel entrance. The man in the woolen hat with the dimple was nowhere to be seen.

Was he watching her?

Avril waited until she saw the pretty blonde receptionist walking down the street toward the hotel.

"Excuse me," she said, approaching her.

The young woman halted, her hand flying to her chest. "Oh, you startled me."

"I'm sorry," Avril said. "I'm an agent with the Federal Bureau of Investigation, and I'd like to talk to you."

The woman's eyes flitted to her ID card. "Actually, I'm late for work."

"This won't take a minute. Please, it's important."

The woman frowned. "What does an FBI agent want with me?"

"To warn you." At the woman's surprised look, she added, "There's a man targeting blonde women in the area. We're asking everyone who fits the profile to be vigilant."

"Oh." She took a step back. Avril realized she was invading her personal space and shifted her position.

"He's already murdered two other women," Avril said.

"Oh, God. Were they both blondes?"

"Yes."

Her eyes widened.

"Have you noticed anyone following you lately? Felt like you were being watched?"

A quick glance over her shoulder. "No, I don't think so."

"Okay, good. Please be careful."

"Er, sure." The woman started moving away. "I should go now."

Even though Avril wanted to stress how important it was that she be vigilant, that the killer was almost certainly coming for her, there was nothing more she could do. Scaring the woman wouldn't help and might get her into more trouble.

"Thank you for your time."

The blonde nodded and hurried into the hotel. Avril imagined she'd be telling her colleagues what had happened. It couldn't be helped. If her warning had made the woman even the smallest bit cautious, that was a good thing.

IT WAS LATE when Avril slipped out of the back entrance of her hotel. Dressed in black, with a dark woolen hat and scarf to hide her hair and as much of her face as possible, she made her way across town.

Nearly a full twelve hours had passed since she'd spoken to the blonde receptionist.

This is crazy, she told herself, but deep down, she knew she couldn't stay in her room doing nothing while the killer was out there stalking his next victim. Even if she had to follow the blonde woman home every night this week, it would be worth it to save her life.

Knowing it was against her doctor's orders, Avril had removed her brace so she had the use of both hands. She had no hope of apprehending a suspect with it on.

The handcuffs Krister had lent her were clipped to her belt. In her jacket pocket was her pepper spray, and even though it wasn't legal for a civilian to carry a knife, she had a small switchblade tucked into the leg of her left boot. No way would she face the killer unarmed.

The bar next to the hotel was bustling, with a long line forming along the wall outside. Girls in short skirts and makeup laughed with tall, Scandinavian men in leather jackets, while dance music pulsed into the street. Two burly bouncers in black shirts, trousers and puffer jackets scrutinized the crowd.

Avril hung back, waiting for the receptionist to leave after her shift. She didn't have to wait long. At ten fifteen, the woman appeared. Tight skirt, court shoes and long black coat. Her hair wasn't quite as neat as it had been earlier, and she looked tired. Twelve hours was a long time to be on your feet.

The woman walked toward the train station. Every now and then she glanced over her shoulder as if checking behind her. Avril nodded in approval. At least her words had sunk in.

The streets leading away from the hotel were relatively quiet. The woman walked past the odd partygoer heading toward the club, but most of the activity was behind them. Avril kept out of sight, hugging the wall, but she kept her gaze locked on the blonde.

Two more streets to go. The blonde turned the corner and increased her pace. It was even quieter down here. A good place for the killer to lie in wait. A knot of anxiety grew in her stomach. Avril found she was holding her breath, waiting for something to happen.

And then it did.

A shadow jumped out of a doorway, lurching at the blonde. She screeched, and tried to push him off, but he put a hand over her mouth, so it turned into a muffled yelp.

Avril broke into a sprint. She raced toward the attacker, reaching for her pepper spray. "Leave her alone!"

The man looked up, saw Avril, and put out an arm to stop her. She sprayed him in the face, and he let out a howl, swiping at his eyes.

"You bitch! You've blinded me."

"FBI, put your hands up!" Avril yelled.

The blonde stumbled backwards, crying. Her purse had fallen off her shoulder and lay on the wet ground. The suspect shoved Avril out the way, reached for it, and took off down the street. Avril gave chase, gritting against the jarring of her shoulder.

Unwittingly, the man was running in the direction of the club. He rounded the corner, sprinted down a side road and emerged at the intersection where she'd narrowly avoided being run over the day before.

"Help me!" she yelled to the bouncers, who realized what was going on and gave chase. They were much faster than her, and she slowed down as they caught up to the attacker. Launching into the air, one of them brought him down in an impressive tackle.

Avril ran up, panting. Her shoulder throbbed from the exertion. "Thank you," she said, flashing her FBI badge. "I'm with the police."

The bouncer hauled the attacker to his feet. He had barely broken a sweat, unlike the suspect, whose chest was heaving.

"This yours, ma'am?" The second bouncer handed her the stolen purse.

"No, it belongs to a woman down the street. He mugged her. Would you mind holding him while I call the police?"

"I thought you said you were the police?" the first one asked, still gripping the suspect by the arm.

"I'm an FBI agent. The police are different." She rang the number she'd been given and got through to Henriksson.

"Agent Dahl, what can I—"

"I've apprehended a man. He attacked a woman in the street outside the hotel."

A pause.

"Is it him? Is it the man you were looking for?"

Avril studied the suspect standing sullenly in front of her. He had black hair, dark eyes and was in his early thirties.

"No, sir. It's not him."

chapter
twenty-nine

The hotel receptionist, whose name was Frida Sørland, appeared on the scene shortly after Avril. She hadn't been able to go anywhere without her purse, which contained her Metro Pass, credit cards and driver's license.

"Thank you so much," she gushed at the burly bouncer who grinned as he handed her back her purse.

"It's my pleasure. Hey, you work at the hotel? I've seen you around."

The woman ran a shaky hand through her hair, which had come loose and now hung down her back. "Yes, I work at reception."

Avril left them to flirt and went to speak to the police officers who'd arrived on the scene. After a brief explanation, they took the mugger into custody. Avril hitched a ride with a young officer back to her hotel. Her shoulder was killing her and all she wanted to do was knock back some painkillers and collapse into bed.

What a waste of an evening. If the killer had wanted to attack Frida, they'd never know because that stupid mugger had gotten in the way.

Would *he* try again?

Maybe he'd seen Avril following Frida and had called it off. If so, it had been worth it. Frida was still alive, after all. It was on this more positive note that she drifted off to sleep.

. . .

"YOU WERE FOLLOWING the woman to the train station?" Henriksson stared incredulously at Avril from across his desk early the next morning. She stifled a yawn. It wasn't eight o'clock yet and she'd been summoned by the Oslo Police asking her to come in and give a statement.

Henriksson had obviously come to work despite it being New Year's Day because he'd heard about the previous night's events and he demanded an explanation. The sun shone lazily across his desk, as if it too had just stumbled out of bed but didn't really want to be there. "I was making sure she got home okay. The third murder—"

"There is no third murder," he cut in, his cheeks turning pink. "You can't go around following our citizens just in case they get attacked. You have no evidence that this man, this Frost Killer, is even in Oslo."

"Except that he tried to run me down yesterday." Or was it the day before? She was so tired, she couldn't even remember how long she'd been in the Norwegian city.

He glared at her. "That was an accident."

Actually, it *was* just an accident, she was sure of it. But he'd been there.

He'd whispered in her ear.

It's not your turn yet.

If she'd told Henriksson that, however, he'd have laughed in her face. Better to go with Krister's theory that he'd been driving the hit-and-run vehicle. It sounded more plausible.

"He's in town," she said stoically. "It's just a matter of time before he strikes again. I may have gotten in the way last night, but I'm sure—" She broke off as a thought struck her. Could he be that diabolical?

Henriksson was watching her.

She exhaled, her brain churning as she considered the possibility.

No, surely not.

But she couldn't let it go.

Henriksson shook his head. "Go home, Agent Dahl. If your mysterious serial killer strikes again, we will notify you."

"Have you interviewed the mugger?"

"There's no need. He was caught red-handed, so to speak. Thanks to you." A smirk. "Besides, he has a record for petty theft. We also have a statement from the club bouncer and the victim, Frida—" He glanced down at his notepad.

"Sørland," Avril supplied.

He gave a curt nod. "Sørland. The mugger is in custody and will be sentenced later today."

"Can I talk to him?"

"Why? I assure you, we know what we're doing."

"Please, it's important."

Another sigh.

"Fine, if it'll get you off my back. You promise you'll leave afterwards?"

"I promise."

Avril followed him to an interview room.

"Wait here."

She took a seat on the cold, metal chair. Like the interview rooms back at the Swedish Police Station, the chairs and table were bolted to the floor. The uneasy feeling that had gripped her made her feel nauseous, or maybe that was the painkillers on an empty stomach. Taking a deep breath, she composed her thoughts while she waited for the mugger to be brought in.

A short while later, a uniformed officer led the sullen suspect into the room. "Detective Henriksson says you have ten minutes."

She gestured for the man to sit down. Six-foot, black hair, with a heavy-set face and bushy eyebrows that met in the middle. His hands were calloused, the fingernails jagged, but not bitten. This man worked with his hands. Manual laborer, construction worker?

He studied her with open animosity. "You're the bitch who pepper sprayed me."

"You're the man who attacked that woman."

Some of the fire fizzled out of his eyes.

Avril narrowed her gaze. "Why did you attack her?"

He glanced away. "I saw an opportunity. What does she expect walking home alone at that hour?"

"So she was asking for it? Is that what you're saying?"

He remained silent.

Avril took a deep breath. "I think you planned to attack her. You knew she'd be there last night. You knew what time she left the hotel, because you were lying in wait. I saw you jump out of that doorway."

He clenched his jaw but didn't answer.

"What about the balaclava? You just happen to have that in your pocket?"

"It's cold."

Sure.

"What about her purse? You only went for that once I got there." At first, he'd simply attacked Frida, ignoring the purse that had fallen to the ground.

"I told you, I saw an opportunity. Times are tough, okay? I'm a carpenter. I don't make much money. I've got mouths to feed."

He was lying.

"You're not even married." She nodded to his lack of wedding ring. Plus, he had a record. This guy was a common criminal.

Another sullen glare.

"Why'd you attack her?" Avril repeated. "Did someone set you up to it?"

"No, why would you ask that?"

Too quick.

"Come on, tell me the truth. It'll help your case if you weren't the one who planned the attack. You could get a much lighter sentence."

He thought about this. A flash of fear crossed his face. "I told you, I saw an opportunity."

"He told you to say that, didn't he? The man who set you up?"

A pause.

Avril sighed. "He's using you. You realize that, don't you? You'll go down for something he planned. Do you want that?"

No reply, just another sulky stare.

"How much did he pay you? Was it worth five years in prison for assault and robbery?"

The muscles in his jaw worked overtime. She was getting to him. Slowly wearing him down. Her ten minutes was almost up.

"How did he contact you? Was it by phone? Or did he leave a message? A letter through your mailbox?" There's no way the killer would have met the mugger in person. Too risky. He wouldn't want the carpenter to give an ID to the police, should the real story come out.

The mugger's eyes darted to the door as if he wished he could bolt out of it.

"You're not going anywhere," Avril told him. "But you might get a reduced sentence if you can prove it wasn't your idea."

A sigh.

Come on.

"Do you really want to go down for someone else's crime? The judge will sympathize with you. Like you said, times are tough. People are desperate. If you can prove you were set up, it'll work in your favor."

He held up his hands in a gesture of defeat. "Okay, okay. Some dude put a letter under my door, in an envelope filled with cash. He said there'd be double that when the job was done."

Avril let out a shaky breath.

She knew it!

It was as she feared. This man had been a decoy. A distraction. Designed to grab her attention so the killer was free to commit murder elsewhere.

A cold fear gripped her.

That meant there was another victim.

It was later that day when Avril got the call she'd been both dreading and expecting. After interviewing the suspect, she'd told Henriksson her suspicion, but he'd been in turns both condescending and dismissive. Unable to convince him a murder had already taken place, she'd left the police station and gone back to her hotel.

Avril was packing her bags when he called.

"We've just received a missing person report." His voice was tight.

Her heart skipped a beat. "Oh?"

"A young hotel worker didn't make it home last night. Her boyfriend called the station this morning to file the report. It just landed on my desk."

"Description?"

"Blonde, late-twenties." He cleared his throat. "She fits the profile."

It was *him*, she knew it. He'd outwitted them. No, he'd outwitted *her*. He'd set up the mugging as a distraction and she'd fallen for it.

Avril gripped the phone until her knuckles turned white. "Where did she work?"

"One block away from the hotel where the mugging took place."

chapter
thirty

"You'll find her body on the Bygdøy Peninsula." Turns out she had needed that visitor's pass again after all.

Henriksson stared at her across his desk. He looked tired. "How do you know that?"

"Because that's what he did before." The detective's lack of knowledge of the case told her he hadn't bothered to read the initial investigation reports.

"You're talking about the murders that occurred fifteen years ago?"

She fixed her gaze on him. "Yes."

His deep frown told her he was at a loss.

"He's copying the same pattern," she explained, trying not to let her irritation show. "The first murder was in Stockholm, a young mother, her body found in the woods north of the city. The second was in Bergen, a ferry worker, her body found in the slopes of the mountain overlooking the city. The third was in Oslo, a hotel worker, her body found on the Bygdøy Peninsula. So far, he's stuck to the pattern with all three murders."

Henriksson was silent, and she could almost see the realization dawning. "Then it's true, we have a serial killer on the loose in this city?"

"Yes."

He murmured something under his breath in Norwegian. Avril didn't respond. Finally, he looked up. "If I send a search team to Bygdøy, are they going to find her?"

"I would stake my career on it."

"It will be my career if they don't."

She gave a tense nod. Unfortunately, that was probably true. After ten years of hunting this monster, she'd had to stand her ground more than a few times. It didn't always work out. Yes, she understood how a career could hang in the balance. She also knew she had to stick to her guns. Why would he deviate now? This was what he'd planned. Now he wanted to gloat.

"She'll be there."

A sigh. "Okay, Agent Dahl. I hope to God you're right."

He picked up the phone.

"THEY FOUND HER?" Krister's voice was incredulous.

"Yeah. Two miles from the Royal Estate. Exactly where Helene Basken was found."

"Holy smoke. Are they sure it's him?"

"Yes, she was wearing a snowflake pendant." Avril knew she sounded breathless. It wasn't anxiety or excitement, but rather frustration. She'd come so close.

There was a brief pause.

"That's three, Avril," Krister said quietly.

"I know." She gritted her teeth. "He tricked me, Krister. He staged a decoy, and while I was distracted, he took some other poor girl off the street."

"I'm sorry, Avril." She could hear he meant it.

It didn't help. "I should have known he'd try something like that."

"How could you have known?"

"I know how he thinks. He's manipulative. Clever. I should have realized that the mugger was a decoy."

"There's no way you could have known," he repeated, adamantly.

She sighed and closed her eyes momentarily. Weariness seeped into every pore.

"What are you going to do now?"

"I don't know. Come home, I guess." She had to regroup, figure out what she should do next.

"That's good. You'll be safer here where I can keep an eye on you."

She didn't reply.

"Sorry, that came out wrong. I didn't mean to be condescending. I know you can take care of yourself."

"It's okay. I know what you meant." He was worried about her. She liked that. Nobody had worried about her in a long time. "How'd it go with Olaf Senior?"

"Oh, you were right about him. There was a CCTV camera outside his office. He didn't leave the afternoon Agnes was murdered. He couldn't have done it."

She gave a nod. Not that he could see.

"How are you getting home?" Krister asked.

Home.

Where was that?

Not Stockholm, where she was living in her father's house. Not D.C., she was hardly ever there. Suddenly, she longed to be far away from here, from *him*. All she wanted was to drop off the radar and sleep for a week. When this case was over, she would take a long holiday, preferably somewhere warm.

"I'll get the overnight train and be back by morning."

"It's New Year's Day. The trains won't be running."

Crap, she'd forgotten about that.

"I'll catch the first one tomorrow morning," she said.

"Avril, be careful. I don't like the thought of you there by yourself. Now he's finished with his third victim, he could come after you. You could be the fourth."

The fourth victim.

Avril frowned, the semblance of a plan beginning to form.

"Avril? Are you there?"

"Yes, I'm still here. Don't worry, Krister. I won't leave the hotel. See you tomorrow."

AVRIL HAD JUST FALLEN asleep when the phone rang. She was exhausted and decided to get an early night. Her head was still tender, and her shoulder ached.

Glancing at the screen, she saw an unknown number.

"Hello?"

It was Detective Henriksson. After not wanting anything to do with her, he'd become her new best friend. The discovery of the body at Bygdøy had elevated him amongst his peers, but now the pressure was on to find the victim's killer.

"Agent Dahl."

"Detective Henriksson, it's late."

"I know." He hesitated. "I'm sorry, but I wondered if I could send you some photographs of the crime scene. We've just got them back, and there's something we don't understand."

Groggily, she sat up. "What?"

Had the killer left her another message? A clue?

"Our forensic team didn't spot it at first, but when the official photographs came back, we saw it."

"What did you see?" She held her breath.

"I think it's better if you see for yourself. I'll send them to your phone."

"Okay. I'll take a look and call you back."

Her phone pinged. With trembling fingers, she opened the message. The photograph was of the third victim lying in a mound of snow, surrounded by trees. Dark, forest-green, and dusted with white powder, they cast long shadows over her pale, lifeless body. With the sun always low in the sky, Scandinavia was the land of shadows.

Avril's eyes were drawn to the victim's face. Glistening with frost, the woman's eyelids and blue-tinged lips had frozen together. Her arms were placed on her body, in a funeral pose. She wore no jacket, and her feet were bare. Around her neck hung a silver chain and at the bottom, the snowflake pendant.

The image was so vivid, so startling, it took her a moment to see what Henriksson had noticed. Instead of undisturbed snow around the body, as was the norm, there looked to be a word carved into it in a semi-circle above the victim's head.

Tilting her head, she tried to make it out. The shadows gave it an embossed effect, making it hard to read.

It wasn't a word, it was numbers.

1993.

She frowned. What did it mean?

Why had the killer carved it into the snow above the body of the third victim? Or, rather, the fifty-fourth victim. Was that year significant for some reason? Did it mean something to him?

She frowned, hitting Henriksson's number on her phone.

"What do you make of it?" Henriksson asked.

"I don't know. When was the victim born?" Avril had been born in 1994, and the victim had looked younger than her.

"Nineteen ninety-nine. She was only twenty-two."

So young.

"She'd had a hard life," Henriksson continued sadly, and Avril got the impression he needed to talk to someone familiar with the case. "Her mother was an addict, and there's no record of her father on her birth certificate. She was in and out of social care, and has a record of misdemeanors, drug use, and shoplifting."

"Did she ever work at a gallery?" Avril asked.

"I—I don't think so. Why?"

"No reason."

Avril wasn't surprised at the victim's tragic backstory. The Frost Killer's original third victim, Helene Basken, had also had a checkered past.

"Has the autopsy been done?" she asked.

"Yeah, and you were right. The pathologist found chloroform residue around her lips."

No surprises there, either.

"We're going to catch this monster," he growled, and she could hear he meant it. Before she'd left, she'd briefed him with all the salient points. His real name is Mikael Lustig, but he sometimes goes under the alias of Nils Henemark. He'd be staying in a hotel or guesthouse somewhere in Oslo, possibly close to where the girl was abducted. He'd have hired a vehicle to transport her.

"My team is on it. He's not going to get away with it this time."

Avril suppressed a sigh. He already had. But she appreciated Henriksson's determination, even if it was too late. "Please keep me posted."

"I will." He hesitated. "What are you going to do now?"

169

"I'm heading back to Stockholm in the morning. I suspect he's already left Oslo."

"If he's following his original pattern, he's got one more kill to make," Henriksson said. If she hadn't felt so desolate, she'd have smiled. He'd finally read the file. "That's how you can catch him. You have to anticipate his next move. We're going to gather as much evidence as possible on our side so when you get him, we can nail the bastard."

His faith in her was sobering.

"Sounds good," she replied, lying down again.

"Happy New Year, Miss Dahl," Henriksson said, before he hung up.

Was it?

She didn't think so. Not until this bastard was behind bars.

chapter
thirty-one

AVRIL FOUGHT BACK THE WEARINESS AS SHE LET HERSELF INTO her father's house. The train ride had taken the better part of the day, and her shoulder ached from carrying her luggage. At least her head had stopped throbbing.

Sleep or coffee?

She chose coffee.

As the high-speed train had raced through the snowy countryside, she'd thought long and hard about how she was going to outwit her opponent. The semblance of an idea had blossomed into something more definite, but she needed Krister's help on this one—and he wouldn't like it.

1993.

That number reverberated around her brain like a pinball in a machine. What did it mean? Then she remembered the record cover. Beethoven. That had a year written on it too. Was it the same one?

Going into the living room, she looked around for the LP. It was still on the record player, the cover lying to one side. Heart slamming against her ribs, Avril picked it up. There, in the middle of the white paper sleeve was penciled the year 1993.

Was that when Mikael had given the record to her mother?

Was that why Olivia had played it so much when Avril was a child? She was thinking about him? The year preceding her birth.

Feeling queasy, Avril raced upstairs to her father's bedroom. She dove under the bed and retrieved the box containing his documents. Fumbling, she found her parents' marriage certificate. It was on thin paper, folded in half. Shaking, she opened it and looked for the date.

May 25th, 1993.

Her breath caught in her throat. She'd been born on January 6th, 1994. Eight months later.

Eight months.

God, no.

It couldn't be.

Her mother must have been pregnant before they got married. They'd been dating for a while, right?

Avril sat on the floor staring at the faded document.

She didn't know.

Wracking her brain, she tried to remember a story about how her parents had met, but there wasn't one. It was blank.

Don't be silly, she told herself.

Obviously, they'd been dating, her mother had gotten pregnant, and they'd decided to get married. Avril had been born eight months later.

It made sense.

She was panicking over nothing.

Exhaling, she caught sight of the photograph of her parents. Her father, dark-haired, strong-jawed, a big man. Her mother, slight and blonde and fragile looking. It was clear she'd taken after her mother.

Standing up, she walked to the dresser and stared at her reflection. Then, she took out the now-wrinkled photograph of her mother and Mikael. It was a pity his back was to the camera so she couldn't see what he looked like. Other than the light brown hair and the dimple.

The thought of you always brightens mine.

That's what he'd said in the card attached to the bouquet.

Feeling sick, Avril looked up. Forcing a smile, she stared at the dimple in her left cheek. It was in exactly the same place.

A SURGE of nausea hit her, and Avril stumbled away from the mirror. She ran for the bathroom and vomited, her guts clenching as the reality of what she was thinking hit home.

No.

Please, no.

It couldn't be. She couldn't be the daughter of a serial killer. There was no way.

Avril slid to the cold, tiled floor, trying to block out the horrendous thoughts swimming through the quagmire of her brain. It didn't work.

In her head, she heard the familiar melody to Beethoven's haunting 1st concerto and was sick again. Her mother used to play that constantly when she was a girl. Now it made sense.

That's why he'd written 1993 in the snow. It was a message. He was telling her to look at the record, to connect the dots so she could figure out what he already knew. That she was his illegitimate daughter.

That's why he was recreating the first four murders. That's why he wanted her attention.

It wasn't just that she'd been hunting him all these years. It was that he wanted to make contact. He wanted her to know what he'd done. He was proud of it.

Another surge of nausea, but this time she managed to keep it down. A slow, cold anger replaced the shock she'd felt at the revelation.

No wonder her father had been so convinced his wife was having an affair. She had. Not at the time of her death, but before. Thirteen years before, to be precise. That's when Avril had been conceived.

Had her mother known her father then? Had they been dating, and she'd met Mikael, had a whirlwind romance, a passionate affair, but then cut it short? Perhaps she'd discovered she was pregnant and begged her father to marry her. Or maybe she'd convinced him he was the biological father.

Perspiration broke out on her upper lip. She could taste the sweat. The cold from the bathroom floor seeped into her bones. Weakly, using the toilet for support, Avril got to her feet. She washed out her mouth, then went back downstairs, taking the box of documents with her.

Some macabre impulse made her lift the needle of the record player and lower it gently onto the LP. As the initial notes of Beethoven's 1st hit her, her skin crawled. Sinking onto the old couch, she clutched the shoebox and stared into the past as the music flowed over her.

She was a little girl. Three, maybe four years old. Her mother was baking, and she was helping her.

"Stir it like this," Olivia said, demonstrating, before handing the bowl to Avril.

As a little girl, she'd had to stand on the chair while she grasped the wooden spoon, stirring it ineffectually. "Like this, Mama?"

"That's it." A warm smile. "You're doing great."

The music soared above them, the piano's bright arpeggios and bold, confident orchestral responses filled the kitchen mingling with the scents of vanilla and cinnamon.

"What music is this, Mama?" Avril asked, seeing the rapture on her mother's face.

"It's the piano, darling. A brilliant composer called Beethoven. You'll learn all about him one day."

"I like it," Avril had said, eager to please, her movements gaining confidence as the piano's lively tempo lent her its rhythm.

"So do I, darling," her mother had replied, a faraway look in her eyes as the music swelled to a crescendo. "So do I."

HOW LONG SHE SAT THERE, Avril didn't know. The record came to an end, the needle scratching on the vinyl, then fading into silence. The sky grew dark, but she didn't switch the lights on. The darkness was her friend. It hid the now startlingly obvious truth, that she shared DNA with the Frost Killer.

No way had she seen that one coming.

Her father had known. That's why he'd gotten rid of all her mother's things. That's why he'd barely spoken to his daughter since Olivia's death. He'd thought his wife and her lover were back together again, that she'd betrayed him.

But he'd been wrong.

If only he was still alive so she could explain. Mikael had come back, but Olivia had refused him. She'd told him to leave her alone, that she was married and everything they'd had was in the past. That argument Anna Frieberg had overheard at the Christmas party, that was the final straw.

Olivia had gone over there in a rage and confronted him. That must have been when her father had followed her and seen them together.

Except Mikael hadn't liked what she'd had to say.

Her rejection had sent him over the edge, and he'd plotted to kill her. Had he stalked her, like he stalked all his victims?

With an icy shiver, Avril wondered if he'd witnessed her party earlier that day. On the brink of womanhood, but still a child. Vulnerable. Innocent.

Had he followed her mother into the woods when she'd gone to walk Roffe? Ambushed her, knocked her out with the chloroform, and carried her back to his car?

He'd destroyed her childhood. She felt sick thinking about it.

That monster had kept her mother unconscious for nearly twenty-four hours. Then, when the search party had been called off and they'd trawled through every part of those woods, he'd moved her back to the clearing and left her out in the cold to freeze to death.

Avril was so tense, she felt like she was frozen in place too.

At some point during the evening, there was a knock on the door, but she ignored it. She couldn't face anyone right now. Krister's figure appeared in the window, peering into the dark interior. She didn't move.

Krister wouldn't be able to see through the gauzy curtains into the dark room, anyway. He'd think she wasn't home yet. After about ten minutes, he went away.

She exhaled.

Hours later, frigid with cold, Avril came out of her stupor. Blinking, she cleared the grit from her eyes and stood up. It wouldn't do to sit here lamenting about the past. There was nothing she could do about it now.

What she could do was check if her theory was correct, as repellant as it may be.

Going upstairs, she went into her father's bedroom. When she'd been cleaning up, she'd seen an old comb in the dresser drawer. Her father had sported a thick head of black hair, and there were a few strands stuck in the teeth of the comb. Using gloves, she extracted them and slipped them into a plastic evidence bag she'd brought with her.

Next, she pulled out several strands of her own fair hair and put them in a second bag. A DNA test would confirm whether or not she was her father's child.

Avril sent Krister a message saying she was exhausted and going to bed and would see him at the station in the morning. She could tell he was upset with her by his one-word answer.

OK.

Early the next morning, Avril took the hair samples to a private clinic in Stockholm's city center. According to their website, they specialized in speedy DNA testing. She filled out the form, paid the exorbitant fee, then took an Uber to the police station.

It was time to put her plan into action.

chapter
thirty-two

"You cannot be serious!" Krister exploded as he faced Avril in the squad room.

"I am." She'd had a long time to think about her plan. Five hours and forty-two minutes from Oslo to Stockholm, and then all last night. "It's the only way we're going to catch this guy, Krister. We have to flip things around. Like you said, we have to make him dance to our tune."

He glared at her, but she knew it was out of concern. The rest of the office was listening in, intrigued by this fiery exchange. Krister was usually so calm and collected, a natural leader. Now, here he was pacing up and down the office, raking his hand through his hair. Avril could only imagine what they must be thinking.

Ingrid watched them from her desk, an unreadable expression on her face.

"It's too dangerous," snapped Krister.

"If you'll hear me out."

"It would mean putting yourself in the line of fire."

"That's the point. You have to use me as bait. It's the only way we'll catch him."

"What if something happens? What if he gets to you?"

"He won't. I'll be wearing a wire, and you'll be there."

Krister continued to pace, his expression a stony mask. The other detectives gave him a wide berth. "I can't sanction it."

"Krister, this is his last kill. After this, he's done. We'll have lost him. It has to be now. Don't you see? We won't get another chance."

She won't get another chance.

"You don't know that."

"I do. That's why he's revisiting the past, and why he's been inactive these last two years. Something's happened, and he's packing it in. This is it."

Krister's gaze burned into hers. "You haven't caught him in ten years of trying, Avril. What makes you think you can do it now?"

She glared at him. "Because I'm smarter than he is, and I know how to play him."

Krister stopped pacing and shook his head. "Look what happened in Oslo. He tricked you. He tricked everyone."

"I've learned my lesson. If you'll just listen to my plan, you'll see that. It's a good one, I promise."

He sucked in a breath, his chest expanding. Everyone watched him expectantly. "Okay. I'll listen, but I reserve the right to say no."

"Fine."

They glared at each other, neither willing to back down.

"I don't know why you two don't just get a room," Freddie murmured, causing a few snickers.

Krister flicked his head toward his sidekick. "What did you say?"

"Nothing, boss." Freddie reddened. "I think you should hear her out. It would be good to catch this guy."

There was a general murmur of assent. Everybody was tired of arresting suspects only to have to let them go. Avril didn't blame them. It was a waste of time and paperwork.

Huffing, Krister reached for his notepad and a pen. "Let's talk in private."

Avril followed him out, ignoring the not-so-subtle kissing sounds.

His outburst had worried her. She hadn't seen Krister this angry since the day she'd borrowed his bicycle and gone off by herself in the woods. It had begun to rain, so she'd taken shelter in a scout's fort she'd come across. Several hours later, she'd returned to find a sodden eleven-year-old Krister beside himself. He'd been convinced some awful fate had befallen her, and despite searching on foot, he hadn't been able to find her.

"Never, never go off without telling me," he'd shouted, his hands curled into tight little fists. "I thought something bad had happened to you."

"Well, it didn't. I'm fine." To be fair, his father had mangled his leg in a motorcycle accident the year before, but this was different. She was on a mountain bike and had taken refuge from the rain.

"You could have gotten hurt, and it would've been my fault."

"Why would it be your fault?"

"It's my bike."

"Krister, nothing happened. Relax."

He'd stormed off into the house, much like he'd done now.

Krister went into the staff canteen at the end of the hall and turned to face her. The aroma of machine coffee and stale cinnamon buns permeated the air. "Okay, tell me this brilliant plan of yours."

Avril smoothed her hair back. "Right, well, you know the fourth murder begins on a ferry. Anna Hollman, a Swedish university student, disappeared while crossing from Stockholm to Helsinki."

"That's a seventeen-hour trip," he said.

"I know. She had a cabin on board, and sometime during the night, he must have snuck in and drugged her. When the ferry docked in Stockholm, she was gone."

Krister cocked his head. "How do you know she didn't get off? Was someone waiting for her?"

"Her boyfriend. He was Finnish. When she didn't emerge, they searched the ferry, including her cabin, but she was nowhere to be found."

He frowned. "What makes you think he didn't throw her overboard?"

"That's what I thought at first, even though that's not his MO. Without a body, it was the most likely explanation. Then, I discovered a wheelchair had gone missing during the voyage."

He blinked at her. "A wheelchair?"

"Yes, one of the ferry officials noted that it had been stolen. My theory is that at some point during the voyage, the killer drugged Anne Hollman, then took her off the ship in the wheelchair when it docked the next morning."

Krister rubbed his forehead. "Wouldn't her boyfriend have noticed if she'd been wheeled off?"

"Not necessarily. He wasn't expecting her to be in a wheelchair, or with someone else. People only see what they want to see. The killer also could have put a scarf on her, turned her face to the side, or pulled on a cap. There are any number of ways to disguise a drugged person."

"Okay, fine. If he took her off in a wheelchair, where's her body?"

Her shoulders slumped. "That I can't tell you. It was never found. That was why they ruled it a suicide."

He frowned. "I thought I read in the report that she was depressed?"

"She was going through a bad patch. Her grades had dropped, but when I spoke to her college friends, they remembered her being distracted during the term. They said she'd stopped going out and developed agoraphobia."

"Consistent with depression."

"Consistent with being stalked."

Krister folded his arms and leaned back. His light brown eyes flickered over her face. "Let's say you're correct, and she was taken off the ferry. How does this help us?"

"I plan to be on that ferry." Krister opened his mouth to complain, but she held up her hand. "Let me explain." He closed it again. "I need to make myself into the perfect target to entice him to go for me. If I re-enact the same trip as his fourth victim, he won't be able to resist."

"You want him to come for you?"

"I want to meet him face to face," she admitted. "I want to know why he destroyed my life."

I want to know why he killed my mother.

I want to know why he's been playing this cat and mouse game with me.

Krister sighed. "It's dangerous, Avril."

"I know, and I'll wear a wire. We'll be in constant contact. When he comes to the cabin, we'll be ready for him."

"He'll be expecting that."

She pursed her lips. "I was thinking about that. We need to throw him off, convince him that the police have lost interest in him as a suspect. Make him believe I'm on that ferry alone."

"How are we going to do that?"

She pushed her glasses up her nose. "What if we leak it to the press that we've arrested Olaf Senior for his daughter-in-law's murder? You could issue a small press release for the local newspapers. The killer will think he's been dismissed as a suspect by the police."

"Olaf is innocent," Krister protested. "Of murder, anyhow."

"Yes, and you can release him afterwards. By arresting him for Agnes's murder, the killer will think you've abandoned me and my serial killer theory, and I'm on my own."

Krister exhaled, but she could tell he was thinking about it.

"I'll stay at home for the next few days," Avril continued. "We'll have no visible contact. I'll purchase a ticket online and board the ferry alone. He'll think we've fallen out. That the coast is clear."

Krister scratched his head. "How am I going to get on board then?"

"You wear a disguise. You and Freddie, or whoever is coming, buy independent tickets and board separately. He won't smell a setup if there isn't one."

Krister was frowning, but she could see his mind working. "How are we going to catch him?"

"I'll let you know my cabin number. We'll stay in contact, and when he comes for me, I give you the word, and you run in to save the day." She spread her arms. "Easy."

Krister stared at her for a long time. "What if I can't get to you in time?" He was that little boy again, worrying about her falling off his bike.

She gave a rare smile "You will. We'll make sure of it."

"I don't know, Avril."

"It's the only way, Krister. You know that. It has to be like this. He's been playing me the entire time. It's time I turned the tables on him."

"Even if it means getting hurt?"

Or worse.

He left the words unsaid.

"I won't."

"You might." His voice caught.

She wanted to take his hand, to tell him it would be alright, that she'd be fine, but she couldn't. "If it means finally catching this monster, I'm willing to take the chance."

chapter
thirty-three

THE KILLER WATCHED AS AVRIL BOARDED THE FERRY AT Stockholm port terminal. Finally, he had her all to himself. It was uncanny how much she looked like her mother. Soft blonde hair, delicate features, slim frame. The oversized coat drowned her as she moved inside to take a seat and open a magazine. He couldn't tell what she was reading.

The police had arrested that other hairy bastard for Agnes Hellgren's murder. How could they be so stupid? He'd stuck to the MO of Olivia Dahl's murder, painstakingly making sure every little detail was correct. The clearing in the woods, the lethal weather slowly draining her life, the pendant around her neck. What more did they want?

Still, he understood how these things worked. The department had quotas to fill. Like everywhere in the world, the police were under scrutiny. Public trust was at an all-time low.

He scoffed.

With idiots like Krister Jansson in charge, it was no wonder.

They'd turned their backs on Avril, abandoned her. The fifteen-year-old serial killer theory was getting stale. Nobody wanted to believe it anymore. Nobody wanted that hovering over their heads.

There were too many other crimes to solve. What was one more? Especially if they could pin it on some other idiot. He shook his head and watched as she paged through the magazine, waiting for the ferry to leave.

Every now and then she'd look up, scan the passengers, and then go back to reading. She was looking for him.

His heart grew warm as he thought about that. Not warm, exactly, but something. A tinge of pride. Agent Dahl hadn't given up. Her persistence was impressive. Had she understood his last message?

1993.

Had she made the connection?

He hoped so.

She'd never known him, not like a daughter should, but he'd known her. He knew how she thought, how she'd react. He knew how to manipulate her.

For ten years, he'd watched as she'd grown into a woman, become an FBI agent, and now an outcast. The FBI didn't want her anymore. The Swedish Police had also cast her aside.

His daughter.

He'd show them how wrong they were. And how right she'd been.

They'd regret not taking her seriously.

He gave a little snort. It was the least he could do.

Slipping into the passenger lounge via a side door, he took a seat two rows behind her. He could almost smell her scent from here. She wouldn't recognize him, not like this. The gray wig, cheek implants, and the walking stick completely altered his appearance. Besides, nobody looked twice at the elderly. They were invisible.

He'd smiled when he'd seen her board the ferry. She'd taken her time, lingering at the boarding gate, making sure she was visible to anyone watching. Clever girl. She was sending a signal. Letting him know she was interested. She'd know he wouldn't be able to resist. It was too good an opportunity.

But he was smarter than she was. He'd meet her, of course. They both needed closure. A career of killing, and she'd been on his back the entire time. A few times, she'd come so close, he'd had to change his plans and get out of town fast.

Chicago was a case in point. His groin still ached when he thought about how that bitch had kicked him. How was he to know she had a black belt in karate? It hadn't come up in any of his vetting processes. She hadn't attended a class in the weeks he'd been stalking her. She didn't have any martial art outfits or medals in her apartment. The defensive attack had taken him by surprise.

A mistake he hadn't made twice.

A few more people filtered into the lounge. Avril glanced up, surveying them. Her eyes—Olivia's eyes—roamed over their faces, then dropped back to her magazine. He was hit by an indignant surge. How dare the police abandon her? Didn't they know how dangerous he was?

Still, the anticipation of what was about to happen made his heart beat that little bit faster. It was still early. He wouldn't strike until later, when the voyage was underway, and she was tucked up in her cabin.

The overnight ferry connecting Sweden and Finland was his preferred method of transport between the capitals. He loved the sea. One regret he had was not spending more time enjoying it. Still, he'd had a rewarding life —and he'd gotten to spend it with his daughter.

He'd always known, of course.

Even if she hadn't.

He saw in her the same relentless spirit, the same meticulous nature that had driven him. In some ways, they were quite similar. In others, they were very different.

He manipulated people. Always had, even when he didn't need to. It was a skill he found hard to set aside. It came with growing up having to fend for yourself. People were objects to be used, not human beings with feelings. He scoffed.

Feelings.

Who needed 'em?

Avril used her abilities for good. She solved murders, brought killers to justice, and gave the families of victims a measure of closure. Cleaned up after his mess.

She was good at it too. Most of the time, she got her guy.

Just not him.

Never him.

He'd always been one step ahead.

The giant ship got underway. The massive engines roared to life and maneuvered the vessel out into the bay. The killer felt an odd kinship with their relentless power, a reminder of his own indomitable spirit that had propelled him through countless challenges.

The port, with its mechanical giants and steel sentinels, retreated into the distance. Soon, there was nothing around but the cold, gray ocean.

At five-thirty, Avril got up and went into the dining hall. The smörgåsbord dinner that the ferry was famous for looked good, but he wasn't hungry. Neither was she, judging by the tiny amount of food she placed on her plate. All the time her eyes wandered around the room, scanning faces, looking for signs he was there.

Her pale blue eyes landed on him, and he caught his breath. Had she recognized him? Did she know who he was? His heart pounded erratically in his chest as he waited for her reaction. A second passed, she blinked, and her gaze moved on.

He exhaled. He was in the clear.

She took a window seat and settled down to eat. Usually the window seats were the first to go, but this time of year, there were plenty available. Most people were at home with their families during the holidays. A boozy, duty-free shopping trip on the high seas wasn't at the top of their agenda.

Outside the window, the ship's lights reflected on the churning waves, creating pools of light in the darkness, only to be swallowed up by the next surge of water. In the distance, the dramatic scenery of the passing archipelago was in shadow, the skeletal trees stretching skyward as they resisted the icy gusts.

Avril ate, then got up and retired to her cabin. The killer followed at a discrete distance, his walking stick clacking on the floor. A few others milled around, looking for their rooms, or staring blindly out of the windows into the darkness. Somewhere in the background, the rhythmic thud of the disco could be heard. He cringed at the intrusion.

Before entering, she glanced up and down the corridor. He bent over his stick, pretending to be looking for something in his pocket. Head down, he sensed, rather than saw that she'd moved on.

He had his own cabin, just in case. It wasn't under his name, of course. Nor was it under a name she'd recognize. He wouldn't give her that big a clue. After he'd noted her room number, he went back to the lounge. Now he knew where she was, the rest would be easy.

At midnight, the ferry made its scheduled stop in the Åland Islands. The killer stayed in his cabin, reading, until they were underway again. He had several hours to kill. There was no point in going too soon, because if he had to sedate her, he didn't want to keep her unconscious for too long before he laid her out in the cold.

His daughter.

His final victim.

Or would he sacrifice himself for her? Give her the chance to bring him in? That would be a fitting end to a frustrating career. It would prove she'd been right all along.

He could see the headlines now. FBI AGENT CATCHES NOTO-RIOUS SERIAL KILLER.

It made him smile.

Self-sacrifice wasn't really his style, though, and it would mean he couldn't complete the cycle. Avril was the closest to Olivia that he could get. She shared her DNA. Killing her would be his greatest achievement.

But he might make an exception this time. After all, she had earned it. It would be his way of saying he was proud of her.

At five a.m., just as the sky in the east was lightening, the killer got up, stretched and made his way to Avril's cabin. The endless beat of the disco had stopped, but the slot machines in the mini casino still jingled and beeped on the upper deck. He pictured Avril waiting for him in her cabin. He appreciated her setting up this little meeting.

Now that she knew...

A surge of adrenaline made his skin tingle, or maybe it was just the icy draft seeping in from outside.

Soon.

Soon they would meet face to face.

The killer detoured past the onboard medical office and took a wheelchair from several lined up outside. Nobody would notice until it was too late. Sitting in it, he balanced his walking stick across his knees and pushed himself toward the elevator.

Two floors down, and he was on the right floor. The wheels squeaked on the hard floors as he maneuvered down the corridor. It was hard work, and by the time he got there, his arms ached. He could feel the hull of the ship rolling over the swells, creaking as it did so. Outside, the wind buffeted the windows, making them shudder.

Room 307.

The killer stopped, listened, then angling his body to block the view from the cameras, he inserted a slim, metallic lockpick into the upper part of the keyhole. With deft fingers, he felt for the pins inside, his touch as light as a pianist's. Each pin offered a different resistance, a tiny obstacle to be navigated with precision. He jiggled the pick, listening for the faint clicks as the pins settled into place. The tension wrench held steady with just enough pressure to turn the cylinder when all pins were aligned. It was a delicate exercise, a balance between force and finesse. One wrong move and he would have to start over. But the killer was patient, his breath controlled as he coaxed each pin into submission, inching closer to the rewarding snap of the lock giving way.

Then, he was in.

Silently, he pushed open the cabin door.

It was the music he heard first. The soft, lyrical melody of the second movement of Beethoven's 5th piano concerto playing in the background. The lamp beside the bed was on, but she'd fallen asleep on her side, facing the wall. He couldn't see her face, just blonde hair spread over the pillow and across her cheek.

The killer got out of the wheelchair, pulled it into the room and closed the door behind him. The woman didn't move. He scoffed. How silly of her to fall asleep when she ought to be waiting for him, for their meeting.

He crept up to the bed. Removing his wig, he stared down at the sleeping woman.

"Hello, Avril." His voice was hoarse with excitement.

This was the moment he'd been waiting for. The moment when he met his daughter in the flesh. He felt like he knew her so well, without having known her at all. It was a strange sensation, and not one he was used to.

The blonde turned and stared up at him.

He blinked, confused.

"Who are you?"

chapter
thirty-four

"I don't like this," Krister muttered in her ear. He watched from the CCTV monitoring room on the same level as Avril's cabin. "He's been in there too long."

"It's only been five minutes," Avril reassured him from her position in the elevator hall at the end of the corridor to the cabins. As soon as she'd seen the old man wheel himself down the corridor she'd known it was him. The wheelchair was a nice touch, and it confirmed her suspicion, that he'd used one to get Anna Hollman off the ferry fifteen years ago. "If we go in now, we won't have anything to pin on him. We have to wait for him to abduct her." Even then, they'd only have him on kidnapping charges. There was no evidence he'd murdered the fifty-five other victims across a fifteen-year span. No DNA, no fingerprints, not so much as a hair. He'd been extremely careful.

"Tell me again why you asked Ingrid to take your place?"

"I want to be the one to arrest him," she murmured, pressing one of the cordless earbuds further into her ear. "It has to be me."

"What if we've placed Ingrid in danger?"

"No more so than I would have been."

"You're an experienced FBI agent, and she's pretty green. She only got her detective badge last year."

Avril pushed away any feelings of guilt. She had manipulated the young detective into it, she knew that. Told her it was a way to make her mark, show senior management she had what it took to be a front-line investigator. "She offered. She wanted to impress you."

Krister gave a soft snort.

"It's a pity he can't lead us to where he buried the fourth body fifteen years ago," Avril murmured. "Then we'd really have something on him."

"No way," came the immediate reply. "I am not allowing him to abduct Ingrid and take her off this ship."

"I wasn't suggesting that."

"Yes, you were. I know you, Avril, but the stakes are too high."

She gave a frustrated grimace, not that he could see it. "It would mean we could get him for more than just an abduction. If he's recreating the first series of murders, he'll take Ingrid to the same spot he took his fourth victim, Anna Hollman. That way we can place him at the scene and pin Anna's murder on him. It might be enough to convince a jury he's guilty of all the other murders too."

Krister's voice was as hard as steel in her ear. "I said no, Avril. It's too dangerous. I'm not putting her life on the line to catch this guy. What we're doing is more than enough."

Avril didn't reply. It wasn't enough. As things stood, they had squat. An old man entering a cabin that wasn't his. Big deal. They needed him to take Ingrid off the ship so they could follow him. That was the only way they would catch him.

But Krister was right. They couldn't knowingly sanction an abduction of a police officer. It was too risky.

She'd have done it, if she was in that cabin, but she couldn't be both bait and arresting officer at the same time. What if he chloroformed her? She'd never get to talk to him before he took her off the ship—and one thing was for sure, after a decade of chasing this man, and suspecting she was related to him, there was no way she wouldn't have her say.

"She'll press the buzzer any minute," Avril whispered.

In addition to the buzzer, they'd equipped Ingrid with a digital tracker in a bracelet fastened to her wrist. The clasp was such that the killer would have to break it apart to get it off. Many of his other victims had been found wearing watches or earrings, so she didn't think he'd care about a bracelet.

"There's nothing to worry about," Avril had told the young detective.

"I'll be right outside the door, and Krister will be watching on camera. As soon as he tries to attack you, press the buzzer, and we'll be there."

It had almost been too easy. Ingrid had jumped at the chance to get involved. Anything to participate in an op with Krister. Avril had known she would and had used it to her advantage.

"Press the buzzer," Krister said in her ear.

At that moment, a siren reverberated around the ship. Loud and constant, it screeched through the quiet night air, and a robotic voice told everyone to stay calm and proceed to the main hall on the upper deck.

"What's happening?" barked Krister.

Avril kept her voice steady. "It's a fire alarm."

Krister yelled into the phone. "It's him! It must be."

Chaos erupted. Cabin doors flung open, and anxious, groggy passengers filled the hallway trying to get to the upper deck.

"I'm going in," Avril shouted, taking off at a run. She zigzagged through passengers coming the other way, feeling like a salmon swimming upstream, until she got to her cabin. Krister would be right behind her. It wouldn't take long to get from the CCTV monitoring room to the deck where her cabin was located.

"Move!" she yelled, dodging the tidal wave of people. Being a petite five-foot-four, she'd lost sight of the cabin door. But finally, she got to room 307.

The door was ajar.

Pushing it open, she darted into the cabin, only to find it was empty.

Ingrid was gone.

"SHIT!" Krister paced the room, stunned. The lingering smell of chloroform hung in the air. "He's got her."

Avril stared at the rumpled bed where Ingrid had lain. "She didn't press the buzzer."

"He must have gotten to her before she could activate it."

Avril pulled out her phone and opened the tracking app. "At least we can still track her."

Krister peered over her shoulder.

Her voice wobbled. "I can't get a signal."

"Goddammit!"

She shot him a worried look. "I think the network is jammed." Everybody on the ship was probably using their phone right now.

"Let's start searching," Krister said, swiveling around.

Avril bit back a surge of panic. They couldn't let him get away. Not without being able to trace him. "Can we get the staff to help?"

"Not with the fire alarm blasting like this. Once they've checked the source of the fire, we can speak to the captain."

Avril shook her head. "Why isn't it working?"

"We should have expected this." Krister threw his hands in the air. "He knew you'd double-crossed him when he saw Ingrid."

Avril didn't reply.

Krister shot her a worried look. "What's he going to do with her?"

"He'll have her in a wheelchair," Avril said, her heart sinking. "It can't be that hard to find them. There's no way he can carry an unconscious woman without being noticed. I mean, we're on a ship."

"He won't go up to the top deck," Krister said.

"The cargo hold is my guess." Avril adjusted her glasses. The ship's bulk rose and fell as it swooped over a swell. The sea was getting rougher.

"Okay, let's split up."

"I'll go down to the cargo hold, and you check the remaining floors. I'll meet you back at the CCTV control room."

Krister nodded, then took off.

Avril watched him go, then exited the cabin. The way the ship was designed meant she had to return to the middle deck before descending one of the two side staircases that led to the cargo deck.

The handrail was cold and slippery, but she slid her hand down it to stabilize herself as she took the metal steps two at a time. By the time she'd reached the bottom, the fire alarm had stopped, and an authoritative voice over the loudspeaker told everybody it was a false alarm and that they could go back to their rooms.

A convenient false alarm.

Below, the cargo area loomed large and shadowy, a cavernous space segmented by containers and machinery, all bathed in the pale yellow of flickering lights. She moved silently, her steps muffled by the constant hum of the ship's engine. The air was thick with the smell of oil and sea salt, a pungent reminder of the open ocean churning outside the steel walls.

Avril weaved through the maze of vehicles and container trucks, each a potential hiding spot, peering into the darkened interiors. She wished more than ever that she had the security of her service weapon in her holster, ready to draw at the slightest provocation, but all she had was her pepper spray and a taser, which Krister had reluctantly loaned her for the operation.

A whisper of movement made her swing around, but it was nothing more than the water slapping against the side of the hull.

Where were they?

She finished her systematic search of the cargo area but saw no sign of Mikael or his hostage. They certainly weren't in any of the vehicles, as far as she could see. Could they be hiding in a container? If so, how had he gotten in? Unless he had help, and like her, had kept that person a secret.

She frowned. No, that was unlikely. Mikael wasn't the type to have a sidekick. He worked alone. He may have coerced someone into helping him, however. That was more his style. Manipulative, persuasive, threatening. He could be all those things.

Another surge, and she clutched the hood of a nearby SUV. The weather conditions were deteriorating. The ship tilted from side to side before righting itself again. The massive steel cargo door groaned as waves broke against it.

Just then, Krister rushed down the stairs. "Anything?"

She swung around. "He's not here."

"You sure? He's not on any of the floors, either. I also checked the security cameras and couldn't find him."

"Did you look inside the other cabins on that floor?"

"Only the ones I could get access to. There are many still locked."

"He could have taken her into one of those," Avril said. "We need to get into them."

"We'll need permission."

"Okay, I'll go back to the monitoring room and keep an eye on the CCTV in case he's on the move."

"I'll speak to the captain and meet you there." Krister ran a hand through his hair. "He's got to be here somewhere. It's a ship, for goodness' sake. It's not like he can get off."

"Not in this weather."

They went back to the main hall where relieved and slightly giddy passengers ordered coffee from the canteen. Avril checked her phone. It was nearly seven o'clock in the morning. Outside, the sky had lightened to a muted gray, but the view through the misted windows was minimal. The ocean was a vast, blurry expanse surrounding the ship, but in the distance she could see a dark outline. Helsinki. They had maybe two or three hours until they docked.

Back in the CCTV room, Avril replayed the video footage from just before the alarm sounded. The old man in the wheelchair heading to her cabin, fiddling with the lock. The flimsy cabin door opening.

It was a good disguise. You'd never know it was him from this distance. Hard to prove in a court of law—just some old cripple heading to his cabin. You couldn't even tell he'd picked the lock, since his upper body obscured that section of the door.

Then nothing until the alarm had sounded.

Avril checked the time. Three minutes. Three minutes he'd been inside before the alarm had gone off. Three minutes to realize he'd been duped, and it wasn't Avril in the bed.

Cabin doors had been flung open, worried faces peering out. A stampede of people making their way along the corridors to the stairs leading to the upper deck. In the throng, she couldn't see the door.

Narrowing her eyes, she squinted at the screen. The door was open, but she couldn't see when he'd come out, or whether he was pushing Ingrid in the wheelchair or holding her as a hostage.

Where had they gone? A wheelchair and an unconscious woman weren't the easiest to hide. He must have ducked into a vacant cabin, in which case he could still be there, waiting for the ship to dock. What of the occupant? Were they still on the upper deck? What if they came back? Would he hold them hostage too?

Frowning, she flicked her hair off her face. One thing was for sure. He wouldn't be able to get off this ship, not until it docked in a couple of hours' time.

And that's when they'd get him.

chapter
thirty-five

"He knows you betrayed him," Krister fumed. "There's no telling what he might do now."

"He's going to do the same thing he does to all his victims," Avril told him, her voice steady. "Keep her unconscious until he can get her to the spot where he'll leave her."

"To freeze to death." Krister swiped at his hair. He was wound up like a spring. "I don't understand where they could have gone. We've searched the entire ship."

"Not really," she argued. "He could be in one of the other cabins, and we haven't searched the staff quarters yet." They hadn't been given permission by the captain, even when Krister had stressed it was a sanctioned operation by the Swedish Police. They didn't have the appropriate warrants.

Krister looked up. "What if he's thrown her overboard?"

"He won't." Avril leaned back in her chair and looked at him. "Somehow, he's going to get her off this ship, and that's when we'll catch him."

"There are only two of us," he reminded her. "There's limits to what we can do."

"I know." The tracker still hadn't come online, and she was beginning to wonder if something had happened to it. It had been working fine when she'd tested it beforehand. Without the ability to trace him...

She squeezed her eyes shut.

"We'll get him. There's only one passenger exit and one cargo exit. Can you radio the police in Helsinki and ask for their assistance when we dock?"

"Already done," he barked.

"Then we'll catch him," she said, wondering if she was reassuring him or herself. "We have to."

The ferry eventually pulled into the harbor and docked, the giant engines straining as it idled, churning the water beneath its hull. Crew members secured the vessel to the berthing. Finally, the massive cargo door lifted, and the passengers hovered, ready to disembark.

Thanks to Krister, the staff held them back until he and Avril had gone ashore and spoken with the Helsinki police officer in charge. Krister explained the situation—that they were looking for an old man and an unconscious woman in a wheelchair.

The officer gave a curt nod, spoke to his men who spread out along the dockside, then signaled that they were ready. Only then did Krister inform the ferry staff, who allowed the passengers to start leaving the ship.

Avril stood beside Krister, scanning faces. Her eyes flitted from one individual to another, analyzing features, searching for the blue eyes, the dimple—details that wouldn't change regardless of the disguise.

"I can't see anyone in a wheelchair," Krister muttered.

Once the passengers had disembarked, the vehicles were allowed to go. A slow cavalcade of cars, lorries and trucks began to crawl out of the hold, each one scrutinized by the waiting police officers.

"Why aren't they searching the containers?" Krister asked a police officer on the dock. All they did was peer inside the vehicles.

"No authority," he replied, subdued.

Avril shook her head. "It's too easy for him to get away like this. He might have a vehicle on board."

"He didn't. We watched him walk onto the ship."

"An accomplice? A paid driver? This man is resourceful. He's avoided law enforcement for fifteen years."

Krister slammed his fist into the palm of his other hand. "Dammit, Avril. I knew this would happen. Now we've lost Ingrid, and we've got nothing. We can't even prove that he broke into the cabin."

"I wouldn't say we've got nothing."

"Huh?"

She smiled and held up her phone. "Signal's back on. The tracker is working."

Krister let out a relieved breath. "Thank God. Where are they?"

"Heading north out of the harbor."

"He *did* have a vehicle," Krister breathed, his eyes following the pulsing dot. It was moving faster than someone on foot.

Avril looked at the officer beside him. "We'll need a car."

The officer wouldn't agree to lend them a squad car but said he'd drive them. They clambered in, and he took off out of the harbor, following the tracker.

"They're heading north, out of the city," Avril said, her phone in front of her. "He's probably got a fifteen-minute head start."

"Looks like they're taking Route E18 towards Turku," the officer said.

"What's there?" asked Krister, from the backseat.

"Nuuksio National Park," the officer replied. "It's a forested area with a lake, fairly close to Helsinki."

"Perfect place to leave a body," Avril muttered.

At Turku, they took a ring road heading northeast. The route was icy, and the sides were piled high with sludgy, brown snow. The officer took a dangerous corner fast, and somehow managed to keep his vehicle perfectly in line. Avril was impressed, but then she'd heard the Finnish produced some of the best drivers in the world.

They passed a sign for Lahti, where they merged onto the E75 highway and kept going in a northerly direction. "Looks like he's heading to Jyväskylä," the police officer said, glancing at the gray dot just ahead of them.

"Can you see him yet?" Krister asked.

Avril scanned the three-lane highway, but there were a lot of heavy goods vehicles, and she had no idea which one they were in. It didn't matter, as long as he didn't realize he was being tracked.

The driver shook his head. "Not yet. He's probably still a couple miles ahead of us."

They kept going, eventually turning onto Route 77, which took them through several small towns toward Joensuu. Krister had been quiet for some time now, and swiveling, Avril saw he'd leaned back against the seat and had his eyes closed. She felt heavy-lidded herself but couldn't sleep. Not when *he* was somewhere up ahead of them.

"I think he's heading into the hills," the cop said, wearily. They'd been driving for nearly three hours. "The Koli National Park is out this way."

"What's that like?" Avril asked.

"Snowy landscapes, lots of open space, forests and lakes. Some good hiking trails in the summer."

"That sounds like it could be his destination." A shiver of excitement ran through her. "Maybe that's where he buried Anna Hollman."

"You set off the fire alarm, didn't you?" Krister said quietly from the back seat.

She didn't realize he'd woken up.

"Of course not."

"Avril, don't lie to me. That's why you gave Ingrid the tracker, isn't it? You *wanted* him to take her so you could follow him out here."

She didn't reply.

"You let him escape." It was a hiss.

Avril swung around in her chair. "I did not set off the fire alarm."

His look said he didn't believe her.

"I swear, I didn't." She hesitated. "But I suspected he might use a decoy to get away."

Krister sucked in a sharp breath. The officer driving them said nothing.

"It was the only way we were going to catch him," she insisted. "If we'd arrested him on the ship, we'd have nothing to hold him on. Breaking and entering?" She scoffed. "We needed more, Krister. Don't you see?"

"For heaven's sake, Avril. Did you even stop to think that you were putting Ingrid's life in danger? That she might die?"

"She won't die. I knew this would work. Besides, she—"

"Don't say she agreed to it," he snapped. "She did not sign up for this. She thought we were going to rescue her before it got to this stage. She trusted us, Avril, and we let her down."

"It's for the greater good," she sulked. "He's a monster, Krister. He has to be brought down. Nothing else would work. It had to be something extreme, something he wouldn't expect."

"So you bet on the fact he'd give us the slip, and you put that tracker on Ingrid's wrist so he'd lead us straight to where he left Anna Hollman's body."

"It was a good plan," she said quietly.

He was silent for a moment.

"You've done some crazy things in your life, Avril, but this takes the cake. If anything happens to Ingrid, it'll be both our jobs on the line. You realize that, don't you?"

"I'm sorry to involve you in this," she said. Her job meant nothing if she couldn't catch Mikael Lustig. She wasn't even sure she would go back to it, but Krister loved his job. He'd worked hard to get there. "If there was any other way—"

"Let's hope your little ploy works." He turned his head and looked out the window. "Or else we're all screwed."

chapter
thirty-six

THE KILLER SIMMERED WITH BARELY CONCEALED RAGE AS THE lorry driver drove them north to the snowy hills of Koli National Park. He'd chosen his spot carefully fifteen years ago, when he'd left Anna there to die.

Located in the North Karelia region of Finland, it was approximately 258 miles from Helsinki, and would take nearly four hours to get there by car. It was also one of the most beautiful places he'd ever seen. He loved it so much, he'd hired a cabin near Lake Pielinen when he'd needed to get out of Stockholm, and before he'd moved to America.

That was a long time ago, in the springtime, but he still remembered the snow-capped ridges, thick forests and meadows filled with herbs and wildflowers. It had offered a pristine sanctuary where he could hide and make plans. It was where he'd crafted most of his snowflake pendants until he'd perfected them.

He had one last pendant. He'd been keeping it for Avril, but now he'd have to use it on this police officer, or that's who he assumed she was. He ground his teeth together, and not because of the frigid conditions in the back of the truck, but because he couldn't believe she'd betrayed him.

His own daughter.

The irony wasn't lost on him. She was smart, she'd played him. But he was smarter. At least the fire alarm had given him the distraction he'd needed to escape. All he'd had to do was light a piece of paper and hold it under the smoke detector in the cabin.

Too easy.

It was a contingency plan he'd used before, once, many years ago when she had come close to discovering him. What a shame he'd had to use it again. Now Avril would never meet her only living relative. He would be gone in a few months, and the murders of fifty-five young women, including Olivia Dahl, would never be solved. That was her punishment, and he knew it would irk her more than anything he could have planned for her.

Not knowing.

A strange sense of nostalgia settled over him as he recalled his daughter's twelfth birthday. He'd watched them through the window. Avril blowing out her candles, Avril opening her presents, Avril playing with her friends.

He ought to have been there with them. They were *his* family.

Olivia belonged to him.

It still infuriated him, after all these years. Olivia's betrayal. And now her daughter had added insult to injury. They were two of a kind.

Well, he'd show her. He'd show them all.

Mikael Lustig would go down as the most prolific serial killer never to be caught. He'd outwitted them all. To think he'd even considered handing himself over to Avril. To give himself up so she could have the glory of bringing him in. His one and only gift to her, his daughter. He'd been prepared to give her what she'd always wanted, to catch the man who'd murdered her mother. To have closure. A gift more precious than anything else. Not to mention the boost it would give her career.

But she'd ruined it. Now, he would leave her to suffer.

She'd never know.

And it would destroy her.

chapter
thirty-seven

"HE'S STOPPED," THE POLICE OFFICER SAID, SLOWING DOWN.

Beside them, Lake Pielinen glistened like a frosted mirror in the subdued light. It was nearly sunset, and the trees that lined the approach road cast long, foreboding shadows over the snowy ground. The landscape was desolate, a vast expanse of white that stretched out endlessly, punctuated only by the occasional evergreen. The air was biting cold, stinging Avril's face and making her breath visible in the frigid air.

"There's a parking area up ahead," the officer said. "What do you want me to do?"

"Park behind him," Krister said, urgency in his tone. "Box him in. We want to make sure we've got Ingrid."

"Okay."

The officer floored it into the deserted parking area and came to a skidding stop behind a large, white van. It was the type used for moving house, with lots of interior space for boxes.

"I'm going to need that gun," Krister turned to the officer, who had already cleared it with his Chief. After unlocking the built-in weapon box in his trunk, he handed Krister a service pistol, a Glock 17, standard issue for Finnish police. Krister checked the magazine and chambered a round with practiced efficiency. They approached the front of the van cautiously, the snow crunching under their boots.

"It's empty," the officer called, peering through the driver's window.

Avril's heart sank.

"She could still be in the back," Krister called, but Avril shook her head.

"Look, there are footprints and sled marks heading into the forest. I think he's pulling her on some sort of sleigh."

Krister came up beside her, his breath visible in the cold air. "They're heavy prints. He's struggling to transport her."

Avril gave a quick nod. "We might be able to catch him. Let's go."

"Whoa!" The officer stared at them like they were crazy. "You can't go traipsing into the woods without backup. It'll be dark soon, the temperature will drop even more. You'll freeze to death."

"So will she if we don't get to her before he leaves her out here," Krister retorted. The officer blinked, confused. He didn't understand what was going on.

"He's got a hostage," Avril explained. "She's still alive, but he's going to dump her body."

His eyes widened, then he gave a hesitant nod. "I've got flashlights in the car, and you're going to need these." He handed them each a walkie-talkie. "There isn't much cell service in the hills."

Avril cast a worried look at the tracker. It was still flashing, but for how long? "Let's go," she urged. "Before we lose the signal."

Krister looked to the officer. "Call the local search and rescue for backup. We'll need it."

"Understood," the officer responded, already calling for support as Avril and Krister set out into the biting cold.

Avril led the way, her gaze alternating between the faint trail they followed and the blinking light of the tracker. The frozen landscape of the national park stretched out before them, a vast expanse of pristine snow broken only by the towering evergreens that dotted the terrain. The forest loomed around them, a maze of frosted trees and ice-encrusted branches that creaked and groaned as they passed underneath, their breath forming clouds of vapor in the frigid air. Icicles hung from the boughs like chandeliers, glinting in the fading light of the winter sun. They were on the clock, not just against the setting sun but also the bitter cold that would overcome them if they stayed out too long.

"Careful," Krister warned, as Avril slid into a deep dip, her foot plunging through the snow and into a hidden crevice. He offered her a hand and pulled her out, his grip firm and strong. She could tell by the tight set of his jaw and the furrow of his brow that he was still pissed at her.

"Thanks." She glanced at her phone as it beeped, the sound muffled by her thick gloves. A random text had come in, probably from the service provider. Swiping it aside with a frustrated grunt, she continued to stare at the dot on the tracker's screen. "We're almost on top of him."

They glanced around, their eyes scanning the frozen forest, but they couldn't see anything. The trees stood like silent sentinels, their branches heavy with snow and ice, obscuring their view.

"What's that?" Krister asked, as they stumbled into a small clearing. The snow drifts were so high it was impossible to stand upright, the powdery snow reaching up to their thighs. In the center of the clearing stood a peculiar sight.

"Looks like a wooden stake," Avril whispered, moving forward, her voice hushed as if speaking too loudly would disturb the eerie stillness of the forest. It was treacherous going, and she slipped and fell several times, the snow filling her boots and numbing her feet. "Two stakes, crossed in the middle."

"X marks the spot," breathed Krister, his eyes widening in realization.

"Oh no." Avril went cold, a chill that had nothing to do with the freezing temperature racing down her spine.

"What?"

"He found it."

Lying in the center of the wooden cross was the tracking bracelet.

chapter
thirty-eight

AVRIL STARED AT THE BRACELET IN THE CENTER OF THE CROSS. "I think this is where Anna Hollman is buried," she whispered. "He marked it for us."

Krister looked around frantically. "But where's Ingrid?"

"We need to get a forensic team up here."

"Avril, where's Ingrid? He's still got her."

Her phone buzzed, but she ignored it. Realizing he was shouting at her, she turned away from the wooden X to face him. "He can't have got far. We were only just behind him."

Krister peered into the shadows beyond the trees. "We have to find her."

Mikael wouldn't let it go this easily. He'd want closure. Someone to witness his grand finale. He'd want her.

The text.

Fumbling, she took her phone out of her pocket.

"What are you doing?"

"Looking to see if we've still got a signal." She read the text message, keeping her expression neutral, then slipped her phone back into her pocket. Swallowing hard, she said, "Nothing."

"Well, we can't just stand here. We need to keep looking."

"Agreed. Let's split up. We'll cover more ground that way."

He frowned. "You sure?"

"Yeah. You said yourself, Ingrid's life is in the balance."

"Okay, but don't go too far or else you might not be able to find your way back." His face was taut with worry. Torn between Avril and Ingrid, she knew he had to put the preservation of life ahead of his fear she'd get lost.

"I'll keep in touch via the walkie talkie. Anyway, search and rescue are on the way. If either of us doesn't make it back, the other will come looking, okay?"

His eyes bore into hers. "Deal."

"I'll go west." She set off into the woods, before he had time to argue.

Very clever, the text said. *Follow these coordinates. Come alone, or she dies.*

Avril stomped through the ankle-deep snow, her breath misting in front of her. Thank goodness for the flashlight. Now that the sun was setting, it was quite dark in the forest, and she could barely make out the footpath. The branches of the trees were heavy with crystalized snow, creating spooky formations that loomed out at her.

Hands trembling, she checked the coordinates. It looked like he was half a mile along this path. She knew she was walking into a trap, but she had no choice. Ingrid's life depended on it.

Finally, they'd come face to face. She wasn't afraid—quite the contrary. Her pulse raced with anticipation as she thought about meeting him, the killer who'd eluded her this last decade.

Her father.

But she wasn't unprepared. Inside her jacket pocket were her two weapons, the taser and the pepper spray, and the knife was still around her ankle. Would they be enough to subdue him if it came to that? *When* it came to that?

Did he have a gun? In all the time she'd been hunting him, he'd never once shot anyone, although this was different. He was on the run now, the police hot on his tail. She had to assume he had a weapon.

The path climbed at a rapid elevation, and soon she was panting. When the trees cleared, she looked out over a breathtaking expanse of blue-tinged snow. About twenty feet away lay a figure.

Ingrid.

Avril hurried over to the police officer's unmoving body.

Please let her be alive.

This had been her idea. If Ingrid died, she'd forever feel responsible. Nobody was supposed to die.

"Hello, Avril."

She froze, every muscle in her body locking up at the sound of his voice.

Slowly, she straightened up. "Mikael."

He laughed softly, a chilling sound that sent shivers down her spine. "You came."

Avril turned around, heart pounding. He was nothing like the photograph of the handsome young man with glossy hair and a charming smile. The man in front of her was thin, almost emaciated, with sunken eyes and a scalp that was nearly bare, save for a few sparse, wispy strands of hair. The only thing he'd retained was his height.

He peered into the woods behind her. "You alone?"

She nodded. Krister was miles away, searching in the opposite direction. He'd never find her here.

He relaxed, his icy blue gaze thawing slightly. "Congratulations. You finally tracked me down."

"You knew I'd be on that ferry."

That dimple, now in sunken, hollow cheeks. "I did. Stupidly, I thought the police had abandoned you. Well played, by the way." He tilted his head.

"It was the only way."

"Except, I got away."

She didn't reply.

"But you knew I would, didn't you? Else why would you put a tracker on your colleague?"

"You're nothing if not predictable. I knew you'd bring her to the place where you buried Anna Hollman."

"Yes, they never did find her body, did they? Then again, why would they? Nobody thought she'd gotten off the ferry." He snorted, a harsh sound in the stillness. "It was so easy. Even her boyfriend didn't recognize her."

"The record, the flowers, the year." Her eyes burned as she stared at him. "Were you trying to tell me something?"

A half smile. "What do you think?"

Abruptly, she turned away from him and focused on Ingrid. "Is she alive?"

"Barely, but there's still time."

"How long?"

"Twenty minutes."

It would take longer than that to get her back to the car. He knew what she was thinking. "You can still save her."

"How?"

"You can take her place."

Avril stared at Ingrid's face, as white as the snow in which she lay. "She already has hypothermia."

"Call your friend. Tell him where she is, and you can come with me."

"We need to get her off the ice."

He nodded, and walked back into the woods where he retrieved a silver blanket, the kind used by the emergency services. Avril spotted the sleigh behind the tree. That's how he'd transported Ingrid's body along the path. He was tall, but not strong.

"You're sick, aren't you?" she said, as he bent down and wrapped Ingrid in the blanket. "You're dying."

Slowly, he straightened up, his movements labored.

"How long have you got?"

A shrug. "Months."

"Is that why you stopped killing? You were having treatment?"

He snorted. "For all the good it did me."

Avril stared at him. Her father. A serial killer. A monster.

"Why?" she croaked. "Why did you kill my mother?"

His face grew hard. "She betrayed me."

"Because she married my father?"

"She was pregnant with *my* child. She should have married *me*. We had something special. A bond. We were in love."

Avril scoffed, her voice trembling with anger. "You can't experience love."

His mouth curled into a snarl. "You might be right, but I recognized it in her. Nobody ever looked at me the way she did."

Avril clenched her hands into fists, her nails digging into her palms.

"You were obsessed with her. You couldn't let it go. Did you stalk her for twelve years, or was it an unlucky coincidence that you ran into her again?"

"It took me a long time to find her," he admitted, walking towards Avril, his steps slow and deliberate. "But when I did, I made sure she wasn't going anywhere ever again."

Rage swept over her, but she held her ground. How dare he take her mother from her. Destroy her family. Ruin her life. "What about all those other women? What did they ever do to you?"

"They were just like her. I wanted to make them pay like I'd made her pay."

"You thought if you kept killing, it would make you feel better?"

"It did."

He stopped right in front of her. A menacing presence with cold, empty eyes, but all she saw was a sick old man. "I'm not afraid of you."

"I know." He chuckled, a sound devoid of humor. "Because you're just like me."

Her skin crawled. "What do you mean? I'm nothing like you."

"What do you *feel*, Avril?"

A shiver went through her that had nothing to do with the cold. "I feel nothing for you."

"You feel nothing. Period. You can't. You're filled with nothingness, just like me."

"You're wrong."

A hoarse laugh. "You can't fool me. I'm your flesh and blood, remember?"

A shiver of revulsion ran over her.

"Now you're going to pay, just like your mother did."

"You're really going to kill me? Your own daughter." Her breath caught in her throat.

"I considered turning myself in to you, did you know that? On the ferry. If you'd been in your cabin, you'd have me in custody by now." He gave a coarse laugh. "But you didn't. You decided to play me."

"Like you've been playing me," she spat out, "for ten years."

"You know why I carried on killing? It wasn't just the thrill, although that was part of it, don't get me wrong. It was because it was a way to see you."

Her eyes widened.

"That's right. I killed those women because I knew you'd come running. Like a moth to a flame. You couldn't leave it alone. Another country, another four victims, and there you were. My Avril, the FBI agent." He laughed, but it turned into a wracking cough.

Avril slipped her hand into her jacket pocket.

She wasn't fast enough. He lurched forward, surprisingly fast for a dying man. His long arms reached out, his hands tightening around her throat.

chapter
thirty-nine

"DON'T EVEN THINK ABOUT IT," HE RASPED, SPITTLE FLYING from his mouth as he spoke.

Her vision blurred, dark spots dancing before her eyes as she clawed at his hands. His grip was like iron, and she could feel the strength draining from her body.

Her knees buckled, and she collapsed onto the snow, the icy coldness seeping through her clothes.

He pushed her onto her back, then straddled her, pinning her down with his weight. His hands tightened around her throat, cutting off her air supply. Panic surged through her veins as she struggled to breathe.

"Stop," she choked out, but it was a mere whisper, barely audible over the pounding of her heart.

His face was inches from hers, his hot breath fanning across her cheeks. "Deep down, didn't you always know it would end like this?"

She gargled a response, her words lost in the desperate attempt to draw air into her lungs.

His eyes gleamed. "I knew it. I had hoped it would be different, but then people always disappoint you, don't they?"

Avril tried again to reach her taser, her fingers scrambling frantically at her belt. Her head throbbed from lack of oxygen, and her vision darkened, the edges blurring and fading. Any moment now, she'd pass out.

"Don't worry, everyone will know you found me," he hissed. "They'll know the FBI agent was right all along. You just won't be around to see it."

"Get off her!" came a shout from the woods, piercing through the haze of fear and desperation.

Krister.

Oh, thank God. Relief flooded through her, even though she was still trapped, still at the mercy of her attacker.

She tried to lift her hand, to signal to Krister, but she was so weak. It was like her body had ceased listening to her brain, her limbs heavy and unresponsive. It was all she could do to cling to consciousness, to fight against the encroaching darkness. Her arm went limp, falling uselessly to her side.

Mikael glanced up and growled, his grip loosening. "How the hell did he get here?"

Footsteps crunched in the snow, growing louder as Krister approached, and then his voice, steady and commanding. "Hands where I can see them!"

Krister had a gun. Hope blossomed in her chest, even as her lungs screamed for air.

"Shoot him," she tried to say, but couldn't get the words out, her voice lost in the wheezing gasps that were all she could manage. A heaviness descended on her, a blackness she couldn't throw off, threatening to pull her under.

"Now!" Krister's voice rang out, sharp and urgent.

A sigh, and Mikael let go, his hands releasing their grip on her throat. She gulped in a breath, the cold air searing her lungs as she coughed and spluttered, the world spinning around her.

Reluctantly, he climbed off her, his hands up. "Seems I was wrong. You get the glory, after all."

She wheezed, but at least her vision had cleared, and her hands had started working again. That's all she needed.

Krister glanced at her. "You okay?"

Still rasping, she reached into her jacket and pulled out the taser. Pointing it at Mikael's back, she pressed the button. The cables shot out and found their mark. He jerked for several seconds, his face contorted in pain, then he fell onto the snow.

Krister holstered his weapon and pulled out his handcuffs. Once he'd secured the unconscious man, he turned to Avril. "Are you all right?"

She nodded, holding her throat. It hurt to talk. "Ingrid," she panted, nodding to the figure in the snow.

"I know. I saw her." Yet he'd come to check on her first.

"I think she's still alive. He covered her up."

Gently, he inspected her neck, that worried look still in his eyes.

She pushed his hand away. "I'm fine. Go and help Ingrid."

He gave a lingering look, but ran over to his colleague. Avril saw him check her pulse and held her breath. "She's alive," he confirmed, picking her up in the silver blanket.

Avril exhaled. *Thank God.*

She clambered to her feet. Once upright, she closed her eyes and took a deep breath. This time it burned less, and she got a proper lungful. "There's a sleigh over there. We can use that to take her back down."

Krister carried an unconscious Ingrid over to the sleigh. They didn't have much time. Hypothermia couldn't be reversed without an external heat source. The blanket wouldn't be enough.

Avril stared at the prostate form of the Frost Killer. Her father. He was still out cold. "What are we going to do with him?"

Krister hesitated. "We'll send someone else up for him. They'll be here any moment."

She wasn't going to give him the chance to get away. Not again. "I'll guard him. You get Ingrid to the car while there's still time."

Krister gripped the ropes of the sleigh. "You sure?"

She nodded weakly. "I'm sure. Go." As he turned to leave, she called after him. "Krister, how did you find me?"

He gave a tight grin. "You were acting weird, so I knew something was up. When I checked my signal, I had four bars, so I figured you were lying. That's when I decided to follow you."

She smiled. "I'm glad you did."

"So am I."

chapter
forty

"Happy Birthday!" Krister said, as she opened the door.

It was January 6th, her twenty-eighth birthday. With the tumultuous events of the last few days, she'd almost forgotten.

Since Michael's arrest, she'd been in something of a daze, going through the motions—eating, sleeping, existing—without any real focus on anything. It was as if her brain was still processing what had happened, and until it did, she had no capacity for anything else.

The press camping outside her house hadn't helped, but since the police had cordoned off the road, things had been a lot quieter.

Avril hadn't had to wait long with Michael on the mountain. The police and emergency services had arrived on the scene just after he'd regained consciousness. The area had been swiftly cordoned off, and she'd been ushered down the hill and into a waiting ambulance, where the paramedics had checked her over. Her throat was still raw where he'd throttled her, a constant reminder of how evil he was. Her father.

The forensic team had arrived soon afterward with their bright portable floodlights and excavation gear. Krister had shown them where Michael had positioned the wooden X. Sure enough, under a decade of compacted snow, lay the frozen body of the Swedish student, Anna Hollman.

Despite the years, she was still intact, preserved by her icy tomb. Her hair had been frosted with ice crystals, her skin tinged with blue, yet smooth and unlined. Long lashes had rested against her cheeks, as if she had been asleep all this time.

Avril had left to accompany Mikael back to the nearest police station where he'd been booked into custody, but she'd studied the crime scene photographs afterward. Anna Hollman had been dressed in the same clothes she'd been wearing when she'd disappeared. Jeans and a chunky knit sweater. The fabric had been encrusted with ice, stiff and unyielding. Her arms had been placed on her chest, a peaceful pose, despite the violence that had brought her there.

Finally, after all this time, her family had a body to bury.

They had closure.

Avril knew what that was like. She'd lived without knowing for so long too, and it had almost destroyed her.

Mikael had been surprisingly docile on the way to the police station. It was as if he'd resigned himself to the fact that the game was over. His prolific career was finished. In the car on the way to the police station, he'd murmured, "You take me in, Avril."

She'd stared at him.

"You won. You deserve the victory."

Like *he* was doing her a favor.

Still, she'd almost welled up as she'd walked him into the police station and handed him over to the custody officer. After ten long years of hunting, she'd finally caught him.

Her mother's killer.

Fifty-five victims spanning fifteen years.

She hoped he rotted in hell.

The night had dragged on. Hours of explanations, statements, reports, until they were finally allowed to go home. Someone else would interview Michael, take down his confession, but it wouldn't be her. Bleary-eyed, she and Krister had boarded a morning flight back to Stockholm, where the media awaited.

Somehow, word had got out that a serial killer who'd been operating in Scandinavia a decade ago had been apprehended. How, she had no idea.

"One of the officers or forensic experts is my guess," Krister had said, as he'd shielded her from pushy reporters armed with probing smiles and telephoto lenses.

Eventually, they escaped the throng and been assigned a police escort back to Stockholm Police Station, where there were more briefings and updates. She'd even had a call from her boss in Washington.

"Congratulations. I heard you finally got your man."

"Thank you, sir." She decided to ignore the patronizing tinge to his voice. He hated that she'd succeeded, that she'd been right all along, and he'd been wrong.

"I have to give it to you, Agent Dahl. You don't give up, do you?"

"No, sir."

"We're proud of you. The Frost Killer is one of the most prolific serial killers in the world, and we caught him. It's all over the news. You're the hero of the hour."

She was inordinately glad she wasn't there.

"But don't worry, the Bureau is issuing a press release. We're taking the line that you were in Sweden on unofficial FBI business, that way your actions are sanctioned, even if you did go a little off book."

Avril didn't know how to answer that.

"If you've got a minute to hop on a Zoom call with our media liaison later today, that would be great," he continued.

She sighed, not having the energy to argue. "Sure, no problem." Let them take the credit. She was still their agent, after all. It didn't matter to her what the press said, only that *he* was behind bars and would never be getting out. Ever.

"We look forward to having you back, Agent."

She stiffened. A month ago, he hadn't wanted her anywhere near the Bureau headquarters.

"Thank you, sir."

She hadn't decided if she was going back yet. The only reason she'd joined the FBI was to continue to hunt Michael. Now that it was over, was there any point?

Ingrid was in a stable condition in a hospital in Helsinki and was going to be fine. Her parents had flown out to be with her. "She'll get a commendation for bravery," Krister had told her, later that day. Avril was glad. The young officer had bravely volunteered to take her place in the cabin, even if she had been manipulated into it.

You're just like me.

After the Zoom call, Avril had gone home, fallen into bed, and slept for twelve straight hours. When she'd woken up, she'd taken her mother's classical records, the old, crinkled photograph of Olivia and Mikael, as well as the snowflake pendant she'd worn since that fateful day and burned them in a drum in the back garden.

As she'd stood there and watched the flames, she'd felt a release so strong it had almost made her cry. Almost.

You feel nothing.

Forcing a smile, she held the door open for Krister. "You shouldn't have."

"How could I not? We need to celebrate."

She didn't feel like celebrating, she just felt exhausted. Suddenly she was free. Free of the nightmare that had haunted her for a decade, and she didn't know what to do with herself.

"Nothing wild," he reassured her, holding up a bottle of champagne. "But we can at least have a toast to Olivia, now that she can rest in peace."

That she could drink to.

"Have you seen the interview?"

"Not yet."

He tilted his head. "Are you going to?"

"I'm not sure." There wasn't anything Michael could say to a police officer that she didn't already know. Still, she'd probably watch it just to make sure.

"Shall I give you the highlights?"

"Okay." Avril got two champagne flutes and put them on the table.

Krister took a seat, still holding the bottle. "It was creepy. He seemed so calm, so relaxed as if he was happy to talk about it."

He was.

This was his moment of glory. Even though she knew he hadn't done it for the infamy, he was still going to enjoy it. It was all he had left.

"After your mother, Michael faked his own death by setting the hostel alight. You were right when you said he assumed Nils identity."

Avril slid into a chair opposite him. "So it was Nils's remains they found in the fire?"

Krister nodded. "That wasn't the only identify he stole. There were several more over the years, one of which he used to travel to the United States."

She'd guessed as much.

"Then there was the MO. You know, the whole burying them in the snow thing."

She bit her lip as crime scene photographs of fifty-four victims flashed through her head. Even now, she couldn't stop seeing them. Deep down, she knew they'd haunt her for the rest of her life.

"When he and your mother were dating, they'd once laid in the snow and made snow angels. He said he used to call her his beautiful snow angel."

She was wrong. There were things she didn't know.

"That's why he posed them in the snow," she whispered.

Krister carefully peeled off the foil around the top of the bottle. "He was recreating that moment, over and over again."

She shook her head. "Do you mind if we don't talk about it anymore."

He stopped, setting the bottle down. "I'm sorry. I didn't mean to upset you. I just thought you'd want to know."

"I know more than enough," she murmured.

"Fair enough. In that case, I'll get on with this." He deftly worked the cork lose until it burst from the bottle with a loud pop and flew across the kitchen.

Krister filled their glasses, before handing one to her. "Happy birthday, Avril. Here's to you getting justice for Olivia and all fifty-five victims."

"It was both of us."

He grinned. "But mainly you."

She raised it up. "To Justice."

It had been a long time coming.

They drank, and Avril closed her eyes as she swallowed, savoring the moment. It tasted good. She thought of Mikael in prison, awaiting trial. It would be swift, and he'd be incarcerated for fifty-five life sentences. Pity he wouldn't even live to serve out one. It was less than he deserved.

She still hadn't told Krister about the DNA test, or that Mikael was her biological father. She'd gotten the results yesterday and had waited a long time before opening the envelope. Part of her had been tempted not to, but she knew she couldn't live without knowing for sure. Just because Mikael thought it to be true, didn't mean it was. There was still a minute chance that it could all be some horrible coincidence.

Please let it be a coincidence.

Except it hadn't been.

There it was in black and white.

Negative.

There was no familial match between her and the man she'd thought was her father—which meant the nightmarish alternative was true. It had to be.

Telling Krister would only make it worse. He'd be shocked, horrified, repulsed—and she didn't want to see her reaction mirrored in his. It was hard enough dealing with the revelation herself.

Besides, it had taken Krister several days to get over her subterfuge. The fact she'd deliberately manipulated Ingrid hadn't sat well with him. He had come around eventually, but only because everything had worked out in the end. A different finale and she doubted he'd ever have spoken to her again.

Avril took a steeling breath. DNA meant nothing. That was how she'd rationalized it.

Her father was the man who'd raised her. Who'd married her mother and supported and loved them both until *he'd* put an end to it.

That monster wasn't her father.

As if to prove it, she'd burned the DNA result and flushed the ashes down the toilet. As far as she could tell, Mikael hadn't told anyone their sordid secret. He'd know it would destroy her professional reputation. Nobody would employ her if they found out she was related to a notorious serial killer, a heinous monster who'd killed fifty-five women.

She'd be a pariah.

Some secrets were meant to stay buried.

"We were right about the galleries, by the way," he said, holding his glass. "Mikael worked for the National Museum as a framer and art restorer. That's how he chose his victims. He watched them come into the museum and followed them."

"What about in the other countries and in America?" she asked.

"Same thing. He was able to move from gallery to gallery, never staying in the same place for long. He had access to staff lists and contact details."

She gave a slow nod. "He confirmed this?"

"Yeah, like I said, he didn't hold back."

Avril suppressed a shiver. Now he was caught, she didn't want anything more to do with him or the case. It was like the little details had ceased to matter. It was a strange sensation, to think that after a decade of living with him inside her head, she was finally able to let him go.

"I got you a present," Krister said. He handed her an envelope with that look on his face that he used to get when they were kids, when he had a surprise for her.

Come and see what I made, Avril, you're going to love it.

She usually did, whether it was a secret fort, an item he'd found, or an abandoned hut in the woods. This time it was an airplane ticket—to a Greek island.

"I thought we could take that vacation together," he said, grinning.

She glanced up, surprised. Those twinkling hazel eyes were shining at her, his face full of expectation.

If he knew who she was. What she was...

But the way he was looking at her... How could she say no?

She realized with a start that she didn't want to say no. It was because Krister knew her so well that he'd been able to see through her lies and come to her rescue. He'd saved her life. She owed him everything.

A warmth flowed through her, and she smiled back—genuinely, this time.

Mikael was wrong. She *could* feel.

She was feeling now.

"I'd like that."

The past didn't matter anymore. She'd put it behind her, and now it was time to look to her future. The nightmare was over.

Avril Dahl's story continues in *Cold Legacy*... click the link below:

https://www.amazon.com/dp/B0DM6Y3P9R

Join the L.T. Ryan reader family & receive a free copy of the Rachel Hatch story, *Fractured*. Click the link below to get started:
https://ltryan.com/rachel-hatch-newsletter-signup-1

also by l.t. ryan

The Jack Noble Series

The Recruit (free)

The First Deception (Prequel 1)

Noble Beginnings

A Deadly Distance

Ripple Effect (Bear Logan)

Thin Line

Noble Intentions

When Dead in Greece

Noble Retribution

Noble Betrayal

Never Go Home

Beyond Betrayal (Clarissa Abbot)

Noble Judgment

Never Cry Mercy

Deadline

End Game

Noble Ultimatum

Noble Legend

Noble Revenge

Never Look Back (Coming Soon)

Bear Logan Series

Ripple Effect

Blowback

Take Down

Deep State

Bear & Mandy Logan Series

Close to Home

Under the Surface

The Last Stop

Over the Edge

Between the Lies (Coming Soon)

Rachel Hatch Series

Drift

Downburst

Fever Burn

Smoke Signal

Firewalk

Whitewater

Aftershock

Whirlwind

Tsunami

Fastrope

Sidewinder (Coming Soon)

Mitch Tanner Series

The Depth of Darkness

Into The Darkness

Deliver Us From Darkness

Cassie Quinn Series

Path of Bones

Whisper of Bones

Symphony of Bones

Etched in Shadow

Concealed in Shadow

Betrayed in Shadow

Born from Ashes

Blake Brier Series

Unmasked

Unleashed

Uncharted

Drawpoint

Contrail

Detachment

Clear

Quarry (Coming Soon)

Dalton Savage Series

Savage Grounds

Scorched Earth

Cold Sky

The Frost Killer (Coming Soon)

Maddie Castle Series

The Handler

Tracking Justice

Hunting Grounds

Vanished Trails (Coming Soon)

Affliction Z Series

Affliction Z: Patient Zero

Affliction Z: Abandoned Hope

Affliction Z: Descended in Blood

Affliction Z : Fractured Part 1

Affliction Z: Fractured Part 2 (Fall 2021)

Love Cassie? Hatch? Noble? Maddie? Get your very own L.T. Ryan merchandise today! Click the link below to find coffee mugs, t-shirts, and even signed copies of your favorite thrillers! https://ltryan.ink/EvG_

Receive a free copy of The Recruit. Visit:

https://ltryan.com/jack-noble-newsletter-signup-1

about the author

L.T. Ryan is a *USA Today* and international bestselling author. The new age of publishing offered L.T. the opportunity to blend his passions for creating, marketing, and technology to reach audiences with his popular Jack Noble series.

Living in central Virginia with his wife, the youngest of his three daughters, and their three dogs, L.T. enjoys staring out his window at the trees and mountains while he should be writing, as well as reading, hiking, running, and playing with gadgets. See what he's up to at http://ltryan.com.

Social Medial Links:

- Facebook (L.T. Ryan): https://www.facebook.com/LTRyanAuthor
- Facebook (Jack Noble Page): https://www.facebook.com/JackNoble Books/
- Twitter: https://twitter.com/LTRyanWrites
- Goodreads: http://www.goodreads.com/author/show/6151659.L_T_Ryan

---

Biba Pearce is a crime writer and author of the Kenzie Gilmore, Dalton Savage and DCI Rob Miller series. Her books have been shortlisted for the Feathered Quill and the CWA Debut Dagger awards, and The Marlow Murders was voted best crime fiction book in the Indie Excellence Book Awards.

Biba lives in leafy Surrey with her family and when she isn't writing, can be found walking along the Thames River path - near to where many of her books are set - or rambling through the countryside.

Download a FREE Kenzie Gilmore prequel novella at her website bibapearce.com.